A DAUGHTER
OF FAIR VERONA

A DAUGHTER
OF FAIR VERONA

CHRISTINA DODD

JOHN SCOGNAMIGLIO BOOKS
KENSINGTON BOOKS
www.kensingtonbooks.com

JOHN SCOGNAMIGLIO BOOKS are published by

Kensington Publishing Corp.
900 Third Avenue
New York, NY 10022

Copyright © 2024 by Christina Dodd

All Kensington titles, imprints and distributed lines are available at special quantity discounts for bulk purchases for sales promotion, premiums, fund-raising, educational or institutional use.

Special book excerpts or customized printings can also be created to fit specific needs. For details, write or phone the office of the Kensington Special Sales Manager: Kensington Publishing Corp., 900 Third Avenue, New York, NY, 10022. Attn. Special Sales Department. Phone: 1-800-221-2647.

The JS and John Scognamiglio Books logo is a trademark of Kensington Publishing Corp.

Library of Congress Control Number: 2024932251

ISBN: 978-1-4967-5016-7
First Kensington Hardcover Edition: July 2024

ISBN: 978-1-4967-5018-1 (e-book)

10 9 8 7 6 5 4 3 2 1

Printed in the United States of America

To Arwen
A daughter of Scott and Christina,
Rich in your generosity and support.
Thank you for your brilliance and kind spirit.
May your days be long and blessed with sunshine.

ACKNOWLEDGMENTS

First and foremost, thank you everyone at Kensington:

John Scognamiglio for his vision and daring.

Lynn Cully, Vice President of Business Relations

Jackie Dinas, Publisher and Director of Sub-rights

Vida Engstrand, Director of Communications, and Jane Nutter, Publicist, who brilliantly created a publicity campaign to present *A Daughter of Fair Verona* to all readers of humor, Shakespeare, mystery, and history.

Kris Noble who designed the bright and evocative cover that inspired the DaughterofMontague.com website and brought so many readers' eyes to the story.

Thank you to:

Authors Susan Elizabeth Phillips and Jayne Ann Krentz for the laughter and encouragement.

Authors Connie Brockway and Susan Kay Law for their brilliant brainstorming.

Shakespearean scholar Mary Bly, aka author Eloisa James, for insisting we Zoom together as we write using the Pomodoro method, and for lending her quote to the project.

Agent Annelise Robey for her unending faith and perseverance, and insisting to me I hadn't gone completely bonkers with my creation.

Thank you to The Husband for patiently watching with me:

Ken Alba, Food: A History

Shakespeare Uncovered

In Search of Shakespeare, Michael Wood

Numerous versions of *Romeo and Juliet* and more of Shakespeare's plays than any one person should see in the space of a few months.

And for going to Verona with me for our Magnificently Large and Significant Anniversary and having a marvelous time.

Thank you to Jeannie Huffman for "canoodle."

Last but not least, thank you to William Shakespeare for creating a play of young love, fateful tragedy, and family strife that has reverberated through the ages and been recreated so brilliantly in so many settings by so many actors. Language sang in your soul. Thank you, sir.

CHAPTER 1

In fair Verona, where we lay our scene

My name is Rosie, Rosaline if I'm in trouble, and I'm the daughter of Romeo and Juliet.

Yes, that Romeo and Juliet.

No, they didn't die in the tomb. Brace yourself for a recap, and don't worry, it's interesting in a *My God, are you kidding me?* sort of way.

My mom was a Capulet. My dad is a Montague. For some reason lost in the mists of time, their families were deadly enemies. Yet my folks met at a party, instantly fell in love—nothing bad ever came of love at first sight, right?—and secretly got married. That very afternoon, Dad killed Mom's cousin in a sword fight, then Mom hated Dad for about five really loud, lamenting moments, then she equally loudly forgave him. They fell into bed and as I heard it, spent the night doing the horizontal *bassa danza*. Papà went into exile because of the killing (in the next town a few hours' gallop away), and Mamma went into a decline. To cheer her up, my grandparents decided she needed to get married. Because in my world, all a woman needs is a husband to be happy.

Has anybody in Verona ever *once* looked around at the state of the marriages in this town?

With typical Juliet melodrama, Mom decided she had to kill herself. The family confessor convinced her to take a drug that put her into a sleep that presented itself as death.

I know, you're thinking—C'mon! There's no such drug!

I promise there is. I work with Friar Laurence, the Franciscan monk and apothecary who mixed it for her. More about that later.

Mom took the sleeping draught, fell into a death-like state, had a terrific funeral with all the weeping and wailing her family is capable of—and let me tell you, that's some impressive weeping and wailing—and was placed in the Capulet family tomb.

She was thirteen years old and to all accounts a great-looking corpse.

While in exile, Dad got the news his new wife had suddenly and inexplicably taken the long dirt nap. Being of equally dramatic stock, he obtained *real* poison, raced back to fair Verona, broke into the tomb, killed Mom's fiancé—my father's an impressive swordsman, which is a good thing considering how many people he can insult in a day—flung himself on Mom's body, and took the *real* poison because his life wasn't worth living without her.

He was all of sixteen years old and in my observations, sixteen-year-old boys are idiots or worse. But again, what do I know?

So Dad is draped all over Mom's supposed corpse, to all appearances dead, and she wakes up and sees him. Can you imagine the theatrical potential here?

I can't. Unless there's someone watching, there's no point in getting all worked up.

But I stray from the story, which I've heard countless times in my life in breathless breakfast table recountings.

Mom grabbed Dad's knife out of the sheath and stabbed herself. There was a lot of blood, and she fainted, but essentially she stabbed that gold pendant necklace her family buried her with, the knife skidded sideways, and she slashed her own chest. She still has the scar, which, when I'm rolling my eyes, she insists on showing me.

What with all that blood, she fainted. When she came to, still very much alive, she crawled back up on the tomb, sobbed again all over Dad's body, and got wound up for a second self-stabbing. It was at this point Dad sat up, leaned over, and vomited all over the floor.

It's a well-known fact you can never trust an unfamiliar apothecary to deliver a reliable dose of poison.

Mom simultaneously realized two things: Dad was alive, and he was tossing his lasagna all over the place. In a frenzy of joy and fellowship, she brought up whatever meager foods were in her stomach.

An argument could be made that she was retching because vomiting is contagious . . . or it could be said I was announcing myself to the world. Because nine months later, I made my appearance into the Montague household.

Did you follow all that? I know, I know. But honest to God, strip away the melodrama and that's what happened.

You might think—why is a girl of Rosie's youth so sarcastic about love and passion?

Let me tell you a couple of things.

1. When you have true love and wild passion and broken-hearted tragedy stuffed up your nose every day of your life, by your mother's family, your father's grandmother, your parents who constantly fight and reconcile and proclaim and monologue and fall into bed and have sex so loudly they keep the whole compound awake . . . love and passion lose a little bit of their gilding. In fact, the whole topic is positively off-putting. Also, I have six younger siblings, and someone with a little sense needs to care for

them, and who else in this madly romantic family is there but me?

2. Actually, I'm not young. My parents have been trying to marry me off to some nobleman or another since I was thirteen years old. As a proper daughter must do, I curtsy and thank them, then I go to work finding these gentlemen wives who they immediately fall in love with and adore forever. I pride myself on my ability to match the aristocrats of Verona with their soul mates, while saving myself from the travesty of love and passion and all that creaking of the mattress ropes and moaning and scratching and . . . You know. Consequently, I'm old, almost twenty years, a heart-whole spinster renowned for the bad luck of being repeatedly jilted, condemned to living in my parents' house until my younger brother grows up, marries, and replaces my father as the head of the household.

He's six. I've assembled all the abilities to remain single, and I've got all the time in the world . . .

Until the day I was summoned to my parents' suite and heard my mother's fateful words, "Daughter, your father and I have excellent news for you."

CHAPTER 2

My heart sank. I've heard the start of this conversation four times before. Although not for the past two years . . .

Yet my parents had once more dragged the subject into the house the way a cat drags in a half-dead rat. A half-dead rat that needed to be killed once and for all.

I made the proper response. "Madam Mother, I eagerly await your bidding."

"We have found you a husband." Seven children had rendered Juliet broader in the hips and rounder around the middle, but in fair Verona, her dark eyes epitomized love. Poets sang of them . . . and found themselves skewered on Romeo's sword.

The problem, as I see it, is that I have my mother's eyes.

Here we go again. I curtsied. "I gladly await your instruction, dear Keepers of my Heart."

With a flourish, Papà announced, "Duke Leir Stephano of the house of Creppa has asked for your hand."

My curtsy knee developed a hitch, and I almost collapsed. "Duke Stephano? Two weeks ago, he buried his third wife!"

"He's had bad luck, it is true," Papà allowed.

"Bad luck?" My voice rose. After all, I am a Montague. I have volume, and I know how to use it. "Titania lies barely cold in her tomb because she ate poisoned eels!"

"They weren't poisoned. She trusted the wrong fishmonger

and ate unwisely." Mamma believed that, or pretended to. "I know she was your friend, but she suffered from the sin of gluttony. Anyway, I don't understand how anyone can eat eels. The texture!" She made a small retching sound.

"I always thought Titania was a bit of a she-wolf," Papà said thoughtfully. "She almost lived here for years."

I reminded him, "Her parents are—"

"I know her parents! Fabian and Gertrude of the house of Brambilia. A miserable match between miserable people devoted to making everyone around them miserable. Why do you think I put up with Titania even after she—" He stopped and stood as still as a hare in a snare.

"She what?" I sensed a story.

Mamma interceded. "She fell in love with my Romeo, which was not a surprise. He's handsome and kind, and he appealed to a girl of her unhappy background. But I had to speak with her and she . . . did not take it well."

I didn't like the sound of that. "How not well?"

"She didn't understand how to graciously take disappointment." Mamma clearly felt uncomfortable. "She threatened me."

"Th-threatened you? *You?*" I was stammering. "You're Juliet!"

"She slammed her fist on the table and spoke with unwomanly vigor, and while I didn't banish her from Casa Montague completely—she was very young and suffered neglect from her parents—I did limit her time with you children and while she visited, I kept her under observation."

"Luckily, she soon transferred her devotion to Duke Stephano and forgot about me." Papà gave a deep sigh of relief.

"I didn't know. I'm sorry, Papà." This whole discussion made me squirm. "Titania wasn't like me. The unhappiness of her home seemed to bring on moments of brooding and melancholy. And her obsession with such an evil man! I understand her loving Papà, all women do, but to move from him to

Duke Stephano? A man renowned for indifference to his own family, who never loved anyone but himself all his life?"

"Poor little girl." Clearly, Mamma's tender heart ached for Titania. "To have died so barren of love."

"She had love. She gave love." I remembered so well. "To me, it seemed like Titania was infatuated with the duke for-*ever*. She was always talking about him and watching him. Following him in secret."

"Did you counsel her?" Papà asked.

I grimaced at him. "You know me, Papà. If I have an opinion, everyone has the right to hear it."

"Only if you think it will help." Mamma was kind.

Papà not so much. "It is one of your most annoying traits, Rosie. Especially when you're right."

"But her devotion to Duke Stephano didn't give him the right to poison her!" I thought of the innocent, laughing, devoted bride I'd seen at the wedding a year before. My voice rose. "As he did his first wife, mysteriously dead after a decade of marriage."

"That action of his surprised me. I believed he loved her, or as much as that wretched man can love." Mamma betrayed her real opinion of him without meaning to.

"Poisoned!" I charged on, louder than before. "Then another wife, also poisoned. Then Titania. All three younger than he. All wealthy. He squanders their dowries and marries again."

Papà's voice rose, too. "Don't bellow at me, young lady! The tales about his spending and his visits to the brothels and what happened to his mistress are no more than society tittle-tattle."

Mom flipped out her fan and used it to cool her face. "What happened to his mistress?"

"Nothing." Papà spoke too quickly.

"You assured me Duke Stephano was not what his reputation proclaimed." My mother was a Capulet and soft-spoken as befits a woman of her station. *Our* station. Whatever. Yet now steel hardened her tone.

"He may not be the ideal man, but . . . look at Rosie!" Papà held his cupped hand toward me. "She'll be twenty ere the summer ends. Twenty and a virgin!"

"This is your fault, Romeo." Mom seldom spoke sharply to him, except on this subject. "You insisted on naming her Rosaline after your first love. Rosaline, who swore to be chaste, and now we have a chaste daughter. Foreshadowing! What were you thinking?"

"I know. I know." Papà had heard it all before.

I gave him the eye.

He picked up his cue. "Rosaline the elder was not my true love, merely a foolish young man's distraction. I have had only one true love, my Juliet."

I nodded at him. *Better.*

Of course, he couldn't let it stand at that. "Although Rosaline didn't stay chaste, so I guess she got over me fast enough." Obviously a point of irritation for him.

Mamma said, "She wed at one-and-twenty. A withered old—"

"She might as well have been dead." I mean, obviously. In a little more than a year I'll be twenty-one, and I feel just fine, thank you.

My bitter observation pulled their attention back to me. My never-ending fault was my inability to *keep my mouth shut.* I made a run at distracting them. "Papà, why did you name me for your girlfriend, anyway?"

His face got all soft and sentimental. "You were so tiny and soft, you smelled good most of the time, except when you didn't, and even then I could tell you were going to be as beautiful as your mother. Your big brown eyes . . . and those lashes! All I could think was of all the men who would want to—" He bumped his fists together. "So I named you after Chaste Rosaline. At the time, it seemed like a good idea. Darling Juliet, even you agreed!"

She ladled blame right back at him. "I was so infatuated with my young husband, I would have agreed to anything."

Papà got his *that's amore* look in his eyes. "Are you still so infatuated? What light is light, if Juliet be not by . . ."

Oh no. Here we go again. I scoffed. "Poetry! How it bores me. What's the theme? What's the plot? Get to the point!"

"Daughter, poetry is the soul of nature put to words!" Papà chided.

"Oh, Romeo, Romeo." Mamma put her hand on his. "We speak not of our love. We speak of marriage; Rosaline's long-awaited marriage, which we will celebrate in hope and belief."

"Rosaline, you always befuddle us," Papà complained. "If I didn't know better, I'd say you were doing it on purpose."

"Why?" I muttered. "Distracting you does no good."

"Two of your younger sisters are already married." Papà was back in full shout. "How is this possible?"

It's possible because my parents had proposed the previous marriages and I'd thrown my beautiful, romantic, accomplished younger sisters into the suitors' paths and I'd been jilted. I'd danced at the weddings, smugly thinking I'd outsmarted them all, and now—this?

I stared daggers of hurt and anger at him. "Papà, how much did you offer him to marry me?"

"Nothing. You're going to him with no dowry. When he proposed the union, I told him I had too many daughters to make a big settlement on my aged, elderly daughter." He grinned conspiratorially at me. "In such circumstances, it makes sense to spit on the merchandise."

I might have been amused, as he wished, but this whole mad series of events made no sense. "Then why does he want me?" I saw my father's eyes shift to the side, and I understood. At least, I thought I did. "Oh. He *wants* me. He lusts for me."

"Rosie. Daughter." Papà lovingly cupped my face. "You know I love you."

"Yes." I did know it. He was a good father who wanted to do for me what was best. The trouble was . . . what was best for every other woman was not best for me, and he couldn't see it.

He brushed his thumb over my cheek. "You're beautiful. Your skin, unmarked by smallpox, the curve of your cheek and your rosy lips . . . when I look at you, I see your mother, the sun and the moon and stars shining all in one."

Papà thinks I'm beautiful because I resemble my mother, and *that's* the problem with my parents. I convince myself that they're the biggest frauds in the lore of romance, then Papà spouts a love sonnet to Juliet's beauty, and Mamma smiles at him as shyly as a maiden, and the love glows between them like a fire to warm my heart.

Damn it. It would be so much easier for me to be a sour old maid if they were frauds. As it is, I cherish a secret hope that I, too . . . But no, they're the only couple I have ever seen blessed with a wild, true, unwavering and eternal love. For the rest of the world, it's a chimera.

"Rosie has your eyebrows, Romeo." My madame mother sounded amused. "Satan's eyebrows."

Men wrote sonnets about my mother. Unsuspecting women gawked at my father. He was one of those guys with the bread, sauce, and cheese stacked in a toothsome order: the hair, the face, the body made the ladies drool. All that saved him from blinding beauty were those eyebrows, and I had inherited those. My eyebrows extended in a slant from my inner eye toward my hairline with almost no curve, and I was the only child to have inherited them. I refused to distress myself about what the meaning of that might be . . .

Mamma continued. "Beloved Romeo, your eyebrows are what first drew me to you. I thought you would be good at sinning."

Papà looked at her and smiled that cocky grin. "Did I fulfill your desires?"

"Later you'll have to prove yourself once more." She beckoned with her words.

In a minor explosion of exasperation, I said, "Would you two *knock* it *off*? I'm your daughter and I'm standing right here!"

Papà dropped his hands to his side, undoubtedly to keep them off his beloved Juliet, and returned to the topic at hand. "Duke Stephano is a powerful man."

A world of pain existed in his words, and I understood at last. "Powerful and dishonorable. A man to be feared by more than merely his wives. You dared not refuse him."

"No."

"Am I to plan my own funeral as well as my own betrothal ball?" A world of bitterness existed in my words.

"Not your funeral. There is hope. We must keep faith." Yet Mamma's chin trembled.

"Why?" I might be resigned, but I was still angry.

"Daughter, you pretend to us, but you can't hide the truth. We know you're"—Papà spoke as if it pained him to say the word—"intelligent."

I looked at my mother. She nodded at me sadly. "You understand mathematics."

"I'm sorry, Mamma." This was a huge point of contention. "I need mathematics if I'm to run the household."

"It's true, lodestar of my heart. She does." Papà nodded at Mamma. "Friar Laurence tells me she's unusually talented, even more than our son."

Mamma fanned herself more rapidly.

Papà turned to me. "Your mother and I discussed this match. Looked at it from every angle. We have no choice. We must accept the offer. Duke Stephano insinuated that if we refuse, misfortune would befall me. Us. My family. The things he said made me fear . . . I can't protect all of you forever. But we know"—urgently he took my hand—"we know we can depend on you to handle this. Somehow."

"Handle *this*. The betrothal ball?"

"That too."

"Of course. When is it?"

"Two nights hence."

Through gritted teeth, I said, "I've given you an exaggerated view of my own efficiency."

"Duke Stephano insists the match happen immediately."

"I'll help," Mamma said brightly. "You know I love organizing a ball!"

She did love it. She was bad at it, but she loved it. "Yes, Madame Mother, I depend on you to arrange the flowers. Perhaps we could have white lilies."

"Lilies? No, those are not for a betrothal ball. They're for a—"

Funeral. The word dangled in the air.

Papà cleared his throat and got the conversation back on track. "I meant that we depend on you to handle the . . . the unpleasant details relating to Duke Stephano."

What did he think I could do? Kill the man? "Because no one else can."

Papà looked down, ashamed of himself. "Yes."

I didn't like to see him ashamed for doing what he must. I'm eminently practical and, in fact, do understand. We're the Montagues. We are important people in Verona. Wealthy. Owners of extensive vineyards and makers of Verona's finest wines. But we're so fertile—not merely Romeo and Juliet, but my aunts and uncles and their husbands and wives and their children—that the wealth is spread thin. Even he, Romeo Montague, the most romantic, least prudent man in Verona, had to make a judgment based on good sense and for the good of the rest of his children. I suggested, "Maybe after Duke Stephano has his way with me, you could challenge him, duel him, kill him."

"Daughter, he doesn't play by the rules. He would never provide me with a fair fight." Papà brightened. "I could assassinate him."

"You could. But it's his way to plunge a knife into a man's back, not yours."

"But for you—"

That imminently practical part of me replied, "Thank you, Papà, but I'm afraid that would trigger another feud and we'd be back at the beginning of your and Mamma's affair, and this time someone might actually die in the tomb—and it might be me. There would be no happy family then."

Mamma gave a sob.

Papà looked wretched. Then, because he's a guy, and unhappy, crying women make him uncomfortable, he lifted his leg and farted.

"Romeo!" Mamma pulled out her handkerchief and waved it before her face.

"Papà! Really?" I hurried to open the window yet wider.

Loftily he said, "Friar Laurence says a healthy person passes gas ten times a day." And he farted again.

"How many people are you, Papà?" I sailed from the room, leaving him sputtering and Mamma giggling into her handkerchief. Which was as I intended; like my worthy father, I didn't like to see my mother cry.

But once in my room, I dismissed my deeply concerned nurse, who like everyone else in the household had overheard all, and went out on my balcony.

At the back of Casa Montague, our garden formed a wilderness of climbing roses and tall trees, polished stone benches, and a wide swing. Old and young alike enjoyed the garden, and I took particular delight in ensuring it remained a place of sweet scents and joyful pursuits. A tall granite wall protected the boundaries of our property and when, as did happen, a thief or scoundrel sought to invade our peace, the thick hawthorn hedge provided an excellent barrier.

Now I stared into the bright sunny garden with its meandering paths, its black poplars, the long columns of green pointed cypress, and the mighty walnut tree outside my window. I needed to instruct the gardener that the roses should be sprayed for aphids—a mild solution of soap should do—and the tall, thorny hawthorn hedge around the outer wall trimmed. With a sigh, I leaned my elbows on the stone railing.

But before the gardening, I needed to organize my own betrothal ball to the cruel and lustful Duke Leir Stephano.

CHAPTER 3

Two nights later, while my brother and still-living-at-home sisters gathered to sit on my bed and make comments about my betrothed, Nurse trussed me into my scarlet velvet gown like a Christmas goose on a rich man's platter.

"He has boils on his bottom!" Cesario, my father's heir, bounced on the bed and flung out insults with all the subtlety of the six-year-old he was.

"His nose hairs and boogers are the most luxuriant in Verona." Eleven-year-old Imogene had begun to mature beyond potty insults . . . but only but.

"Pimples in his ears!" Cesario shouted.

"Extend your arms," Nurse commanded me.

I did, and she pulled the pearl-encrusted silk sleeves up to my shoulders and laced them onto the gown's shoulders.

"His nose tells a lie." Thirteen-year-old Katherina had moved from childish insults to insults so tactful they could be uttered in public . . . a man's nose was supposed to be an indication of his masculine endowments, and Duke Leir Stephano's nose was an impressive edifice indeed.

"He smells his own farts!" Cesario said.

"You are truly our father's son," I told him.

Seven-year-old Emilia, the wittiest of us all, added her long-awaited, deadly insult, lisping with the loss of her two front teeth. "I can't quite remember his name. Is it Duke Leir Stephano? Or is it . . . Duke lo Sterco?"

The children cheered and bumped shoulders and slapped backs for, in the vulgar tongue, *lo sterco* means dung, droppings . . . shit.

As they celebrated, I said, as an older sister must, "You should not insult such a powerful and wealthy man." Yet I smiled at them, touched by their loving support.

Cesario stopped bouncing and flung himself at me. "Rosie, please don't marry him. Please, don't. Stay with us. We need you. We love you!"

My sisters joined him, hugging me while I embraced them with tears in my eyes, and Nurse squawked and admonished them to not undo her hours of labor. We were a family, no doubt of that. We looked like one another. We looked like our parents. We wore the same expressions, used the same gestures, smiled the same smiles, shouted with the same voice. How dear they were! How much I would hate to leave them for another house or, worse, for the next world.

Nurse shooed the children out, promising to take them to a hidden place in the ballroom where they could watch the festivities. Shutting the door behind them, she turned to me with her eyes round in her practical, square face—and burst into tears.

I hurried to her side and embraced her. "Dear Nurse, does my appearance displease you so much?" I was teasing; trying to get her to puff up in indignation that I had maligned her labor.

Instead, she sobbed. "I'll go with you to your evil husband's house as your maid. I'll defend you against all cruelty." She showed me the dagger she stored at all times in a scabbard up her sleeve. She claimed it was her dinner knife, yet no mere eating blade had ever been made of such fine steel or kept so oiled and honed.

I was touched and appalled at the same time. My nurse was of a great age, perhaps even as old as sixty years. She had been my mother's nurse as well as mine, and her caring heart should not be sacrificed in my cause. We had both etched enough lines on her dear face. "Good nurse," I said, "let us not talk about murder before marriage. I might yet escape Duke Stephano's perilous yoke."

She took my proffered handkerchief and blew her nose heartily. "I buried your mother and saw her resurrected. I fear I wouldn't be so lucky with you." She hurried to find me another elegant cloth of snowy linen.

"Tonight will be a glorious celebration of life. Let us eat and drink while we may. Promise me you'll get your share and enjoy the fruits of your labor." For my nurse was always my right hand during party planning.

"Once I get the little louts to bed," she promised, and produced the ornate, lacy white cuffs that would adorn the ends of my sleeves.

I extended my hands to her, one at a time. "You shouldn't speak of them so. They do adore you, and you know you couldn't leave them."

She laced with more vigor than was necessary. "I go where the need calls me, and when you marry the dread Stephano, you'll need me more than they do."

I rested my hand on Nurse's dark gray linen sleeve. "My mother will need you." I shook my arms to settle everything into place. "She's breeding again, you know."

"No. Has she told you?"

"No."

"But you know. How do you always know?" Nurse scrutinized me, her headdress firmly in place and the sash that framed her face a flattering shade of blue that tinted her winter-gray eyes.

"She glows." I cleared my throat of the emotion of the moment. "So no more about coming with me to my new home.

With you and me both gone, and mother going into confinement, this place would fall into ruin."

"Yes. What awful timing she has!" Nurse leaked tears as again she straightened my skirt, tied my lace cuffs onto the ends of my sleeves, and tucked a wild curl of black hair beneath my pearl-encrusted cap. "You're even more beautiful than your mother."

"No, I'm not. I look too much like my father for that." I waggled my Satanic eyebrows at her.

"True. But why Duke Stephano has fixated on you, I do not understand."

I wasn't offended. "Nor do I. I've lived this long without any man wildly desiring me. Why him? Why now? Duke Stephano is not the type to move the earth for love or passion. He wants wealth. I can't give him that."

Nurse's eyes narrowed. "That's true, little madam. I wonder what drives the devil's apprentice to seek your hand."

At once I was alarmed. "You're not to snoop."

She pretended not to hear me. "Go to your parents and enter the ballroom with them."

"You could get yourself killed," I said more urgently.

"Make sure you stay close to their sides and never let Duke Stephano get you alone."

"Good nurse, I'll not let that beast near me, but you must also promise you'll not risk your neck in pursuit of some imaginary evil plan when all the man wants to do is despoil another virgin."

"You'd think he'd had his fill," she said in disgust.

"You would think. I understand the initiation is quite painful."

"Where there is love—" Nurse said, clearly thinking of my parents and their constant, loud, frenzied lovemaking.

"There won't be."

"No. But a man of skill is to be cherished."

I started to disparage Duke Stephano, but the memory of Titania's glowing face and whispered confession after her wedding night choked off my words. He had pleasured her, she said, again and again, and I had no reason to disbelieve her.

"Go on, now. You know you must check my lady's flower arrangements. Sometimes I believe she sees colors like a man."

Flawed, she meant. "I have wondered," I conceded.

Nurse glanced at the light outside my window. "Best to hurry. The guests will arrive soon."

I hurried.

The Montague house was constructed (as were many Veronese homes of the wealthy) with a fortified façade on a cobbled city street. Families feuded, their fortunes rose and fell, their servants included armed mercenaries. Eleven years ago, and I well remember that uncertain time, the Acquasasso family had sought to overthrow Prince Escalus Leonardi the elder, the podestà of Verona, by stealth and deception. They failed, but only after he had sacrificed his life for his wife, who was with child, and his son and heir, Prince Escalus the younger.

The Acquasasso family was exiled. Their allies were much reduced in circumstances. Prince Escalus the younger had risen from the ashes, scarred, determined on revenge and then on enforcing peace on the city. He did so by whatever ruthless means necessary.

So the Montague home had its forbidding exterior defenses, but within hid a passion for beauty and luxury. Verona had grown on the banks of the Adige River and two other crossroads, and those routes brought the city wealth and opulence. Our spacious home was built around an open square of gravel paths and potted plants, leafy trees and places where a fire could be laid on a cool winter's evening. Mosaic tables and sumptuous lounges invited one to take a meal at one's leisure.

The three-story house itself was all long, open corridors and decorative columns, on the ground floor rooms for entertaining, the second floor for sleeping and family leisure, and the top floor for the kitchen and the servants' quarters

As you can tell by my adoring description, I loved my home and wished only to remain under its roof and tend to its needs until the house could pass to another Montague generation.

Now I hurried down the corridor toward the ballroom, and a realization seized me. My nurse, in her guile, had distracted me before I could extract her vow not to snoop into Duke Stephano's reasons for wanting this marriage. What's worse, I'd made her realize she couldn't come with me to my new home to help me survive the wicked duke. What risks would she take to secure my safety?

As I remembered the blade she carried, I turned the corner and ran into a man walking backward at a rapid clip.

Under the force of the impact, he staggered.

Being of lesser stature, I lost my feet and smacked hard on the marble floor. The impact forcibly expelled my breath. Although I gasped, I couldn't get it back. Damn the tight-laced bodice!

When I finally started breathing again, the man was on his knees beside me, gingerly patting my back, stammering apologies. "I apologize, fair lady. I was distracted. I was—"

I took a big breath in and at last could speak. "You were walking *backward.*"

"I thought I heard someone sneaking behind me." He extended his hand to me.

I took it and he hauled me to my feet. I looked down one corridor, then down the other. "There seems to be no one."

"No, but I imagined . . ." This gentleman half turned away, the way Cesario did when he was guilty of something.

I looked down at myself and huffed in disgust. All Nurse's ministrations had been for naught. I was disheveled. My gown was wrinkled. My hair hung in waves around my face, and when I put my hands up, I discovered my beaded cap was eschew. As I tucked and pinned, I looked up to my assailant.

He was staring at my bosom, splendidly displayed by my neckline. Of course. A man will look if he can.

Then . . . oh, then, dear reader, he looked into my face. His green eyes grew dazed, then intent. In an instant, the heavens opened, the angels sang, and our two souls united *for all time.*

In some sarcastic corner of my brain, I noted that it didn't hurt that he was gorgeous. But I shushed that part and allowed the moment to sweep me up.

"My lady." He passed his hand over his eyes as if he couldn't comprehend my beauty or how to respond to it. "I am a clumsy beast to have so overturned a creature as bright and lovely as the silver stars in a black satin sky."

Keep talking. His voice was deep and warm, vibrant with sincerity, yet he had a little squeak as he said the last words that warmed my heart.

His straight dark blond hair was streaked with strawberry. His complexion was clear, his ears a little too large, his clothes were of the finest make and cloth, although someone should have told him not to wear that color of magenta on his cap. His lips were full and soft, made for kissing, and I realized this was the moment I hoped would never happen yet secretly dreamed of.

Holy Mary, Mother of God, I had fallen in love at first sight.

CHAPTER 4

Me, Rosaline Montague, who prided myself on my good sense, loved a man who I had never formally met for the beauty of his countenance and because he saw into the depths of me, a woman of flesh and blood and mind and spirit, and so seeing, didn't take to his heels.

It was a miracle . . . and I never felt so foolish in my life.

I was a Montague. I was a Capulet. I was Rosie, and I loved . . . "What did you say your name was?"

He whipped off his cap and bowed deeply. "Fair lady, I am Lysander of the house of Marcketti."

I ran the checklist in my mind. "You weren't invited."

"How would you know?" he countered.

"The Marckettis of Venice are traditional enemies of the Montagues. Furthermore, I wrote out the invitations for the guests."

He cocked his head and looked me over from head to toe. His tone challenged me. "You're Juliet?"

"I'm Juliet's daughter. I'm Rosaline. Rosie."

"Rosie. Rosie fair." He spoke my name the way one would speak of a loved one doomed by a death sentence. "I'm crashing your . . . betrothal party."

"At least you admit to imposing where you weren't asked. And yes, you are."

"You are betrothed?"

"So I am told." A good reminder this conversation was proving to be.

"To Duke Leir Stephano?"

"Indeed."

With every expression of concern, Lysander said, "Lady, you cannot marry him. He will put you in the grave ere a new day dawns."

So many good reminders. Thank you, Lysander. "My father has made the betrothal. I'm an obedient daughter. I'll wed as I'm told."

"Lady, you are innocent, unknowing." He tried to take my hand. I refused to let him, so he gestured wildly as if to make his point. "Duke Stephano is a beast, a man who kills his wives—"

"His last wife, Titania, was my friend."

"I would save you from such a fate as she suffered!"

I would have you do so, too. To fall in love on the very night my betrothal is announced to another—how the ancient Roman goddesses must laugh! But that deep chuckle I thought I heard must be God himself, the deity who had given us his only son . . . and they were both men.

I waited to see if lightning should strike me, and when it did not, I responded with good sense. "You must know that saving me would be a difficult feat to achieve." But oh, how I wished Lysander would argue.

He did. "True love will find a path." This time he managed to capture my hand. "You must come away with me now and—"

A door behind me creaked open. A man's voice spoke. "Lysander!"

Both the gorgeous Lysander and I jumped guiltily and turned to face—the Prince of Verona.

CHAPTER 5

No one could call Prince Escalus a handsome man.

His harsh countenance was marked from the Acquasasso family's tortures: a knife had nicked him beside his right eye and above the same eye, red ripples in his skin gave testimony that red-hot something had been held close to burn and scar. Even years later, his brown complexion held a gray tinge of dungeon. He limped slightly from the iron bar they had used on the bones of his right leg. He was now but twenty-four, but at the temples his shoulder-length black hair contained streaks of premature white, and he had a reputation for moving silently and appearing suddenly when he was least wanted.

For instance, now.

Prince Escalus gazed upon me and in the reflection of his critical eye, I saw myself as I must look: glowing with the first flush of love, disheveled by the fall to the floor, and worst of all, unchaperoned.

Hastily I tucked my hair and straightened my gown.

Prince Escalus then focused on the young lover. "You *are* Lysander, aren't you? Lysander of the Marcketti of Venice?"

"Yes, Prince Escalus." Lysander whipped off his badly chosen cap and bowed a little too deeply. He was nervous—as was I.

"I'm glad you've chosen to come to this celebration and end

the difficulties between the prosperous Marcketti and the noble Montagues." Prince Escalus pushed the door wider and spoke into the shadowy room, where I could see his three steadfast companions and bodyguards, Dion, Marcellus, and Holofernes, and—"Are you pleased, also, Lord Romeo?"

Shit. This situation could not possibly be more ruinous.

"I'm overjoyed at this unexpected turn of events, the announcement of my daughter's betrothal." As my father moved forward into the light, he spoke with intensity and in warning tone—for someone else shoved his way forward.

I knew who it was even before I saw his face.

My soon-to-be spouse and murderer, Duke Stephano. He was red faced, perspiring—and livid.

Woe, for ruin is now my middle name.

I bowed my head to shut out the sight. By all that was holy, I had betrayed myself to my betrothed. I would be shunned, condemned, forced to take the veil as a penitent, a fallen woman.

But hark! Prince Escalus spoke surely, slowly, commandingly. "Romeo, I know the tradition is that the prospective bride should follow her parents into the celebration where they will make the appropriate announcement. But since I am without issue and I'm fond of both the Montagues and Duke Stephano of the noble house of Creppa, may I assume the privilege of leading the bride and groom into this blessed occasion and introducing them as a couple to the people of Verona?"

I kept my head bent, yet looked through my lashes.

My father's mouth hung open, as did Duke Stephano's.

Lysander looked like a recently kicked puppy.

Prince Escalus seemed to find his intercession nothing out of the ordinary, yet when my gaze touched his, his stern expression commanded me, and I turned my eyes to the floor, where they remained.

In haste, my father recovered himself. "My wife, Lady Juliet, and I are grateful for your support and generosity, and to have your public benediction on this union makes it doubly blessed. Indeed, my prince, I yield my place gracefully." He put his arm around Lysander's shoulders. "Let me guide you to the party, *boy*, where you can find friends your age and frolic like the unmarried, frivolous, silly youth you are." As Papà forcibly led Lysander away, he emphasized each of the adjectives, and I foresaw a blistering lecture delivered in a furious undertone, for as any fond father would do, Papà blamed Lysander for the disgraceful state of affairs.

Nurse was summoned to erase all trace of my fall to the floor.

Prince Escalus excused himself to take a piss and strongly suggested Duke Stephano join him. Apparently he feared that without supervision, the duke would flee into the night and the scandal he sought to avert would overtake us all.

The men vanished toward the garden, where I'd had installed a series of portable Leonardo's Lavs. (I was tired of drunk men pissing on my beautifully tended roses.)

Nurse arrived; she'd obviously been apprised of what had happened, for she pushed me into the now-empty chamber and worked in haste, whispering that I must say as little as possible, speak to no one in confidence and to remember, unfriendly ears eagerly awaited further scandal.

I reminded her I was wise beyond my years and knew what was expected of me . . . and abruptly shut my mouth when she glared and said, "Like your parents, you have proved yourself to be feckless, irresponsible, made mad by a full moon and a handsome face and figure."

What could I say? While I never would have believed it possible, every word was true. "All I did was talk to him," I muttered.

"Without the supervision of your parents and his! If report tells true, you held his hand!"

"To be precise, he held mine—"

"Shut your foolish mouth."

I did.

By the time I was refurbished, the prince and the duke had returned, one dour, one surly, neither speaking.

So it was I found myself pacing along the corridor toward the ballroom, Prince Escalus between my betrothed and me, and my hand on the prince's arm.

The silence was crushing in its weight.

As we stepped in, Prince Escalus said to me, "Smile."

He was right, and I smiled, chin lifted, joyously, proudly, carrying myself like a queen as my mother had taught me.

All of Verona was here in the magnificent Montague ballroom.

Drops of belladonna made eyes bright. Plucking revealed long, noble female foreheads and bleaching creating golden hair where formerly raven hair had reigned. Male hairlines also revealed long, noble foreheads, although that was more from hair loss than any human intervention. Musicians played light songs of dance and cheer, and troubadours crooned of romance and thwarted love. Thick blue curtains embroidered with the Montague arms concealed alcoves where a man and a woman could enjoy an assignation. In short, everything was as it should be . . .

Except where was Lysander?

Walking in with Prince Escalus meant that officially, I was still a respectable woman of society.

Yet unfortunately, Duke Stephano dragged me down into the stink of suspicion, and he would never forgive me for my part in his humiliation.

I wished I could assure Duke Stephano his humiliation compared nothing to mine—not that he'd care. I had fallen in love with a pretty face who abandoned me at the first whiff of challenge and scandal. Lysander should be here, staring at me longingly, not cavorting with youths his age or kissing other girls.

The prince did as he had promised; he lifted his glass and

proposed a toast to our upcoming nuptials, and his patronage made it impossible for Duke Stephano to denounce me. But as soon as we had been politely cheered and insincerely congratulated, Prince Escalus moved on, leaving me alone with my furious betrothed.

Not alone *alone*, you understand. Montague servants practiced invisibility while carrying out their duties, yet glanced worriedly at me and consulted with one another. They would do what they could for me, bless them. Guests milled all around, watching eagerly for rumblings of trouble.

I flatter myself it was not me society so enjoyed seeing flayed like a sardine on a platter, but rather my betrothed, Duke Stephano. He treated his own kin with appalling indifference, allowing his aging parents no more than a retirement in a cold country home at the foothills of the Alps. Orlando, his younger brother and heir, lived in exile, afraid for his life. His servants despised him. Three dead wives equaled three families who loathed him. If I were a gambling woman, I'd bet his horses and dogs wished him dead. Certainly every guest and servant here rejoiced to see him dishonored.

Duke Stephano grabbed my arm and squeezed hard enough to raise a bruise.

I struggled, but a hand appeared on his shoulder, squeezed just as hard as he'd done with me, and spun him around.

Rescue! And from a most unexpected source.

Duke Stephano faced Fabian and Gertrude of the house of Brambilia, the people who made him look like a saint.

Titania's parents.

CHAPTER 6

Duke Stephano attempted to knock the hand off his shoulder.

Fabian tightened his grip. In no way did he match Duke Stephano. His squinty eyes were the color of unlit coal. Despite his age, his oily hair remained a midnight black, his skin the blaring white created by lead powder, and an unnatural red tinted his lips. His meager height and rotund frame made him unimpressive, yet he wore only the best velvets, silks, and jewels, and all formed a symphony of coordinating colors. Rumor claimed he had risen to wealth from the docks of Venice, which accounted for the extraordinary strength of his hands and arms.

I saw Duke Stephano struggle in his mind; should he wrestle with the smaller man and take the chance of losing? Only a fool would take that gamble. "Fabian, what are you doing here? What do you want?"

"I was invited, and I'm here to get what is mine."

"It is not yours!"

Interesting. Duke Stephano knew of what Fabian spoke, and he sounded both defiant and guilty.

"I promised you a trunk of gold for every year my daughter lived with you, and you killed her at the start of the second year. I want my money returned!" The merchants of Verona claimed Fabian could pinch a coin until the emperor squeaked, and here was the proof.

"How many times do I have to say it? I didn't kill her. She ate those eels and died." Duke Stephano glanced around at the crowd that gathered, wine goblets in hand, ready to be entertained. He abandoned his feeble defense and returned to the real issue. "It was a small trunk, barely large enough to hold a woman's earrings and in any case, there was no provision in our agreement to give the gold back if the girl turned up her toes!"

The sentimentality of these two men brought a tear to the eyes.

No, wait. It didn't.

"The gold was to keep my daughter properly." The pincher of coin leaned forward, coal eyes lit by a red spark.

Gertrude could wait in silence no longer. In her sweet, high, girlish voice, she said, "Duke Stephano, you're not keeping her except in the tomb of your family, and that requires no cash."

Gertrude . . . ah, Gertrude Brambilia. Titania got her looks from her mother, a tall, curvaceous woman with wide blue eyes, long lashes, and blond hair inherited from some Viking visitor of the long past. She had the face of a cherub, the voice of an angel . . . and the temperament of the Great Beast.

Fabian swung his fat hand within inches of her face. "Shut your maw, woman. I'm handling this."

Seemingly without fear, she retorted, "You've said that ever since Titania was envenomed, and yet the cash remains in his pocket, not ours."

Husband and wife despised each other with ever-increasing vigor, if such a thing was possible, and to be close felt like hate slicing with a thousand knicks of a blade.

"For eternity, Titania will lie in the Creppa tomb on a slab of noble marble. Does the girl deserve better than my other wives?" Duke Stephano demanded.

I assure you I had no wish to distract from this entirely enjoyable quarrel between despicable people, but I felt forced to intervene. "Her name was Titania."

Both men glanced at me as if I was speaking the language of the infidels, without comprehension.

"Titania," I repeated. "Not The Girl. Not your Daughter. Her name was Titania."

The men and Gertrude made dismissive noises and turned back at the disagreement with renewed vigor. I thought, I hoped, they would all kill one another.

Instead my father, Lord Romeo, and Prince Escalus, podestà of Verona, swooped down upon the two men and separated them, for only lords of distinction could exert the control to halt the quarrel.

After a few insulting gestures, the men parted.

Before she stalked after her husband, Gertrude grabbed me by the wrist. Her grip was as cruel and strong as her husband's, and the vitriol that spewed from her lips was all the more frightening coming from that sweetly rounded face. "With this betrothal, death has put its seal on your forehead. I told my stupid daughter thus, but she shrieked her defiance, and my greedy husband wished to be allied with a duke, so the deed was done. I hope your death is quicker and less painful than Titania's . . . but I doubt that it will be. He'll make sure you suffer. He will!" Those large eyes glittered with icy blue diamond delight.

She was a savage in silks, and the terribleness of her ill wishes wiped away my pleasure in seeing Duke Stephano so humiliated. Poor Titania, to have been raised with such fiends as these.

A man's deep voice spoke at my shoulder, "Lady Rosaline."

I turned at once, eagerly imagining Lysander had at last arrived at the party.

Instead, Dion of the house of Bellagamba stood there. "Prince Escalus commands that you accompany me."

Although he was a pleasant looking young man, as he offered his arm, I fear my face fell. He was not Lysander. As far as I could tell, Lysander hadn't arrived. Should I worry for Lysander's safety?

I took Dion's arm warily, for while I recognized him as one of Prince Escalus's three long-time companions, younger sons all, I didn't remember ever speaking to him. "What is it?"

"Prince Escalus believes as a lady of the house of Montague you should distance yourself from such a vulgar argument between those two men." As he led me through the guests, his voice was low and absolutely deadpan.

Yet when I glared at him, he was smirking.

"Your beaming smile may have determined Prince Escalus's course of action," he finished.

I was indignant. "The podestà advised me to smile."

Dion looked directly at me, eyebrows raised.

"Although possibly not in those exact circumstances," I admitted, "and not with such joy at two gentlemen making fools of themselves."

Dion chuckled. "Wasn't it a pleasure to see a fight between those most vile and loathsome two, defilers of—"

"Remember who you are, Dion, and who you represent. You speak too freely and too loudly." Marcellus of the house of Parisi and another one of the prince's companions, interrupted us. "I'll take her now."

That wiped the smile from Dion's face most entirely, and he relinquished me with a bow.

As Marcellus led me away, he said in a low tone, "You must forgive my compatriot. He's young and brash, more adept at fighting than at diplomacy."

"Surely both are important to the podestà," I protested, for I liked Dion's humor and honesty.

"Fighting men he can have, as many as he wishes, but in Verona, diplomacy is a rare virtue and most needed as Prince Escalus negotiates the constant danger which surrounds him."

Marcellus was a severe man, no older than Dion or the prince, I felt sure, but with a dark and brooding countenance that even good food, dance music, and cheerful company did not lighten.

"Constant danger? Even now?" In the relative stability of recent years, I'd come to believe Prince Escalus controlled Veronese politics with the strong hand in the velvet glove. "He was barely more than a boy when he beat back the rebels and for many years has wielded power."

Marcellus dismissed my question with a curl of the lip. "It's not the place of a woman to concern herself with the politics of a city-state."

Briefly I entertained myself in imagining the woman with whom I would match Marcellus. Gertrude came to mind. Too bad she was already spoken for.

"It is not for me to judge Prince Escalus for his choices as friends and stalwart companions." I could deliver a back-handed slap as good as any *man*.

Marcellus stopped his parade through the guests and viewed me with stern disfavor. "What reason possesses my prince to—"

Now Prince Escalus's third companion, Holofernes of the house of Negri, arrived to offer his arm. "Come, let us walk."

Marcellus bowed and gladly we parted.

Holofernes I knew; he was, like the others, no older than Prince Escalus, but unlike the others, he was a native of Verona, and bore the marks of a man who'd fought for the house of Leonardi and spent time as a captive, held for a ransom that never came, and tortured by the Acquasasso for his family's lack of funds.

"Why this constant changing of my partner?" I asked him.

Holofernes paced through the crowd, smiling at me like a man willing to be charmed, in other words, like a conventional party guest. "Prince Escalus did command us to make sure you were prey to no more gossip and scenes, and to ensure that we take our turns to walk with you, never slowing enough to allow anyone to engage you in unnecessary warnings or cruel taunts. At the same time, this changing of the guards ensures no one can claim you allowed a man not your betrothed to occupy your thoughts and time."

"How . . . thoughtful of the prince. He kindly makes sure this marriage with Duke Stephano takes place." I wanted to say, so wanted to say, *I hope he takes as much interest in the funeral that follows.* I refrained; Holofernes answered me squarely and behaved with gentlemanly respect, and he deserved better than my hostility. "When do we stop walking?"

"When your betrothed has returned to your side."

"Then let us walk on!" At first test my bitterness overflowed.

Punishment followed swiftly; Duke Stephano loomed at my side, and Holofernes released me and melted into the crowd.

I was surrounded by guests, and at the same time I was alone with Duke Stephano, and obviously his temperament had taken a turn for the worse.

Yes, I know—how was that even possible?

CHAPTER 7

As one does, I made conversation with my betrothed. "How beautiful the flowers are tonight. My mother chose them and arranged them. She's invariably a style setter." By that I meant the flowers were a hodgepodge of wild blossoms and blinding colors combined in ways they should never be . . . and yet such was Juliet's cache that I knew tomorrow morning every noble lady in Verona would be following her lead.

Duke Stephano paid no attention to my conversational gambit. Grabbing my wrist, he hauled me toward a concealed corner of the room, and despite a flutter and a flurry, no one intervened.

I'm not a large woman, but I have many appallingly rambunctious siblings and I know how to set my heels.

When Duke Stephano realized he could haul me no farther, he released me beside the long table filled with marvelous dishes of artichokes roasted in breadcrumbs and cheese, blushing peaches baked in custard, gilded pastries, pickled pheasant eggs in many colors, pies of calf brains, and crusty breads accompanied by herbs and oils.

I nodded at the chef who waited at the end of the table for my approval. The Montague kitchen was the envy of Verona, and with the help of our trusted cook, I had made it so. Foolish

Lysander for abandoning me so soon. I would have made him a good wife. Not that I'd planned so far ahead . . .

At the center stood a sugar sculpture of a loving couple surrounded by tweeting birds. The female resembled me. The male, unfortunately, resembled a goblin. Our sculptor, it appeared, held an unfavorable opinion of Duke Stephano.

I had the presence of mind to pick up a sturdy silver bowl that would bruise if slammed down on Duke Stephano's broad-knuckled fingers. I wandered along the table, choosing a tidbit here and a tidbit here, smiling at guests who lingered near, inquiring of children and elderly relatives.

Duke Stephano followed on my heels, snarling like a mad dog. "If you keep eating so much, you'll be fat as butter. Like your mother."

Some would say I should have done the proper thing and applied tact and flattery. I can, you know, if I have the time to think through my words. I'm as trained as any other virtuous maiden of Verona.

Yet with no chance of appeasing him and more than a little incensed that he should so insult my beloved mother Juliet, I stopped and boldly looked him over from head to toe.

He was a tall man, once mighty and handsome, but dissipated living had rendered him outsized in all the unfortunate spots and, it was rumored, he suffered from gout. My critical gaze flayed him, and he flushed even ruddier yet. When I felt I'd made my point, I answered in kind. "I will never be fat, for with your wives you cannot breed children, you breed death."

"No more. That part of my life is done. You and I, I pledge, will live long together, with many children." He cast a glance around at the guests and the healthy number of Montagues and Capulets among them. "You should be fertile. God owes me that."

I crossed myself. "Sir, you blaspheme and tempt the fates. The deaths of your wives—"

"The deaths of my wives weigh no more heavily on my soul than your marred reputation weighs on you. After your display of immodesty in that corridor with that . . . Marcketti youth, I should renounce you. And prancing all about the ballroom with Prince Escalus's men." He made himself plain for all to hear—and guests and servants did linger near, ears cocked. "Yet I have good reason for marrying you."

Aha! The truth loomed, waiting for me to ferret it out. "Pray tell me, good lord, what reason would that be?"

"Power, my stupid trollop. Power and revenge." He laughed, a deep, infectious laugh that startled me with its warmth. . . .

And sent a chill up my spine. "Power? From marrying me? What power would you find in this unholy union?"

"Don't worry your fool's cap mind about that. You are nothing but a female, a pawn. Be grateful for your part in this, my stratagem."

Behind him in the ballroom, Lysander swaggered in, cap askew, arms draped around some of the most disreputable youths in Verona.

I saw his drunkenness. I despised it and me for longing so keenly. Lysander was still the most handsome, shapely, and exhilarating youth I had ever seen, and if he would come to me, I would welcome him in my heart and in my arms.

Duke Stephano turned as if my gaze had provided him with a map. He observed Lysander, then turned back to me and thrust one stubby finger in my face. "Come to me in the garden when the belltower strikes the evening hour, and I'll teach you how a good wife should speak and behave. Do not fail to meet me at the fountain, or tomorrow's sunrise will never be witnessed by your cheating eyes."

I curtsied deeply, courteously. "My lord, I come at your command." I watched him walk away, then pulled the strong, slender carving knife out of the roast duck.

CHAPTER 8

As I had seen my industrious nurse do, I tucked the knife securely into my sleeve and stalked after Duke Stephano toward the garden.

I paid no attention when the young widow Porcia sought to waylay me. "Rosie!" When I didn't stop, she yelled "Rosie!" and rushed to block my path.

"I don't have time for a friendly conversation right now, Porcia. I have been summoned by my future lord to attend him." If Porcia had the wit of the gnat that haunted my wineglass, she would have taken note of the steely glint in my eyes and stepped aside.

Of course, she did not. She was my age, a simpering idiot who heartily, loudly, and repeatedly pitied me my single state while patronizing me for being a virgin and so frequently left at the altar.

She put her hand on my arm in a sisterly gesture that made me want to punch her between her plucked bald and badly redrawn eyebrows. She said, "One must make allowances for your pure state and how it affects the balances of the humors, but please take the advice of one who has joined the legion of womanhood—you should not pursue Duke Stephano to the garden. He could have nefarious designs upon your treasured virginity and after waiting so many years to wander among the pleasures of the marriage bed, it seems unwise to prematurely venture forth."

Bless her shriveled wit, Porcia could always use a hundred words to say what others could say in five. "Your matronly headdress proves the depth and breadth of your experience." I eyed the mammoth contraption askance.

She flushed; she'd always had extravagant and dreadful taste in fashion, and this one left her looking like a galleon in full sail. She threw back a blue curtain and indicated an alcove. "In here!"

It was easier to give in than to have her chase me across the ballroom and shout my business to the world. I entered. "Be brief."

She shut the curtain behind her and advanced on me. "On your wedding night, the pain is dreadful. There's blood!"

"Is that how your husband, Troilus, introduced you to the marriage bed? I feel sorry for you if that's true." It wasn't true, and well I knew it. Troilus had been the most gentle of men who was much missed in Veronese society.

Sourly she said, "Troilus was a courteous gentleman who graced my bed too seldom."

"Ah." The source of Porcia's discontent was revealed.

Her eyes lit up. "But I hear Duke Stephano is a heartless man who hurts all who come close, especially those he places beneath him and rides to a froth."

"Are you speaking of his horses or his wives?"

"He rides his horses cruelly?"

I did not grin. I did not. But it was a close thing to realize Porcia cared not a tweak about the women he had murdered, only about his livestock.

"As a virgin, I'd think you'd be terrified!"

"Since that is what you intend, perhaps?" She might have sensed my amusement, but before she could attack again, I said, "Titania loved him with a mania." A mania I had privately thought unnatural.

Porcia said petulantly, "She died so recently. She's barely cold. And what a miserable funeral. Barely anything to eat. Bad wine. Her parents fighting the whole time. No one mourning except—"

"Me." Not that funerals were ever festive, but Titania's had been epic for its haste and lack of lamentation. Although after her marriage our relationship had grown distant, I grieved for the years she'd spent playing in our garden. When we were mere children, Mamma had brought Titania home, explained to me in private that her parents knew not how to love, the little girl needed a friend, and she put her in my care. I took the charge seriously, and she became a friend who clung to me and pitifully appreciated every kindness. As she grew, so did the household's knowledge of her strange games and steadfast pretenses. Her memorial had not celebrated her life, but too clearly showed the bare ripple her passing made in Verona's quiet pond.

"And me. She was my friend, too." Porcia made a show of dabbing her eyes with her sleeve. "Although the things she knew about . . ."

"About what?"

"She was very like you, sometimes. Odd. Odd in the way she'd stare, as if she could see my thoughts." Porcia flinched.

A light thrown on Porcia's thoughts would probably illume a twisted pile of eels.

"Best not to speak ill of the dead." Briskly, Porcia returned to the subject nearest to her heart; since I wasn't dead, she didn't hesitate to speak ill of me. "I don't understand why Duke Stephano is rushing into this marriage. Why would that man want an untutored virgin who knows nothing of love?"

I contemplated a drinking game; a glass of wine every time Porcia used the word "virgin." I felt sure I could scarcely stagger to the garden should I indulge.

I may have smiled, for I could see the change come over her thin, cunning face. Her pretense of caring had ended. Her lace cuffs came off, and she was ready for battle. "A woman like me"—she smoothed her hands down her amply padded hips—"knows ways to satisfy and pacify a raging bull like Duke Stephano. If I were to be his wife, he'd be mellow with pleasure."

"You could be his wife. Your husband has left this mortal coil and you are a wealthy widow." I suspected Troilus couldn't stand that shrill voice one more day and had instead chosen to contract the plague.

She didn't appreciate my unspoken sentiment; that Duke Stephano had ignored her and instead made the offer for me. "When he's killed you as he killed his other wives, I'll take up the challenge and teach Duke Stephano to be gentle and tame." She tossed her head.

With a headdress that size, I was surprised she didn't wrench her neck. "He won't kill me tonight, for I assure you, I do not go alone to the garden." I pulled the knife from my sleeve and showed her. "My chaperone."

Dear reader, let me pause to assure you I had no intention of using the knife on Duke Stephano in a deadly way. I merely wanted to pointedly make it clear to him that I was not a woman who would put up with his abuse.

Pointedly. Heh.

Obviously Porcia could never grasp the subtlety, and even more obviously showing her the knife was the act of a fool and a clear sign the stress of this event had worn away my good sense, for at the sight of the shining blade, Porcia gasped so loud the cardinals in the Vatican in Rome turned to see from whence such a gust of ill wind had been generated.

I slipped the knife back into its hiding place . . . and nicked myself.

That sharp pain was a wakeup call. *Calm down, Rosie, use your vaunted intelligence. Wiliness must win the day.*

She put her hand to her skinny bosom and said, "It's against the laws of man and God for a woman to deny her husband!"

"He's not my husband yet, so neither the law nor God could be offended." I tried again to stalk away.

She grabbed my arm, which drove the knifepoint into me again, and demanded, "How much did your father have to pay Duke Stephano to relieve the Montagues of the burden of keeping you?"

I should have said, *I'm not privy to that information, that is the province of men.* Or even, *Ask my father, bitch.* But Porcia had seen the knife and knew squeezing my arm could result in an injury; she enjoyed that, and she wearied me with her constant harping. In pain and disgust, I took my revenge. "My face and figure are payment enough. Duke Stephano takes me without a dowry."

"You jest!" she said incredulously.

Payback!

"Do I?" I smiled a Mona Lisa smile, swept the curtain aside—and knocked one of the fragile old widows off her feet.

So much for my grand exit.

The elderly woman was no more than a small pile of black silk and veiling on the floor. Remorseful, I helped her to her feet and said, "Lady, I beg your pardon. May I help you find a seat where you can recover yourself and have a servant bring you a plate?" For although her veil hid her face, through its deep folds I could see how gaunt she looked; I suspected she was one of the widows of a wealthy Veronese family who perhaps neglected their lesser relatives and left them to the charity of the street.

"That would be lovely, dear."

Her voice quavered so much, I feared I'd done her an injury. Although she smelled of unwashed woman and the faint odor of decay, I put my arm around her scrawny waist. "Are you hurt? May I send my nurse to care for you?"

"How kind. No, I thank you." Her pale linen gloves had once been expensive, with colorfully embroidered gauntlets, but now they sported dark damp blotches that looked as if she'd fallen hands first into a pile of rotting garbage.

Porcia surveyed her and me, pointed her little nose in the air, gave a disdainful sniff, and pushed past us.

The old lady's dark, shadowed eyes followed her, then returned to me. She covered my face with her gloved hand as if she were blind and reading my features. "A seat, a plate of food, and a glass of wine will restore me. What a lovely child you are."

I signaled one of the Montagues' faithful servants and gave him instruction, then returned to her. "I must be away, but I leave you in Giotto's hands. All you have to do is ask, and he'll see to your needs."

Giotto made an elegant bow. "I'm honored to do as you wish, lady."

I again offered my wishes that she be well, and hurried toward the garden, toward the confrontation with my betrothed. As I swept through the ballroom, the whispering behind fans, murmuring behind handkerchiefs, and knowing stares clearly indicated that the tale of my interlude with Lysander was now the subject of malicious gossip. One of Galileo's cannon balls dropped off the Tower of Pisa could not have caused such a shock, and for what? Lysander was even now slipping into an alcove with the fair Lady Blanche.

A pox on them both!

My heart, so recently given, was now broken, but I had no

time to weep and wail as a proper daughter of Romeo and Juliet should do. Instead I prepared to meet Duke Stephano. I needed to be wary. I needed to be on guard. I needed to be shrewd.

He had said he wanted me for *power and revenge.*

Power over me, I assume, but revenge? On whom?

CHAPTER 9

Because the Montague staff had unfolded the feast across a myriad of tables in the ballroom, the garden was empty of guests. The full moon hid behind towering clouds that lumbered across the sky on a gentle breeze. Strategically placed flaming torches lit the veranda and the back of the house, but as I moved farther along the paths, deeper into the maze of boxwood hedges and cypress trees, the area loomed in shadow. I silently cursed the darkness, for that gave Duke Stephano the advantage of surprise, and I had no doubt he'd gladly use it to do me an injury or, as Porcia warned, rape me.

As I glided along the edge of the gravel paths, I kept on the grass to avoid the betraying crunch of my footsteps. I neared the center of the garden, breathed the cooling night air, listened to the music and laughter from the party, wished I was back among the guests and not out here with a knife up my sleeve and the hope I would come out alive. When I heard the tinkle of the fountain where cupid shot water out of his arrow of love, I knew I had arrived at the garden's center.

But where were the torches? At least one should burn out here to light the way of any guest who strolled the paths. Had Duke Stephano doused them as part of his evil plan to frighten me, grab me, despoil me? I slowed my pace and scanned the area, trying to see Duke Stephano's bulky outline in the dark, but I observed no trace of him.

Did I trust him?

Of course not. As I inched forward, I pulled the knife from my sleeve. The handle was sticky with blood. *My* blood, and I was struck by the stupidity of stowing a sharp, unprotected blade on my person. Sadly for me, no one had left a sleeve scabbard lying around the roast duck.

I would obtain such a scabbard should I live through this night. Surely even a *virgin* had the right to protect herself from a monster.

At my own wit, I snorted in unseemly amusement. Porcia's everlasting drumbeat insistence on my purity had taken root against my will.

As I neared the far end of the fountain away from the house, I could discern the tall, trimmed shapes of the hedges, and the water in the pool began to shimmer. The moon sought to break through the clouds. My eyes narrowed as I inched forward.

My foot in its soft slipper kicked something that obstructed the pathway. The warm remnants of a torch, recently extinguished. I pushed it out of my way with my toe, took another step, and struck something large, long, heavy, inert like clay, growing cold . . .

A corpse. Dear God, a corpse!

I admit it, I screamed, a thin sound in the dense night air, and in my haste to back away, my weight overbalanced. I fell forward. I hit hard on the . . . on the *dead body.* My knife flew out of my hand and skidded off into the dark. My palm landed in a sticky pool that felt too much like the blood in my sleeve. I groped and found the hilt of a knife buried in . . . in the chest of this corpse. The large male dead corpse. All instinct and revulsion, I pushed myself to my feet and backed up—and ran into a living man, my back to his front.

He grabbed me, clapped his hand over my mouth.

The killer!

I bit down hard.

He yanked his hand away. "Woman! I'm trying to protect you."

The prince. Prince Escalus. His voice. I was relieved, but only for a moment. "Protect me? From whom? Whoever this is, is dead!"

"Whoever it is? Do you not know?"

Then . . . then the moon burst through the clouds and I saw who had been slain by a knife—not my knife—in his chest. My betrothed. Duke Stephano, his eyes wide and staring, a look of terror contorting his features.

Confused thoughts chased through my mind. I felt guilty, as if I'd killed him with my hatred. Relieved, because he was dead. And frightened because . . .

"Did you kill him?" A logical question, I deemed.

"I did not. I don't sneak up on a man in the dark and put a knife in his chest." The poised, cool, unemotional prince took umbrage at any insinuation he would act with such dishonor.

But I wasn't wrong. "In his chest. Not his back, in his chest. This was no sneak attack. Look at him. He saw something, someone, and failed to defend himself! Who else but you—?"

Nearby in the garden, drunken young men laughed and hooted.

Prince Escalus caught my hand. "Let us not be caught hovering over the body."

Right. Right. The prince was right. The Montagues had thrown a party. They'd invited everyone in Verona. Now that the initial hungers had been satiated, guests would be wandering everywhere. *Were* wandering everywhere.

I hovered on the edge of hysteria, but I still had my wits about me. "Wait." I wrestled myself free, groped, searched the bushes, found my knife, and joined him.

I wanted to run, but he said, "Slowly, with dignity."

Quite right. It wouldn't do to look suspicious. Using the utmost care, I tucked the blade into my sleeve, then allowed him to place my hand on his arm. He led me on a leisurely stroll along the shadowy garden path lined with yet more tall boxwood hedges. About halfway down the walk, shouting arose behind us. Boisterous young men raised their voices in consternation. "Murder most dreadful!" they yelled, and, "Duke Stephano is stabbed through the heart!"

My heart beat quickly; would we meet someone, be implicated in the death?

We reached a cross path. Prince Escalus stopped and in a low voice said, "We need a discreet way back to the festivities."

I knew the garden. I'd grown up in this garden. "This way." As we walked toward the kitchens, the shouting grew fainter with distance. My heart began to beat at its normal rate and my mind to work in its usual rational manner. I thought carefully about my words before I uttered them. "I mean no disrespect to your good name, my lord, on reflection I realize my mistake in thinking you would have stabbed Duke Stephano on a dark night when he was undefended. But the question remains, what *are* you doing out here?"

"Porcia—" he began.

"Porcia." I slapped my forehead. "Of course, Porcia!"

"Who has more headdress than wit, was loudly declaiming to her group of chin-wagging cronies that you'd gone out to the garden with a knife and with the intent of killing Duke Stephano and freeing yourself of—"

"That infinite and endless liar!"

"You did not tell her that?"

"No. I was foolish, but not that foolish." I didn't want to explain, but I had no choice. "I showed her the knife."

"That *was* foolish, a trait I had not previously noted about you. Previously, you seemed to be quite sensible."

"Thank you."

He cleared his throat. "What brought on this particular recklessness?"

I sighed. "I lost my temper."

"I had noted the temper."

He had noted? He had noted . . . *me?* Yes, he visited homes, spoke to men both common and renown, called each person by name. He was the consummate prince. Yet he never revealed anything of himself, never received the Veronese in his private chambers, only in the public parts of the palace. His sister, born months after his father's murder, had been seen so seldom rumors claimed he had reason to keep her hidden. He kept everything about the Leonardi family secret and private, and I hadn't imagined he watched others so assiduously. Certainly not me, an aging spinster of a family loyal to his reign. "Sometimes it seems as if it can do no harm to loose the fiend of my temper. I am taught better now."

"No person of influence can ever release their personal demons without unexpected repercussion."

"I'm not a person of influence, my prince."

"So you have become." Before I could protest, he continued. "Fortune smiled that I overheard Porcia, for I told her I had caught you on the terrace and as prince, reprimanded you for even thinking of such impropriety. . . . She smirked."

"As prince, did you reprimand her for filling gossips' bowl?" I asked icily.

"I did. Her pleasure vanished in a gobble of peahen indignation. Promptly I slipped away and hurried to apprehend you before you did harm, and stumbled on"—he pointed back the way we came—"that!"

"You could have stopped me before I fell on him!" I flexed my hands, sticky with blood.

"I wanted to see how you reacted."

My voice rose. "How I reacted?"

"Hush." He waited until I had calmed. "You may not have

done the deed, but you might have instigated it with your lover."

"My lover?" I may have shouted, for the prince pulled me to a halt and once more put his hand over my mouth. I didn't bite him this time, but I tasted the blood on his hand. "Whose blood is that?" I asked quietly.

"Mine. You broke the skin."

"Good."

The prince frowned at this honest statement.

We listened. Although we'd moved away from the hubbub created by the discovery of Duke Stephano, clearly word had spread. We could see a glow of many torches at the fountain, the yelling of voices spreading throughout the garden, and on the terrace, one shrill female's commentary.

"Porcia," I said in loathing.

"Indeed. When we're inside, we must break apart and both enter by different means."

"We're almost there." I led him toward the chapel and pointed down the candlelit corridor. "Take a left. You'll enter the ballroom and from thence you can navigate to the terrace. I'll come from the direction of the ladies' facilities."

He nodded and started down the corridor.

"My lord prince."

He stopped and looked back, a brooding-browed man in dark, elegant clothing who carried night's aura like a weight.

I said, "I do not have a lover."

"Young Lysander is handsome, from a good family, kind-hearted, and infatuated with you."

"Is he?" I fought the irresistible smile that wanted to form on my lips.

"As I'm sure you know." Prince Escalus crushed any maidenly pleasure with his cool tones and smooth countenance. "He would be a good match for you and as such, you two would form the bridge across the disagreement between your

families. Do you wish me to speak to your father about insti-
gating marital negotiations?"

"Thank you, my lord prince, but that would be premature.
This evening we met for the first time." I recalled Lysander's riotous entrance into the ball. "He seemed easily recovered from
any unhappiness about my upcoming nuptials. I doubt if I'll
see him again."

"And of course, this evening you lost your . . . what? Fourth
betrothed?"

In less than twenty-four hours I'd been betrothed, fallen in
love with another, been scorned by that love, and left before
the altar with only death as a bridegroom. Yet when faced with
the knowledge of Duke Stephano's murder, I thought only of
Lysander. What did this indifference show about me? That my
affection should be engaged before my body was bargained?

Yes, my parents bore witness to the success of that union.
"Duke Stephano was my fifth betrothed."

"You lost him, although not in the usual way."

"No. No, the others did not choose death, but another mate."

"How fortunate for you that each of the others discovered
his desire before the two of you were one in the eyes of God."

"Yes . . ." Fortune had nothing to do with it. The young
men hadn't married me because I'd arranged for each of them
to find their one true love, which was not me. But it would
hardly do to say so.

My eyes narrowed on Prince Escalus. He was a handsome
man, if one discounted his scars and dour demeanor, and fit, if
one discounted the limp, a renowned swordsman and a force-
ful statesman. Yet he lacked a family of elders. Someone needed
to help him find a wife to support him in his duties.

Who better to arrange a match than me, who had already
arranged four successful unions?

The young lady should be accomplished, of course, but more
than that, she should bring him joy and passion. She should be

tactful, able to advise him on matters relating to womanly issues: charity for the poor, widows and children in need, those invisible issues of benevolence and generosity. She should know her place, and never speak of things having to do with the law and the duties of a prince's rule.

My sister Katherina would be a good mate to any man, but she was thirteen and Prince Escalus was twenty-four, for eleven years already the Prince of Verona. I hesitated to condemn my own sister to the onerous task of supporting a man so driven by duty. But there were others, all eager to marry into such a noble family, and I knew with judicious thought and a little scheming I could find a woman for Prince Escalus who would make him the happiest of men . . . if I survived this night without accusation and imprisonment.

When I ceased my plotting and returned my focus to Prince Escalus, I found him observing me with a cynical twist to his lips. It was almost as if he read my very thoughts and did not appreciate them. Yet he said only, "Make sure you bring the knife with you to the terrace."

I curtsied. "As you command, my prince."

CHAPTER 10

I hurried upstairs to my empty room; Nurse remained with my brother and sisters. I stripped off my cuffs, poured water from the ewer into the basin, and washed my hands and the small cuts the knife's point had made on my arm. I tossed the bloody water into the walnut tree that grew beside my balcony, used a rag to wrap my wound, laced clean cuffs to my ornate sleeves—a task that was best done by two—and following Prince Escalus's commandment, I slid the knife up my sleeve once more. I then paced downstairs past the ladies' facilities and onto the terrace.

A milling and a shouting greeted me. Guests gestured widely, speculated loudly, buzzed and hummed. Fabian and Gertrude of the house of Brambilia sneered and smiled and informed, and I knew each word from their lips dripped of poison and shamed their angel daughter as she was held in the bosom of our beloved Madonna.

I slipped through the crowd to my father's side. I tugged at his sleeve. "Papà, what's happening?"

My father clasped me in his arms, looked at me with such joy and relief, I almost cried for I realized he'd feared I was lost, too, a body out there in the darkness of our garden.

I couldn't reassure him; I had to keep up the ruse of ignorance. "Why is everyone shouting about murder and guilt? Who's dead?"

Papà looked around as if frantic. "There. There's your mother. She should tell you. Stay close to her. She's the most beloved woman in Verona, and she'll keep you safe regardless of . . . what madness takes the crowd."

Too late!

Like the baying of hunting dogs, the guests began moving in, circling, saying in a cacophony, "There she is. There's Rosie. She was his betrothed. I remember hearing she argued against marrying him. She got a knife. She stabbed him in the chest. She killed him!"

I pressed closer to my father.

Fabian and Gertrude of the house of Brambilia stood in the crowd, smiling nastily as they joined in the jeers. Located in different parts of the crowd, I saw Prince Escalus's men, Holofernes, Marcellus, and Dion, watching and listening. The elderly woman was there in her heavy black veils, her eyes glittering as she watched the scene, and I hoped Giotto had coaxed her to eat, for she looked eerily like a corpse.

Papà put his arm around me and loudly said, "I'm sorry you had to hear such sad news in so public and sensational a manner. I would your gentle mother had had the opportunity to tell you in private, where you might mourn." He glared balefully at Porcia. "A foul deed has ended the life of Duke Stephano."

"He is no more? The lord to whom you betrothed me has . . . gone to his just reward?" I buried my face in my hands and pretended to weep while thinking Duke Stephano's just reward would involve a bumpy ride through all of Dante's nine rings of hell ending with a perpetual *balletto* under Satan's sharp hooves.

One shrill voice rose above the rest. "I saw her take the knife. She confessed to me her intentions. She's guilty of Duke Stephano's murder!"

I should have plucked the blond hair with the dark roots from Porcia's forehead while I had the chance. I held the evidence that the blade buried in Duke Stephano was not my knife, but the crowd was rapidly becoming a mob. Who knew if I would have the chance to prove my innocence?

Where was Prince Escalus? Had he left me to my own devices?

But no. His calm, commanding voice rose above the cacophony. "Good people of Verona, let us take dispassionate counsel before we unfairly judge this noble lady."

No one wanted to take dispassionate counsel. Everyone wanted someone to be declared guilty so they could go home and sleep in their beds unafraid that a sharp blade would next find its way into their chests.

No one had the audacity to naysay the prince—except Porcia.

She pushed her way into the center of the crowd. She pointed her skinny, knobby finger with its long red pointed fingernail at me . . .

All right, fine. Her finger isn't knobby and her fingernail isn't long and red and pointed, but I'm rightfully irritated at this woman who so genuinely desired to see me take a dive into a boiling-hot pool of hellfire for no reason other than—

"She's a virgin!" Porcia cried.

I looked to the heavens for patience and gestured with my upturned hands.

"Virginity is a state much to be required in a young, unwed woman," my father said.

"Unwed, anyway." As nasty as Porcia was being, you'd think I mocked her matronly headdress.

Oh, wait. I had.

"How many times has she been betrothed and yet never wed?" Porcia waggled her shaved eyebrows suggestively.

The prince joined my father and I, standing at my right side.

Porcia continued. "Rosie is warped and bitter with the weight of her aged virginity!"

Guests scrutinized me as if searching for obvious signs of deformity caused by purity.

While Porcia drew a deep breath, preparing for her next blast of venom, I muttered, "How many times will she work the word 'virgin' into the conversation?"

Prince Escalus got a funny look on his face. I didn't know what to make of it. On that narrow, still, aristocratic face, it looked oddly like . . . a smile. Not a full smile. A quirk that lifted his eyes and one side of his mouth.

I had never witnessed such a thing, and it vanished as quickly as it came. I tried again, still muttering, "If she calls me a virgin five times, you owe me a florin." At first I didn't think he'd heard me.

Then, "Seven."

"Six."

"Done."

"We're already at two," I advised.

"Unless she has given herself to God, it's unnatural for a female to be unwed at such an advanced age!" Porcia continued in full sail. "I tell you, this is by her design. She confessed to me she was going to the garden to meet Duke Stephano—"

"On his command!" I said.

Porcia paid no heed to my interruption. "And I saw her take a carving knife from the duck!"

"Which I still have." I pulled it from my sleeve.

Guests gasped and backed up as if expecting me to go on a slashing rampage.

That fingernail pointed again. "It has blood on the blade!"

"It's my blood!" I didn't know I could unlace my sleeve that quickly, but I did, and I showed the two cuts on my arm. I decided I was done being on the defensive. "You caused this. All this!" I gestured around.

With unerring calm, Prince Escalus plucked the knife from my waving hand.

I advanced on Porcia. "Porcia, explain to the kind citizens of Verona why you believe you should have been betrothed to Duke Stephano and not me."

She pulled that finger back to her chest. "I never said that."

Heads swiveled between her and me.

"Why did you think *you* could keep him happy?" I asked. No, I *demanded.* "Tell them what you told me. Tell them!"

In a lofty tone, she said, "A kindly warning that on her wedding night, an uncaring husband can horribly hurt his virgin wife by tearing through her flower!"

I lifted three fingers toward Prince Escalus. *Virgin.* "Then he should ask, 'She loves me, she loves me not?'"

Porcia understood the reference to the ancient silly love rhyme, for she made an unattractive moue even as amusement rippled through the crowd.

"Then you told me . . . ?" I prompted.

"What I said was an intimacy between two women." She glared like an adder about to strike.

"You made free with my words. Shall I do the same with yours and tell these good people why you're also a suspect in Duke Stephano's death?"

"I am not!"

I faced the crowd. "She compared him to a raging bull and claimed when he had killed me as he killed his other wives, she'd take up the challenge and teach Duke Stephano to be gentle and tame and—how was it you said it, Porcia?—mellow with pleasure."

She blushed so hard she had blotches of red on her cheekbones and her nose. "You stupid virgin!"

I lifted four fingers and was gratified by a small cough from the prince. A hastily stifled laugh, perhaps?

"Rosie, while those words are not becoming for such a recent widow, I don't understand why this would give you cause to accuse Porcia of murder." Prince Escalus did understand, I could see that, but he wanted me to spell it out for those among the guests who were less quick-witted.

I spoke clearly so that those on the fringes could hear. "She wanted him for herself, and she was dismayed to discover he took me without a dowry."

"I still don't believe it," Porcia fussed. "Who would take such an old virgin without payment?"

Five fingers.

She didn't even seem to realize that, even if not everyone agreed she had a motive for murder, through her own speech she had revealed herself to be vapid and grasping.

Until Troilus's lady mother said, "We will return you to your father's house, Porcia, and hope you discover an appropriate grief at the loss of my son, your young husband, and modesty as befitting a grieving widow."

Porcia scanned the guests and observed that sentiment had turned against her, and she hurried to her mother-in-law, her hands upraised in appeal.

"It would be best, Porcia, if you say no more tonight," Prince Escalus said. "I command you to silence until you go to the priest and confess to the sins of vanity and pride."

My mouth dropped open. I could have got her to call me a virgin one more time. I know I could. But Prince Escalus had plainly cheated, and now I owed him a florin. I crossed my arms and huffed.

"Where is Stephano's body?" Prince Escalus asked my father.

"We carried it to the chapel."

"Did you remove the knife from his chest?"

"No, my prince. We left him as he was found."

"Then this knife and this woman are innocent of the deed."

The father of Duke Stephano's first wife, Anna, spoke up in

fierce and jubilant tones. "The knife, perhaps, but not necessarily the woman. She had good reason for killing him. Kill before she was killed. Who here wouldn't do the same?"

A babble of agreement rose from the families of Duke Stephano's deceased brides and an equal furor of disagreement from others in society, mostly men whose wives occasionally excused themselves from functions because of bruises and contusions.

"I discovered Rosie's plan to meet Duke Stephano in the garden. I forbade her and sent her to her room." Prince Escalus smoothly told the lie. "Yet someone did kill Duke Stephano. Tonight let us take counsel with all men who have reason to know anything about this crime." He turned to my father. "The ladies should go hence to their homes and their chapels and say solemn prayers for the soul of Duke Stephano."

As with all the women, I curtsied to the prince and the assembly and exited, and as I did Anna's mother caught my eye, gave me a huge smile and that ancient Roman gesture of approval, a thumbs-up.

I shook my head at her and spread my hands, palms up, in innocence.

Gertrude glided up, all beauty and grace, and in a voice pitched to carry, she said, "I didn't know you had it in you."

When counseling me to control my temper, my mother frequently said, *If you wrestle with pigs, you get muddy and the pig is happy.* Almost certainly she'd been speaking about Gertrude, and I didn't bother to argue.

In the corridor an older man wearing Stephano's livery rushed forward and knelt before me.

I came to a halt and viewed him warily.

Forcibly taking my hand, he kissed it. "*Gràzie*, thank you. My name is Curan, and I speak for all the servants in Duke Stephano's house, Lady Rosaline. You freed us from painful and onerous service."

"Don't thank me. I didn't kill him."

"I know. I know! Of course not." He respectfully lowered his gaze. "Why would you kill such a cruel master and murderous husband? You, a gentle creature of modesty and virtue?"

I yanked my hand free. Guests and servants were watching . . . and listening, and he wasn't helping. Taking my skirts in my hands, I hurried away.

He called after me, "It's good that you never have to enter that household where sad and vengeful wife-ghosts weep and watch, there to die a dreadful death at Duke Stephano's hand."

As I walked down the corridor, I knew that I should have stood still and let Curan speak. At least then his trumpeting cheer and approval would have attracted a smaller audience and some sideways glances would have been diverted.

Clearly, despite Prince Escalus and his testimony on my behalf, I wasn't yet reprieved in popular opinion.

CHAPTER 11

The appropriate action for Duke Stephano's grieving betrothed would have been to go into our chapel to say the
prayers that Prince Escalus had commanded. I had experience
with death; in this world of infection, plague, and woe, expo-
sure to its effects was impossible to avoid.

Yet I had fallen on the corpse, a horrible remembrance
that made me want to wipe my hands again and again on my
gown. I'd seen that expression of terror—or was it disbelief?—
contorting the duke's face.

No, I would not go pray in the chapel so others could witness my piety. No one believed my earlier grief, and while I
would say prayers for the repose of that man's twisted soul, my
piety was not for show.

With a shiver, I hurried past the chapel door and saw, ahead
of me, Mamma waiting with a fleece to throw around my shoulders. At that sight of her concerned, sweet, motherly face, I realized that while I might not grieve for Duke Stephano, I was
frightened and unnerved. "Mamma!" I burst into tears and
rushed into her arms.

She wrapped me around in the fleece and helped me up the
stairs, and as we walked I heard Gertrude cynically announce,
"A touching demonstration to convince us of her innocence."

In my room, Nurse waited with a posset and fond words, and I buried my face into a linen towel and sobbed. The stress of the last few days had taken its toll.

When I lifted my head, my mother had disappeared. The door remained open, Nurse stood on the threshold, and I could hear a voice I knew as well as my own—but I had heard that tone only a few times in my life, and each time had been a moment of consternation.

For my gentle mother, Juliet Montague, had descended the stairs, faced off with Gertrude, and told her to count her legs, and when she got to two, she should run away and never again look back at the Montague palazzo because if she did . . . she would no longer have two legs to count.

Nurse listened with a smile on her face. "That's my girl. Your mother, *femmina*, is a force of nature, and no one ever threatens her little chicks."

Juliet's little chicks. That was me and my siblings.

My tears dried, and I nodded at Nurse. Yes, my mother was fearsome. When Mamma came back upstairs, she accepted a cup of broth while I changed into my most plain nightgown. I'd had enough of glamour for one night.

Mamma and I sat together and talked, not about the night and the murder, but about her stunning flower decorations and how the staff was defusing the ongoing crisis by serving wine and laden plates to the men of clearly superior intelligence who remained to seek out the killer. When we were done laughing about that, through the open window we heard the men dispersing. Nurse hung over the balcony rail and listened, then returned to impart the news that Prince Escalus's testimony had created a bulwark around me that no man dared assault.

"This is the news I've waited to hear." Mamma rose with a stagger of exhaustion, kissed me on the forehead, and retired to the master suite. Nurse accompanied her, her arm around her waist while I watched and thought about who my mother was and how much she meant to me.

I was tired, but not sleepy. Too much had occurred in the past few hours, and I mentally answered accusations and conducted conversations and wondered who had in fact killed Duke Stephano, whether the killer was in our household, and if so, who was in danger under our own roof.

Then . . . oh, then, dear reader, came the moment the fates had foretold for me.

"Rosie . . ." The sound was no more than a kiss of air on a warm summer night. "Rosie . . ."

CHAPTER 12

I hadn't imagined it. I grabbed a flowing white robe and ran toward my balcony.

There, at the top of the walnut tree outside my window, the most handsome man in the world laid along a broad branch, peering through the long green leaves.

That would be Lysander of the house of Marcketti, if you're in any doubt.

I thought one of us should be sensible, so as I thrust my arms into the loose sleeves, I pretended to be. "Lysander, do you know what proprieties you offend with your actions?"

He inched forward, leaned his chin on his palm, and flirted with his handsome, knowing eyes. "Proprieties be damned if I may once again gaze on the sunrise of your countenance."

I waved a hand in front of my face as if his flattery left a stench. (I loved it.) "Do you know what dangers you court, what my kinsmen would do ere they found you here?"

"Death. Dismemberment. Torture. A rude scolding."

I gazed on that handsome laughing face in the midst of the tree and realized he teased. "Do you have so little respect for the blades of the Montagues?"

"I have more respect for my own ability to skulk. I climbed the tree and surprised you, did I not?"

I securely tied my belt around my waist—surely by now, with the light behind me, he had seen enough—and settled into flirtation. "You do skulk well, I admit."

"If my skulking fails, and your kinsmen and their blades do indeed discover me, you'll have the chance to admire my running and bleating like a baby goat."

I smiled for what felt like the first time in days. "You almost make me want to see this spectacle"—my humor failed me—"especially since I saw you slip into an alcove with the pleasing Blanche."

"She is not so pleasing up close." Lysander's lips curled in a most satisfying sneer. "She smells like overripe fruit."

I snorted, used my handkerchief to blot myself dry, and resumed the conversation with much increased pleasure. "Then why bother?"

"Camouflage, my lady. Over a pitcher of wine, I was given that rude scolding for so endangering your reputation and your betrothal."

"Ah." I nodded my understanding. "By my father?"

"By Prince Escalus. I do not know what kind of alliances your marriage would have created, but I know that he feared civil disturbance if I acted without wisdom and caused a schism in your heinous betrothal to Duke Stephano."

Tonight I had rather liked the prince. Now I experienced a cynical displeasure. "So the good prince is willing to sacrifice me for peace in the city." Peace in the city was his task and he had good reason for his insistence; his father's death, his own torture, the memories of battles in the streets, his mother's sad passing, and his little sister's loss of both her parents. Yet when my life was the tribute to be offered up, I found myself without understanding. For all my skill and intelligence, I was, after all, not yet twenty, and life stretched before me like a new and richly hued Persian carpet.

Lysander blithely continued. "Prince Escalus assured me he

wouldn't allow Duke Stephano to harm you. He insinuated all was not as it seemed."

"Huh." I leaned my elbow on the railing, which encouraged Lysander to stare fixedly at my chest as if the fire in his eyes could burn away the fine material and reveal what lie beneath. I pretended not to notice as I attempted to delve into the prince's thought process. "What could he do? Breaking a betrothal is no snip of a thread."

"Some kind of diplomacy, I thought. He seems an honorable lord with a strong contempt for Duke Stephano, and more important as Verona's podestà, the well-being of his people is closest to his heart." Lysander indicated me meaningfully. "All his people, Rosie."

I grinned at him. "Even insignificant me?"

He grinned back. "Even most exquisite and glorious you. When he did swear to me he would intervene on your behalf, I gave my word I'd eschew your beguiling companionship until you were free of that most evil pact."

"Now I am free." I twirled in a circle to express my joy, but his words had stirred my suspicion. Coming to a stop in front of the branch, I asked, "Lysander, did *you* kill Duke Stephano?"

"Fair lady, I did not. Did you?"

"I'm flattered that everyone thinks that I could, but alas, no."

"If we are both innocent, let us discuss who did, for although Prince Escalus forced the men to pronounce you innocent, the ladies are not so easily swayed. They hold a power men cannot hope to match, and I would rather confess to the murder myself than allow you to be disgraced and . . . and exiled."

One moment Lysander was the handsome, laughing boy of my dreams, and the next he seriously offered to sacrifice himself for me.

I adored him. How could I not?

"I didn't kill him." I felt as if I'd been saying that for far too long.

Lysander answered in all seriousness. "Someone did. Who? If we can discover his murderer, you'll no longer live under the shadow of suspicion."

Nodding, I fetched a pillow off the lounge, knelt beside the railing, my arms resting on the stone and my face level with Lysander's. "Who was at the party who hated him?"

Eyes dancing, Lysander laughed.

I laughed, too. "I know. Who didn't hate him?"

"There are so many people at whom to point the saber. His former mistress was there, did you know?"

"No! Why? How?"

"I don't know why, but as to how—I climbed the wall. She probably walked in with the rest of the guests."

I may have sounded critical when I said, "One thinks that method would have worked for you, too."

He drew back, an offended hand to his chest. "That would have been too easy. The Marcketti pride themselves on their lurking and I will take the family prize."

"Of course. Forgive my obvious error. In the future, lurk to your heart's content."

"So long as it be outside your window?"

"You read my thoughts, my lord. We are well matched, indeed." That had been too bold, too presumptuous, and hastily and with embarrassment, I said, "Tell me more about Duke Stephano's mistress."

Lysander sat up, straddling the branch, and once more inched forward. "Miranda once was the darling of the *trovatori*, a singer of great renown. Now she has the mark of a knife on her throat—and it's rumored Duke Stephano put it there."

I had a flash of memory of the wedding of Titania and Duke Stephano, and at the following celebration a dramatic-looking woman with brown curly hair loosened around her face singing a wild lament of love. Her dark-ringed green eyes had made it memorable, and haunting. "She was there? At the party? You're sure?"

"You were very focused, my Rosie, on resisting Duke Stephano's cruel grip and savage intentions."

I looked at the bruises forming on my wrist. "Yes. I don't know what he intended in the garden, but I know he meant me harm." My fingers trembled as I remembered, a reaction much delayed, but sincere nonetheless. Lysander leaned forward and for the first time since we met in the corridor, our hands touched. Comfort flowed from him to me, and my lips curved in a shaky smile. "I'll put that aside, for he'll harm no woman ever again."

"Many prayers have winged their way to heaven, imploring the Madonna and all saints to end Duke Stephano's reign of terror. Mine, for one." Lysander's voice quavered with sincerity. "Surely tonight's result is heaven's intervention."

"Lysander." I gripped his fingers tighter and squeezed them. "I don't think the blessed Mother of Heaven carries a knife to dispense justice. By my troth, the deed was done by human hands. Once more we're back to the question of—who?"

"You are both exquisite and logical." Lysander released me and sat up again. "I saw Miranda with my own eyes, and she did indeed have a scar on her throat. She drank much strong wine and watched you and Duke Stephano with deadly malice."

A chill crept up my spine. "Yesterday as the pork arrived, my lord father's provider mentioned to me that when I had wed Duke Stephano, he trusted I'd pay the household debts, for his debts caused much hardship among the merchants." So much hate and grief caused by Duke Stephano, and my unwilling betrothal meant I had caught the backlash of that whip.

"The sentiments among Duke Stephano's other wives' families must match the grief and anger of his first wife's family."

"Anna. Yes, Anna's mother is angry, hurt, vengeful." I pushed my fingers through my hair. "Surely she's merely happy he's dead. Surely she didn't kill him?"

"I don't know. Would your mother kill for you?"

I swallowed. And nodded. "Yes. Yes, she would."

Lysander was acute and intent. "Forgive me, lady, but your family seems loving and kind. Why would your father give you to such a beast as Duke Stephano?"

That was an easy answer. "Duke Stephano is powerful and when insulted, apt to hire an assassin."

"*Was* powerful," Lysander reminded me.

"To be out of this betrothal—I should now be the happiest woman in the city. Yet how did I become the target of so much trouble? I didn't ask to be wed to anyone, much less Duke Stephano. When I seized the knife, I wanted to protect myself and perhaps frighten him away, not kill him. Now he's dead and I'm the object of suspicion." *It isn't fair.*

In my head, I heard my mother's voice chide: *Life's not fair.*

Lysander heard my complaint and answered to soothe my dejected spirit. "I would vanquish your troubles with the gift of my hand holding yours ever elevated above the world of gossip and censure." Again he offered his hand, palm up.

I gazed at it, noting the length and strength of the fingers, the calluses caused by dedicated sword practice, the prophecy of good fortune that stretched all along his lifeline. I longed to put my hand in his and promise forever, but I was not as young as my mother when her Romeo visited her balcony, and the wisdom of the added years gave me pause. "Do you think our families can heal their enmity?"

"Your parents have proved the success of a marital alliance as a bridge across troubled waters." Still he held that hand out, and he smiled invitingly, his face so handsome the moon itself wept with envy.

I put out my hand and leaned toward him.

Clutching the branch with a one-armed embrace, he inched closer and closer. "A clasp of your hand and a kiss from your lips, and all my dreams past and forever will be fulfilled. I'll never again wander lost among the heavens looking for that one star to guide my heart."

"Shhh." I put my finger to my lips. I leaned toward him as he leaned toward me. "Speak no more, but grant me my first kiss as a memory to cherish and a warm seal of red wax on our hope for the future."

He stopped moving forward. "You're bad at this."

"This?" As if I didn't know.

"Romantic, lyrical paeons."

I sighed. "I haven't the knack for spouting amorous nonsense."

"That seems as if it would be a crime in your family."

"Not a crime, but from their lips words spring like butterflies and—" I couldn't figure out a lovely simile to describe the innate and instinctive perfection of the Montague family's language.

Lysander came to my rescue. "From their lips words spring like butterflies, ascend toward the cosmos, and drop tiny turds on your shoulders?"

I fell backward onto the marble floor of my balcony and laughed so loudly the nightbirds winged away in alarm. Swiftly I covered my face with my robe to muffle the sound. The picture Lysander created in my head, of a swarm of Montague-faced butterflies in all their colorful glory rising toward heaven's radiant light while irreverently raining poo on my earth-bound self . . . was so apt, so true to their amorous aptitude and my practical personality that I couldn't quite push it away enough to recover.

When, many long moments later, I at last gained control, I looked up and observed Lysander, his elbows resting on the branch, his chin leaning on his hands, his gaze on me. He was, of course, grinning, cocky and well pleased with himself, and in this Lysander, beneath that face of perfection, I could see the remnants of the mischievous lad he'd been.

That sent me off into another gale of laughter. When I could, I staggered to my feet and gripped the marble railing. "No turds," I told him. "And sometimes the words aren't like butterflies. Sometimes they're like horns blown discordantly or giant drums pounded without rhythm."

Lysander lifted his brows in inquiry.

I explained, "The other things my family does well is lose their temper and shout."

"Are you a member of that part of the family?" he asked.

"Indeed I am, and while I don't like to be modest, I'm probably . . . nay, assuredly . . . the Montague who is swiftest to anger and loudest of voice." It struck me I'd held this discussion with someone else on this fraught day . . .

Verona's podestà, Prince Escalus.

Right now, I didn't want to think of the prince's cynical quirks, or the manner he let me stumble on Duke Stephano's body to clear his suspicion, or the florin he won through unfair means that I now must find a way to repay. It was a pleasure to transfer my attention back to Lysander. I smiled at him, conscious that merriment lit my flushed face, and well aware of that homily that my mother had taught, that the swiftest way to make another person like you was to laugh at their jokes.

I had done more than laugh. I had guffawed. Even now my lips trembled with amusement, thinly veiled. "Do you think we could try again to exchange a—"

"Warm seal?"

I cackled.

His face grew grave. "After such a tumultuous evening, a kiss between us will vanquish the shadows of the night and prepare our world for the dawn of happiness."

He was no Capulet, no Montague, each phrase placed and

turned and admired. But his sincere sentiment and tender tone swept away the haunting detritus that cluttered my mind and gave me something new on which to focus.

A kiss. A simple kiss.

He inched forward.

I leaned out as far as I could.

His eyes closed.

My eyes closed.

And—the branch released a thunderous crack.

CHAPTER 13

Lysander yelped.

I heard a hard thump below followed by a crackling rain of twigs and leaves.

I opened my eyes, leaped back, stared in disbelief.

The branch had splintered halfway toward the trunk.

I leaned over the railing, seeking enlightenment about Lysander from the dwindling torches that illuminated the palace's exterior.

In the shadowy garden, he lay flat on his back, unmoving, covered with the remains of the branch and the tree's debris.

I called him softly.

He didn't move.

I panicked.

Wouldn't you?

"No. No, don't be dead. Please don't be dead." I gathered my fleece and wrapped it around my shoulders. "You can't be dead."

From the door, Nurse said sharply, "Lady Rosie, what are you saying? Doing?"

"He fell. He fell. No, he didn't exactly fall, the branch broke. I don't know how, but it broke out from underneath him and he plunged—"

Nurse's eyes grew round with horror and the memory of the last time a man had wooed at her mistress's balcony. "Not again!" She brushed past me onto the balcony and looked over the edge.

"Is he still there?" I wanted to cover my eyes. I wanted to have an attack of the vapors. I wanted to turn into a hysterical female when I was a sensible woman. Always. Always. But today I had celebrated my betrothal to Duke Stephano by finding him dead, and tonight I did not want to discover the man who a few hours ago had become my One True Love had perished in a fall.

I lived an uneventful life. How had all this happened now?

"That's young Lysander, I assume?" Nurse pulled back from the edge. "You'd better hope he's not dead."

"I do. Of course I do!"

She swept on her dark cloak, pulled the hood up, and as if I hadn't spoken, she continued. "Or you two will have started a feud between the Marckettis and the Montagues that makes previous strife seem amicable, and all of Verona will call for your blood, and you'll be sentenced to a nunnery—or a burning at the stake!" She started for the door.

I followed. "I'm coming, too!"

She rounded on me. "No, you are not. You're going to climb into bed and pretend that visit"—she gestured at the balcony—"never happened."

I was wringing my hands, a most un-Rosie activity. "What are you going to do?"

"I'm going to revive him, if I can, and send him on his way." She pointed at the bed.

I obeyed, climbing in and pulling the blankets up to my chin. "What if he can't be revived?"

"Then I'll drag his body onto the street." Nurse pointed her finger at me. "Stay!"

Like a lapdog, I stayed, quivering, waiting, hoping, pretending to be asleep and yet awake to every cry from the night, every creak from the house, to the distant sounds from the kitchen at the far end of the garden and . . . God's teeth, would Nurse never return?

When she did at last, I bounded up on the bed. "Tell me."

She removed her cloak, a puckish twist to her mouth. "When I got down there, he was gone."

I flopped back in relief and closed my eyes in relieved prayer. "Thanks be to all the saints. He revived."

She shut the door behind her. "No."

My eyes popped open. "What do you mean, no?"

"I mean I saw the marks in the dirt. Somebody dragged him away. I followed until I reached the maze. When I ran out of light, I returned to the house."

I sat straight up. "You must go back—"

"Out into the garden where an unknown creature dragged an insentient man's body?"

"If you will not, then I must—"

"No." Nurse dragged the dressing chair in front of the door and seated herself, arms crossed. "No."

"You . . . can't . . . keep . . . me . . ." I was sputtering.

"My lady, you know I do everything you wish of me with a willing heart. But about this you cannot sway me. A wild young love is all well and good, but you're nearly twenty and should know better." She closed her eyes wearily. "Although perhaps a woman is like wine and the longer her cork remains intact, the more intoxicating she becomes."

I was incredulous. "Did you just call me a virgin?"

"I did."

I pulled a pillow over my face and screamed and drummed my heels on the mattress.

Nurse yanked the pillow away and leaned over me. "He's a young strong man. He landed in the moist earth. I vow he's not dead, but I will be before I allow you to do anything more to

bring disgrace on your name and the names of your parents."
She shook my shoulders. "Go to sleep, Rosaline, and do not
test me further." As she stumped away toward the chair, she
said, "Just like the last time."

"It wasn't just like the last time. It wasn't anything like my
parents! There wasn't any—"

"Canoodling?"

"There was not."

"Not even a canoo?"

"That's not a word, and no, but not for lack of trying! Also,
there was no—" I huffed to a halt.

"What's worse for a maiden's reputation than canoodling?"
Nurse demanded.

"There was no poetry."

"What a relief that is." Nurse's tone left me in no doubt she
scorned my discontentment. She settled into the chair,
wrapped blankets around her chest, pulled the stepstool close,
and muttered, "I'm getting too old for this."

As was I, apparently, for although I swore to myself I'd
sneak past her as she slept . . . I instead fell hard asleep until
morning's light shone in my window and the sensation of being
watched roused me.

CHAPTER 14

I opened my eyes, turned my head, and saw my sisters lined up beside the bed, oldest to youngest, staring fixedly at me. I turned my head the other way and Cesario began bouncing on the mattress beside me.

"Rosie, what happened last night?" he begged.

Katherina said, "Yes, Rosie, last night, what happened?"

I looked at Nurse, who spread her hands as if she was innocent of their presence. Like I believed her. Nurse was an early riser, regardless of the circumstances, and if she had spent the night in that chair guarding my virtue, she was grumpy enough to let the kids in to wake me before *I* knew what happened.

Being the oldest was sometimes enough to make a stallion cry.

I pulled a pillow out from underneath Cesario's rump and stuffed it behind my head. I patted the mattress and asked, "What have you heard?"

Everyone piled on, shoving and sitting on my feet until I pulled them back, and when they were settled down, Katherina said, "In the garden, Duke Stephano was dead of a knife in the chest. A convocation of noblemen led by Prince Escalus discussed the evidence and although it was believed you had motive and a weapon to stab him, Prince Escalus testified that he stopped you before you went into the garden, and it was agreed you must be innocent. Thus whoever killed Duke Stephano is still at large."

I flung back the covers. "There's been no more disturbing discoveries, then. Nurse, has aught come to your ears?"

Nurse looked at me sideways. "The kitchen gossip this morning is all about you and your ill-fated matches. There is some argument about how many there have been. Apparently some of our less astute staff have lost track."

"We'll have to see what we can do to turn that tide." I turned on her. "A branch on the tree outside my window seems to have broken last night."

"So I heard." When she chose, Nurse could sound dry as an old bone in the mouth of a hungry wolf.

"Rotted, I deem. Someone could get hurt."

Folding her hands primly in front of her apron, Nurse said, "Only if they climb the tree."

Picturing Lysander's inert body, I put my hand on Cesario's head. "No one will climb the tree. Will they, Cesario?"

Cesario exchanged horrified glances with Emilia.

I exchanged equally horrified glances with Nurse. How many times had those two climbed that tree? "Perhaps the tree should be removed."

"No!" "No!" "No!"

I gazed, startled, at Imogene, then turned to Katherina. "You too?" She was so sensible, the sister most like me! So of course she had scaled that tree.

She shrugged. "The branches are broad and face outward. We can shimmy up and down and watch from above."

"We play in the storage room," Imogene boasted.

"And eat what you want!" Nurse cried.

"Maybe." Katherina grinned. "All right, yes."

I turned to Nurse. "Perhaps we now have an explanation for

the incident with Aunt Gemma and the infestation of cock-roaches in her bed."

Cesario said fiercely, "That yappy little dog of hers bit Imo-gene and Aunt told her it was her fault because she was a hoy-den and a disgrace to the Montagues and if she wasn't careful—"

Katherina cut him off. "And other stuff."

And if she wasn't careful, she'd be forever unwed like me. I could hear Aunt Gemma saying it now. "Next time Aunt or anybody says anything that deserves cockroaches in the bed, please let me know and—"

Nurse cut me off. "And I'll make sure the cockroaches are delivered."

My sigh was loud enough to make a statement, and I seated myself among my tumultuous siblings and gathered them in my arms. "However, you must promise you won't climb that walnut tree, the one that grows against the house." It was good to be specific when extracting a vow from these children. "That branch was rotten. Another branch could fall."

"Don't take it down, please, please, Rosie. We love that tree!" The clamor from the children deafened me.

"I can't promise anything. If it's rotten to the core, there's no saving it." Rotten to the core brought Duke Stephano to mind again. "But I love that tree, too." In days of yore—and by yore, I mean last week—I'd climbed the trunk, dreamed in the branches, and found quiet from the constant tumult of the household. "Nurse, please tell Gardener to check the condi-tion of the tree and do everything he can to preserve that mag-nificent old wood and give it health." Before Nurse pushed for more strenuous measures, I pointed out, "The offending branch close to my room is sadly gone. There will be no more balcony scenes for me. No one lurks in the garden, do they, to play the part?"

"Any lurkers have departed, apparently on their own two

legs," Nurse assured me. "They've gone elsewhere, and may they stay elsewhere so someone's nurse can rest her weary bones in her own bed!"

Lysander had regained consciousness and left the Montague estate and was . . . somewhere in Verona? I didn't know, but he was alive and relatively unharmed and that gave me hope and comfort.

Katherina watched us as if her dark eyes could see the undercurrents between us. "All the gossip has been about Duke Stephano and his death and the knife you had and the knife in his chest. Is that really all?"

"What else could have happened?" I asked.

"We also heard you fell in love with Lysander of the Marcketti." Katherina gave a forced laugh. "You didn't, did you?"

When I didn't answer right away, Emilia pronounced, "Ha! I told you it was true, Katherina. The rumor has never before been bandied about. Not about Rosie! Look at her. She did fall in love!"

My complexion did not oft reveal my thoughts, so when my color bloomed and my eyes fell, my sisters reacted in all the ways little sisters should, with laughter and jeering and thumping.

Cesario stared, horrified. "No. No. No! You can't. You're the Montague keepsake!"

The girls stopped cheering.

Imogene shoved at his shoulder. "Shut it, boy."

Startled, I said, "What? Cesario, what did you say?"

Cesario sidled away from Imogene and kept talking to me. "That's what Papà says. You're the sister we get to keep."

I was the one who would remain in the backstage and at home forever, unmarried, childless, the aunt, the sister, the female goddess of wisdom who answered the questions and advised on relationships.

Was that what I wanted?

Previously I'd been insistent on that role, then . . . last night happened. Then love and passion had struck like lightning, setting all aflame, showing me a different Rosaline who could use her gifts to command an onstage role. I would be goddess and heroine and lover all in one, and one man most of all would worship my glorious being.

I rose and began to dress. "Perhaps Papà is right. Perhaps not. Now I should go to our mother, who has borne up so bravely in the face of murder in her own home."

CHAPTER 15

I walked toward the double doors of my parents' suite—one did not enter the bedchamber of Romeo and Juliet without abundant caution—and noted that one of the stones creaked when I stepped on it. In the winter, I'd told Papà he needed to have it fixed, and he said he would. I'd do it myself, but Papà had laid claim to the Casa Montague building repairs, and Papà worked on his own, leisurely schedule. When I mentioned it again in the spring, Papà told me not to nag.

Then I pushed him down the stairs.

I didn't really, but I thought about it really hard and he always immediately fixed something completely different. Apparently he simply couldn't stand to do as I asked.

I knocked and entered at my parents' call. My mother sat in her special, comfortable chair with her feet up on a well-padded stool. My father stood close to her, gently stroking her hair.

He had been given the news, I thought. That made my errand easier.

I wore my street clothes and held my black cape over my arm.

"Here she is!" my father said jovially. "Our Rosie!"

"Your keepsake?" I suggested.

He flushed. "Young Lysander would not have it so."

"Papà, what happened between Lysander and me was no more than a moment. He's not the only youth who has fallen in love by moonlight and regained sense with the rising sun." If Lysander had somehow gotten away from our garden, then no need to mention my post-party walnut tree visitor, or his sudden descent and abrupt landing.

"I don't understand you, Rosie. Don't you *want* to be wed?" Papà looked at me the way my siblings stared at the paintings of exotic animals in the books I read them.

Poor Papà. Four—no, five—blighted betrothals and he was only now wondering? "I love only one man, and he is splendid, but my mother is already married to him." It was only a little lie, one that made Papà preen, and avoided for the moment the subject I wished a little longer to hug close to my heart. Before he could regain his baggage train of thought, I said, "Madam Mother, these last few days, I've been distracted with the betrothal, the party, and the, um, murder. I wonder, do you need a tonic to stop the illness of morning?" My gaze lingered on Juliet's waistline.

Juliet put her hands on her belly in a betraying gesture. "Do I show so soon?"

"Not at all, Mother. Only to those who know and love you."

Juliet collapsed with a wail of anguish.

I called for a cool cloth to lay on her forehead, patted her hand, and glared significantly at my father.

He understood and came to kneel beside his wife. He grasped her other hand in both of his and pulled it to his chest. "*Amora*, I'm a good father, am I not?"

Juliet nodded and pressed her handkerchief to her eyes.

"I care for our children, I frolic with them when they're small and as they grow, I teach them swordplay—"

Juliet's eyes snapped open. "I forbade you from teaching the girls. Your mother forbade you from teaching the girls. You listen, do you not, my lord husband?"

"Of course, *mi amora*. Regardless of how much my sweet little girls beg, I won't let them handle my sword."

"I would hope not. It's too long and they could hurt themselves."

"Exactly."

My father and I did not exchange glances. When my mother chose, she could be fierce in her defense of her children and should she discover that years ago, her dearest Romeo had purchased two miniature swords for his daughters and taught them and a few of their closest friends the use of them, she would be most displeased. That they were blunt would make no difference to her, and indeed when used by inexperienced hands, the edge and the point could leave a bruise. As I had discovered, both offensively and defensively.

Releasing Mamma's hand, I stood with my hands folded at my waist, the picture of feminine serenity and propriety.

Such decorous behavior may have cued my mother's suspicions. She dabbed her drying tears. "Romeo, Cesario is too young and your sole heir. You don't teach him yet, do you?"

"No swordplay," Papà said firmly. "After the incident with Paulina, I'm teaching him to defend himself with his fists."

Last year, Cesario had been teasing our five-year-old girl cousin and she'd given him a black eye.

"That's good." Mother hid a smile.

"Better to teach him not to torment a younger child," I said.

"That too. Montagues are never bullies. We're the good guys, and Cesario now understands that." Papà returned to comforting his wife. "The child in your belly will be as loved as all our other children."

Juliet gave a watery smile. "I know. Put simply, I'm very old to be bearing children."

Papà laughed. "Barely thirty-three and still as beautiful as the dawn." He leaned in for a kiss.

Time to forsake this place before they remembered that

when Mamma was already with child, they needed no restraint. I slipped out the door and donned the cloak.

Papà followed sooner than I expected. "You're going to Friar Laurence to make a tonic to stop her sickness?"

"Yes, Papà."

"Get her a strengthening potion, too." Romeo pulled his money pouch off his belt and handed me coins. "I fret when she's tired and ill."

"She'll feel better in a few months," I assured him. "But honestly, my Lord Father, do you have no control? She's already borne seven children!"

Romeo threw his hands into the air. "What do you want me to do? She takes seriously what I poke at her in fun."

"You're not funny!" I shouted.

"Shh." He put a finger to his lips. "Gently. I jest because I worry, Rosie. Each baby, I worry, and we do count the days between her menses, but sometimes . . . God has a soul He wishes to deliver and He chooses us." Romeo looked in equal parts thrilled and afraid.

I hugged him hard. "I know, Papà. I nag because I worry, too. God chooses you and Mother because He wants the child to have a loving home. Mayhap you'll have a second son!"

"Mayhap." He pinched my chin. "Or another daughter of my heart."

I stopped him before he put his pouch away. "Papa, I need a florin."

He frowned at me. "May your father know why you need a florin?"

"I lost a bet with Prince Escalus."

As if disappointed, Papà sighed deeply. "Rosie, if you want to buy yourself a *sorbetto* on the way to see Friar Laurence, you can buy yourself a *sorbetto* on the way to see Friar Laurence. There's no reason to lie about it."

"Yes, Papà." I kissed his cheek.

"You'll take the sedan chair?" He sounded anxious.

"Please don't make me. It's so boring. People stare. The bearers jostle me around. I get seasick."

"I know you don't like it, but—you'll take Nurse? For a woman like you, it's dangerous on the streets of Verona."

"Like me?" I reared back in offense. "I did nothing wrong, and yesterday the streets were safe enough for a woman like me."

"Yesterday, daughter, you had not stumbled on your betrothed's body in our garden while you were holding a knife."

"Why do you think that?" I asked sharply. "Prince Escalus testified that he caught me before I went out."

"I'm your father. How many times have you successfully lied to me?"

"Lots of times."

He sighed in exasperation. "How many times have you successfully lied to your mother?"

My mother, Juliet of the Capulets, detector of untruths. "Mamma enlightened you."

"She told me what she believed was the truth. You've now confirmed it."

"Ohhh." I put my hand to my forehead. An amateur's mistake, and how unlike me! Yet . . . my abhorred betrothal was over. The love of my life had visited my balcony and somehow escaped without harm. My cheer would not be diminished. "Papà, Verona believes Prince Escalus."

"Verona contains a sample of all the peoples of the world. Surely you've met some who love to dispense misery."

His doleful tone rasped at my good spirits. "It's not as bad as all that!"

"Am I not allowed to worry about you, too, Rosie?" he chided.

"I'm very capable."

He knew that, and still he was concerned. "A lady of worth and beauty occasions much envy. Please allow me to know more about the evils of the world than you, daughter." He kissed my cheek. "Ease my mind. Take Nurse."

"As you wish." I watched fondly as he went back to my mother. For all their loving and fighting and making up and emoting, they really were a cute couple.

CHAPTER 16

Many times had I trodden the path from the Montagues' glorious compound on a paved Veronese square to Friar Laurence's humble establishment on a narrow, shadowed alley lined with apothecary shops. Today I kept my hood up and my gaze down as Nurse walked before and shoved people out of the way.

As always, the market square bloomed with riotous flowers, the sellers shouted and the housewives jostled. Rows of rosy apples, blushing pears, yellow onions filled the carts hung with garlic braids, and wheels of thick-rind cheeses could be bought whole or cut as the buyer wished. Wine merchants filled jugs, reunions occurred, arguments flared. Women fetched water from the towering Madonna fountain. Every person could be met here, every staple of food and drink and cheer could be bought here. And the waiting livestock gave off the kind of barnyard odors that made me press my nosegay to my face.

I love this town. It's old, so old, with a tall arena where once, it is said, lions feasted on Christians. The arena had been in use as a theater until a few hundred years ago an earthquake (*the* earthquake, as it is called) knocked down one of the walls. In truth, the earthquake of 1117 had obtained a mythical quality in the telling, and if the old folks were to be believed, most of *my* Verona had been built on the ruins of the old city.

My Verona was raucous and smelly and elegant and dear. All it needed to be perfect was young Lysander striding toward me, a smile on his handsome face and his hand over his generous heart.

Instead a grand horse cantered into the square with a nobleman on its back. The youth was a stranger to my eyes, and a rare sight in this place; aristocrats had servants to do their shopping. He looked about him as if delighted in every act and object that made Verona, and behaved as if he'd passed his life in prison and only now on his release could he see the sunlight in the world. He was so charming heads turned to watch, and Nurse and I stopped in our tracks. I tossed back my hood and smiled at such infectious joy.

"Who is he?" I asked, for Nurse knew everyone and never forgot a face.

"I don't know. He reminds me a little of—" She gasped and spread her cloak as if to conceal me from his gaze.

Too late. His gaze narrowed on Nurse, then his gaze found mine. "Lady Rosaline!" he called. He took care not to trample anyone as he rode toward us. "It is Lady Rosaline, isn't it? And her fearsome nurse who I remember from the life I once enjoyed in Verona?" He dismounted and gave his reins over to the beggar boy who ran up to hold his horse.

I recognized this young man now. Orlando, Duke Stephano's brother and heir, who had been in exile and in hiding. He had been a lad when he fled in fear of his life. Now he was a man; leaner, stronger, someone who watched behind him and in front at the same time. I gasped. "Orlando? I hadn't thought—"

"That I could return from exile once my wicked brother was dead? Yes." Orlando took my hand and kissed it. "And I have you to thank for it!" For good measure he kissed Nurse's hand, too, and she was so overcome she blushed, possibly for the first time in her life, and was speechless, also for the first time in her life.

He'd already been the focus of attention; now passersby had heard him, and looked at him and me. *And me*, and in a way that made clear my father was right; the city wasn't safe for me alone, not until the furor of Duke Stephano's stabbing had died away and the rumors of my guilt forgotten. I pulled up my hood again. "No. Really! No, I didn't kill him. How could I, a feeble woman, overcome a grown man such as Duke Stephano?"

Fiercely he replied, "Believe me, if I knew, I'd have done it years ago."

I tried to divert the subject. "You're here to arrange your brother's funeral."

"Throw his body in a plague pit! What do I care?" He was unshaven, and a sprinkle of hair formed a dark shadow over a jaw shaped of angry derision. "No one can light enough candles to save that man's soul from hellfire, and no one on this earth cares enough to try."

"Hush, sir, I beg you," Nurse said in an undertone.

He noted my expression and her fright, and smiled again in that charismatic manner that had first attracted notice. With his hand on his chest, he bowed. "My pardon. I've forgotten how to behave in polite society. How is your family, Lady Rosaline?"

"They are well. And you, sir? How are your parents?"

"I've sent for them. They're traveling in from the stony castle where brother Stephano forced them to live in hopes they'd develop a cough or a fever of the lungs, and when they arrive we'll unite and sweep all the horrors of the serpent's reign away." Orlando took the reins of his horse and tossed the boy a coin. "I keep you from your errands, but God put you in my way so that I might wait no longer to render my thanks. *Addio*, fair Rosie, our paths will cross again."

As Nurse and I watched him ride away, I said, "He is a Janus, two sides of a man, laughing and dark in equal parts."

"Being seen with him could be dangerous to you. Let us get away." Nurse pushed me ahead of her, and I knew she now carried her knife hidden in her hand. We turned into the alley lined with tall buildings that shut out the direct sun.

Each apothecary had a carved sign above the door, the traditional bowl entwined by a serpent, and some indication of a specialty. On Friar Laurence's sign, a cross marked the bowl, showing his dedication to God.

At the far end of the dead-end alley, in the darkest corner on the left, the bowl looked more like a cauldron that steamed and bubbled. The two women who ran the shop, Agatha and Nunziatina, kept their faces covered in public, and in times of public unrest the shop remained closed and locked; a stench of witchcraft lingered about all of the herbal arts, but Toil and Trouble advertised their knowledge. A bold move, and one that made Friar Laurence worriedly shake his head.

His shop stood first on the right where the light shown brightest. Nurse opened the door for me. The bell over the door tinkled its announcement. She handed me the basket, packed with a meal for Friar Laurence and me, and as I entered, she shut the door behind me. Then, as always, she slipped back onto the streets to shop and visit with her friends.

I entered the dim hush of the narrow shop, lit only by two grimy front windows. I took a deep breath and smelled old books of parchment and paper, dried herbs, ground pastes, fresh flowers and dusty bottles, and for the first time in days, I relaxed. Here on the packed dirt floor and among tall counter tables I was at home.

From the back room, I heard the rumble of men's voices. Friar Laurence I recognized instantly, but the other voice puzzled me, for it sounded very like . . .

Prince Escalus threw back the curtain that separated the rooms and stepped out, holding a bottle and wearing a worried frown.

We both did a double take.

"Lady Rosaline!"

"My prince!" I stumbled into a curtsy.

He observed the mud stains on my cloak, and his already solemn expression stilled into displeasure. "You came here unescorted? Through the streets?" He asked as if he had the right, which although I prickled at the assumption of authority over me, in all honesty he was the keeper of the peace and wished no person to be assaulted or kidnapped in Verona.

I did understand that, and assured him, "My nurse brought me hence."

"A fragile woman to protect a lady of means?"

I laughed. Possibly not the best response when dealing with royalty. "No, Prince Escalus, I promise there's nothing fragile about my nurse. All of Verona knows and fears her. She carries her eating knife, and she *never* has to use it to protect herself or others. She's like the spring melt on the river; if met unwarily, her slap will knock you off your feet." I lowered my gaze so as to not seem as impertinent as I belatedly realized I sounded.

Prince Escalus's cool tone made it clear he was spectacularly unimpressed with my explanation and my feeble gesture of respect. "Nevertheless, when you've completed your business with Friar Laurence, my sedan chair will take you home."

"That won't be for some hours."

"Is the potion you seek so complex?"

"I come here in search of more than a potion. Here I learn craft."

"Craft from a Franciscan monk?" The prince looked around at the dusty shelves, the labeled bottles, the stone mortar and pestles. "What craft is this?"

I suspected from the severity of his tone he wouldn't be pleased with my answer. "I work as his apprentice."

"Lord Romeo allows this?" He gathered outrage about him like a dark cloak.

"Friar Laurence has been a true and loyal advisor and caretaker to our family, and I'm merely the elderly daughter who no man of Verona would now wed." As I spoke, I realized that was true; where before some merchant or aristocrat in need of a wife might have looked on me favorably, now I carried the taint of not only broken betrothals but also a betrothal that ended with the grave. Duke Stephano's murder had ended my chances for marriage as surely as the knife had entered his heart and ended his life. All would shy away. Surely, I had become unmarriageable to all . . . All except, perhaps, Lysander, and some might say he was none too bright in his continued pursuit of a woman under the shadow of suspicion.

Yet last night in the tree he proved a man of intelligence and sharp wit, something I hadn't expected. And why?

To be frank, because his handsome face and manly figure so attracted me and the admiration of other women, I believed he must be a dolt. What kind of person was I to so allow appearances to influence my opinions of character? In the future, I resolved, I would think about a man's character without making assumptions based on beauty.

"You should take care, Rosaline, you allow your thoughts to control your expression." Prince Escalus's warning tone sounded dire in my ears.

How could he see my expression in the light of the dingy windows?

Before I could ask, Friar Laurence bustled through the curtain. When he saw me, his face lit up. His gentle brown eyes searched mine. He hurried toward me, embraced me, said, "Rosie! Rosie! I had such fears that . . ."

He loved me, I knew. We had been good friends since my birth. But this greeting seemed out of proportion with my arrival. Or perhaps . . . "You heard of last night's events?"

"The city is abuzz, and my dread and horror was that you, too, had been harmed."

"I am, as you see, very well in health."

He took a step back, and his mien changed from friend to holy friar. "As your confessor, I must ask—do you have anything to acknowledge?"

I knew what he was asking. "I have no great sins on my soul, Father. I've broken no commandments."

He sighed in relief. "I thought that would be your answer, but as a confessor, I've heard things that—" He looked down as if grieved, then up again into my eyes. "Come to me at any time for any sin."

"Friar Laurence, have I not always trusted you with my sins?" So I did, even though because he recognized my voice I had no chance to remain anonymous. "Last night I was much maligned and perhaps today the speculation continues, for as Papà has rightly declared, some people live to dispense misery as best they can. But sometimes misery turns on them and gives back the bite." I told him what had happened with Porcia.

"Foolish woman. Her parents will be displeased with her return." With a glance over my shoulder, Friar Laurence realized the prince was still there, a lapse out of the good friar's character; he was always alert to the sound of the bell on the door. He started, and bowed. "Is there more you require, my prince?"

"No." Prince Escalus extended his bottle to the good monk. "Send this to my sister via my man. Give him instructions to pass on. Request that he bring my sedan chair back with him, for Lady Rosaline will return to her home in that manner."

Friar Laurence took my shoulders in his chubby hands and looked into my face. "Dear girl, did you feel unsafe on your way here?"

"No, but—"

"A fragile woman, weaker in the mind than a man, is not fit to make these decisions for herself." The prince was crushing in his certainty.

Friar Laurence loosened his grip and stepped away. "You're right, as always, my prince."

I should also agree with Prince Escalus. I should. But I couldn't choke the words through my constricted throat. Yes, I'd heard that and words similar all my life, and shooed them away, ignoring their bite. But when spoken in his coolly aristocratic tone, they burrowed beneath my skin like serenity-sucking ticks.

Friar Laurence looked between us uncertainly.

Prince Escalus pulled a tall stool up to the counter under the window. "In your absence, I'll stay to care for Lady Rosaline and watch her learn your trade."

I shrugged at Friar Laurence and with a sideways nod toward the door, agreed that he should go. I thought it likely the prince wished to discuss last night's events without an audience, and I, too, wondered what information he'd since discovered.

Friar Laurence took the bottle and stepped out the door.

As I tied on my apron, I swallowed my impatience. "My prince, if your equipage is not at hand, how did you get here?"

"Like you, I walked."

That would account for his high leather boots that showed signs of wear.

He continued. "Because I am a man, trained in weaponry"— he touched the dagger at his belt—"the risk is minimal. Furthermore, I bring a trusted bodyguard well trained to protect me."

Furthermore . . . My irritation was back, multiplied. *Furthermore* . . . I was well aware of the honor the prince afforded me with his company. But . . . *furthermore?* That haughty tone and crisp enunciation made me want to empty a jar of stinkweed over his badly inflated head.

"Have you forgotten what you were doing?" Prince Escalus asked.

I realized I stood stock-still, hands on the tie behind my

back, staring at the appropriate jar and its smelly contents. I released the bow and looked down at my palms. With such uncharitable testiness coursing through my veins, I should not make a potion for my mother, for fear my mood would taint its efficaciousness.

"Which of your bodyguards?" I asked. "Marcellus? Holofernes? Dion?"

"In fact, Marcellus accompanies me today."

"Ah." My memory of Marcellus was not fond.

"Why would the *who* be of concern to you?"

"Marcellus is a gentleman of much propriety." I had gathered that the previous night from his withering dialogue.

"And possessed of valuable fighting skills," Prince Escalus told me. "The very day my father released me from the dungeon, Marcellus appeared in Verona with the spoken intent of serving the house of Leonardi. My father recognized his flare with a sword, and also the need to protect me, for I dwelled in the lingering darkness of torture and imprisonment. Papà himself hired him. Now Marcellus commands my guard and the respect of all."

"Then I do respect him." Indeed, I must, for on the subject of propriety and fighting, I acknowledged that Prince Escalus was Verona's lord. Dragging my mind back to the subject at hand, the prince and his superior walking ability, I asked, "Do the people of Verona recognize you?" I asked.

"Indeed. They like to know I wander among them, hear their business and their complaints. I would not have another revolt harm my family or my city, so I listen and I harken to their words."

That was good of him. In my eyes, his actions made him a good podestà, and perhaps explained why he was concerned about me today. I took a long breath and released it—and caught it again when he said, "I wish to speak with you about this shadow that hangs over the death of Duke Stephano."

"I didn't do it." I was more and more defensive.

"I of all people know that."

Yes, rather than stopping me from stumbling across the body, he had observed me. He was a very observant man. Yet—I glanced at his hand—his fingers showed the mark of my teeth, something to remember when he patronized me. I had made him bleed.

Selecting one of Friar Laurence's salves, I pushed the clay jar across the table to the prince. "Put this on that bite."

He opened it and wrinkled his nose at the smell. "Will it sting?"

"Don't be such a baby. A bite from the human mouth can easily poison the humors of the body. As you walk the streets among possible ruffians, you want to be able to defend yourself, don't you?" As I watched him smear on the ointment and wince, I felt I'd repaid him a coin for his condescension. "Has the weapon been recovered from Duke Stephano's chest?"

"It has. It was a small knife, easily hidden, sharp, the blade about the length of my middle finger."

He had long hands, so—"Long enough to reach his heart."

"Yes, and well aimed to do so. The killing thrust was an assassin's thrust, up between the ribs."

"By the look on the duke's face, he recognized his killer, and was surprised. Terrorized, even." I smoothed my apron and pulled my mortar and pestle close.

"Who made Duke Stephano into a coward?"

"He seemed so unafraid of evil deeds and retribution that he could have challenged the devil to a duel." I looked at Prince Escalus in horror and crossed myself. Prince Escalus followed suit. I spoke the truth, but to speak of the devil was to invite him in.

"I understand you witnessed an altercation between Duke Stephano and Titania's parents."

I viewed the prince with surprise. "I did." I told him the details.

He nodded. "Very much what I heard, and for money,

Brambilia is capable of any deed." Did his friends do all the spying for him? Or were there others who informed him of events in Verona?

I pointed out, "But he has no way to recover the money now that Duke Stephano is dead. Although . . ." My recent encounter had to be mentioned. "His brother and heir Orlando has returned to Verona."

"Already? That is . . ."

"Yes." The word *suspicious* hung in the air.

"When we ask who would profit from Duke Stephano's death, Orlando is—"

"Yes. Last, first, and always." Although I liked Orlando, I agreed. He had left unwillingly and come back much changed. "He said he'd sent for his parents, and together they would"— I squinted to remember the exact words—"sweep the horrors of the serpent's reign away."

"I'll summon Orlando, ask him questions and if I'm satisfied, tell him to watch his words and to whom he speaks."

"And warn him about Brambilia."

"That too. I will have peace in Verona. There will be no war over a dead and despised duke."

Before the prince could tell me and once more send me into a frenzy of irritation, I assured him, "I also will be careful what I say and to whom."

His approving nod was not quite as exasperating as his chiding—but only not quite.

"Looking back at the events of the last few days, I must declare I understand nothing about this entire affair." Going to the dusty shelves, I chose the bottles I needed to ease Mamma's morning. "Prince Escalus, do you have any idea why Duke Stephano made an offer for me?"

"You're beautiful." He spoke as if that could be the only explanation.

I brushed that aside. "And have been for most of my life."

The prince barked. It might have been a laugh . . .

I viewed him with surprise. "I'm not conceited, my lord. I'm outshone a thousand times a day by my mother and sisters."

"Beauty is a hallmark of your family," he agreed.

"The fresh bloom is off this rose"—I indicated my almost twenty-year-old face—"and until a week ago, Duke Stephano ignored me. Then the most greedy, despicable, deadly man in Verona took me without a dowry. Coerced my father into giving me to him. Why?"

The prince took a breath. "I fear that's my fault."

CHAPTER 17

Prince Escalus had my complete attention. "How so?"

"As you know, Duke Brutarious of the house of Acquasasso sought to overthrow my father, the podestà of Verona, by stealth and deception. Through the loyalty of our household, my father caught the stench of treachery and sent my mother into sanctuary in a nunnery, where in time she gave birth to my sister, Isabella. I was captured and . . ." He indicated his leg and his face.

"I know. I'm sorry for your suffering."

"My suffering was over long ago, but the shadows of the attempted coup still stretch long across the streets of Verona."

The shop's dim light complemented Prince Escalus's brooding severity. It smoothed out the scars and as I looked, I could see what a handsome man he would have been . . . and still was.

Yes, a wife to cure that brooding. I nodded. He deserved to be happy. I suppose, as did we all.

"My father, Prince Escalus the elder, rallied our allies and taught Duke Brutarious to embrace the long chill of death and exiled his wife, Lady Pulissena, and the entire Acquasasso family to the damp hospitality of Venice. My father freed me from their dungeons, counseled me on what next should happen to consolidate our power—and that night as he slept was murdered by perfidy unknown." Anger and sorrow laced his slow-spaced words.

I thought I knew the story, but I hadn't heard all. I leaned across the counter toward him. "Did you discover who killed your father?"

"Never." Frustration knit the prince's brow. "The assassin slipped away in the night."

"You have your suspicions?" I wasn't really asking; of course he must think and watch and listen, knowing the assassin was out there, a threat to his sister, himself, and the city he loved.

"The Acquasasso weren't alone in their treason, yet after the coup was quelled, those traitorous houses came to me, pledged loyalty on bended knee, paid a hefty fine, and I forgave them even as I confiscated their powers. Duke Stephano's house of Creppa was among them." He watched while I measured ingredients for my mother's morning sickness—dried ginger, peppermint, lemon zest, and cinnamon—into the mortar.

"I find myself unsurprised." With the pestle, I ground the herbs, fruit, and spice into a fine powder. The scents rose and filled the room, lightening my heart.

Not so, it seemed, for Prince Escalus. He kept his somber gaze on my hands as if fascinated by my prowess. "I would never trust those leaders who participated in the attempted coup d'état. Yet with death and struggles within the houses, family patriarchs do change. As each new head takes his place, I assess him and his loyalty to me and Verona, and restore favors accordingly."

I was both fascinated and flattered. Prince Escalus had been patronizing and infuriating, yet now he spoke to me as if I had a mind, as well as a heart. That was a novelty, and a novelty repeated twice in the last day with two different men. Had the world suddenly become as round as the heretics claimed? "Duke Stephano took over for his father, Duke Pietro."

The prince nodded. "Duke Stephano claimed the old man

suffered from senility, that that was the reason Duke Pietro joined the coup, and he sent his parents away to a place in the Alps, where, he said, his father would heal in the fresh air."

I lifted the pestle and stared at Prince Escalus. "Freeze to death, according to Orlando."

"I also heard that, and my investigations have proved it true. He put his parents in a miserable old castle, stripped away all but the most loyal of retainers, and left them to fend for themselves in that cold, hard place. Once they had left, Duke Stephano came to me and oh so obsequiously begged to return to favor." The prince lifted one shoulder. "Should I trust a man who treats his father and mother so callously?"

I thought of my parents and their wild impassioned love for each other and their deep affection for their children. I also remembered the distance between so many of my friends and their parents. "Is his father so bad a man?"

"Duke Pietro, I believe, is weak and easily swayed. His sincere contrition for his part in the rebellion seemed to my eye to be genuine, as did his assurance he'd been told my father and my family would be unharmed."

"I remember Duke Pietro. He was a kind man, at least to the young girl I was. He listened when I spoke. So few adults do."

That must have struck a chord in Prince Escalus, for he gave one of those facial quirks he used for a smile. "I remember him, too. I thought he listened because I was the son of the podestà. It's good to know he was so—"

Thoughtlessly, I interrupted. "Genuine."

The prince seemed unruffled. "Yes. It'll be good to see him in Verona once more."

We were silent. The only sound was the scraping of my pestle against the stone. The only scent was the medicine I mixed for my mother. I felt oddly peaceful here with Prince Escalus, safe and warm. For such an exasperating man, he had an unpretentious air. I glanced up and found him watching me, my face, which made me more aware of the sound, the scent, the peace, our isolation—and suddenly anxious to clarify something he had said. "You haven't yet told me, have you, why it's your fault that Duke Stephano offered for me?"

He lifted his finger. "Patience."

"I am patient." *But could you get to the point?*

A lift of his brow told me his opinion of my patience, but he made no comment. "When Duke Stephano came to me and begged to take up the Creppa duties relating to Verona's governing, I smiled at him and promised him I would reassess his responsibilities. I proceeded with caution. Then young Orlando sent me a frantic message before fleeing Verona in the dark of night."

"What was the message?"

"That he feared for his life. He was fourteen, ill-equipped to fend for himself without family or money. I sent a man to find him, give him money and counsel, advised him to wait patiently."

My gut burned as I considered the plight of young Orlando. "Should you trust Duke Stephano, who not only exiles his parents, but makes his young brother run from all he's known, from safety and home?"

"My thoughts exactly. I hoped Duke Stephano would make a move against me. Against Verona. Then I would know, and deal with him accordingly." Prince Escalus lifted his hands as if he couldn't believe what happened next. "He must have realized I watched him, for instead, his first marriage ended in an unfortunate death, and he married again. And again."

"And almost again."

"Almost. Your escape came close to the impossible."

I was well aware of the irony of sitting here discussing the horrors that had happened and that could have happened.

I wondered how I had been so lucky to escape the Creppa family's eerie tomb, where so recently Titania had been laid to rest among his previous dead and moldering wives.

The prince continued. "In the meantime, Orlando languished in exile, became a mercenary, became impatient with me."

"Six years is forever to a youth."

"It can be forever for any man. Women are more patient."

I lifted my eyebrows at him.

"Or not?" He lifted his eyebrows back at me.

In as neutral a tone as I could manage, I said, "I'm sure what's true for one woman must be true for all."

He leaned back and scrutinized me, and again I thought what a careful and vigilant man he was. "I lost my mother not long after Bella was born," he said. "She never recovered from the birth, and that was a source of great grief for me, and a loss unimaginable for my sister, who sore needs a woman's guidance. Again I lost my young wife with the birth of my son, and my son as well. You eloquently tell me your thoughts without saying the actual words, and in the future, I'll not try to disentangle the complexities of womanhood without your guidance."

He spoke honestly, and I replied as such. "There are no complexities of womanhood. Every woman is complex in herself, as is each man. You are not the same as Duke Stephano."

"What a compliment. I'll try not to allow conceit to overcome me."

I kept my head down but couldn't contain a smirk. He did have humor, our prince, but hid it beneath a cloak of austerity.

Prince Escalus said, "I don't even understand a man who thoughtlessly and willfully makes so many enemies. How is a prince to discover his murderer?"

"Does anyone in Verona clamor for justice?" I meant, why bother finding his murderer?

"None, when they believe I'm not listening, they seem content to blame you for the murder—"

I gave an explosive sound of vexation.

"But I'm the podestà. My directive is to seek the truth. And . . . in this case, the truth could be a seer."

CHAPTER 18

I comprehended the prince's meaning. Was the Duke Stephano's stabbing an act of ill will to the dead man? On casual inspection, and in the words of his servants and enemies, it would seem so, but if political forces were at work, Prince Escalus needed to understand those forces.

"You don't truly suspect Porcia?" He seemed truly interested in my reply.

"No." I scraped my mother's nausea medicine into a linen bag, tied it tightly, and placed it beside me. "Porcia's a sodden wit, but she's not a killer sodden wit. I almost feel sorry for her, condemned from her own mouth to return disgraced to her father's house."

"You're kind, considering how much she contributed to the belief in your guilt."

"She's wretched in herself. Surely that's punishment enough." I opened a jar, removed a handful of dried leaves, and mashed them.

"What's that?" the prince asked.

"Comfrey. It eases bruises, sprains, and aching joints." I would give it to Lysander when next I saw him, for he should indeed be bruised after last night's misadventure. To the prince, I warned, "It's also a poison, so it is to be used in a poultice only."

"You know the effects and uses of the contents of all these jars?" Prince Escalus gestured around him.

"Not all. I am an apprentice only. I have not the skill to mix such complicated medicines as does Friar Laurence." I thought of the potion he had given my mother, the one that put her into a sleep of death for two and forty hours. That was indeed a difficult potion, and one that required a delicate touch. "But when he agreed to teach me, his first and most serious task was to show me where he kept the plants that were not to be ingested. He warned that an accidental poisoning was taken as seriously as a deliberate one."

"Why does he keep poisons?"

I tamped down impatience. This was the prince. He was ignorant of the details of household and garden. And as prince, he naturally had a suspicious bent to his nature. "Ask the steward of your palace and he who tends your garden. Rodents and insects get into the storeroom and wreak havoc with the food stores. Squirrels steal the nuts. Moles dig up the garden, and rabbits eat from above. Friar Laurence says they all spread disease. We can't ever win against the pests, but we can curb them before they breed."

"Ah." He relaxed. "Poisons are in every household."

"Every household," I assured him.

"Friar Laurence—you trust him wholly?"

"I do, indeed. My family owes its existence to the good friar."

The door opened, the bell jingled, and Friar Laurence's great bulk filled the doorway. His humble brown robes declared his order, and the three knots on his corded rope cincture stood for poverty, chastity, and obedience. "The bottle is gone to your sister, my lord, and I took patience with your man to give the proper instructions for her health." The good monk looked anxious and nervous; although he was deservedly a famous alchemist, the honor of having the Prince of Verona in his shop appeared to overwhelm him.

Politely I inquired, "Your sister is not ill, I hope, my prince?"

"Not ill. She's eleven." Prince Escalus seemed to think that explanation enough.

Perhaps it was. "I have younger sisters. Is there aught I can do?"

He stood and leaned across the counter. "Would you?"

His eagerness startled me. "Of course."

Friar Laurence hovered in the background. With a slight hand gesture, I indicated he should return to his labors, and he crept around the shop, or as much as a man of his girth could creep.

I seated myself on my own stool and spoke to the man who had reluctantly showed emotion . . . until now. "What help can I offer?"

"As a small child, Bella was sweet, affectionate, and loving, and I felt acutely the loss of our mother in guiding her footsteps into womanhood. When my wife died bearing our son, sorrow filled us both and we clung together." Affection and worry threaded his voice. "I thought we were close and loving, brother and sister, a family. But lately she has become—"

I chuckled. "Yes, I know. That age for young women is fraught with tempest."

"You know? You do? You understand?"

"One moment she's a child, the next she's a woman, the next a termagant, the next a penitent."

"Yes!" He looked honestly shocked at my insight. "How did you know?"

"It's perfectly natural. The place between childhood and womanhood is a wilderness of briars and monsters we all must cross." When we cross as girls, we're slashed by thorns and whipped by awkwardness, and on the other side, we're one with womanhood, but we're never as we were before. We are, in many ways, strangers to ourselves. Yet I could see no reason to tell Prince Escalus that truth; he would probably, as most men did, turn his gaze away and imagine the princess, his sister, was merely a girl grown into a woman rather than a girl grown into wisdom.

"This month she has pain. I think . . . um . . . I think . . . you know." He was so embarrassed.

Which was charming in a small family sort of way. In my household, poor Papà tried to ignore the female monthly travails, but with so many of us mostly cycling at the same time, the fighting and weeping made that almost impossible. Even Cesario knew to walk softly when the moon was full. "I understand."

"She's crying and won't let me near her."

"Poor child." Suffering in that big, dark, formal palace. "Does she have not a nurse?"

"When Bella was but five, I found her nurse overcome with wine. I dismissed her, and my little sister confessed it happened all too often. I blame myself. I was unobservant."

I scrutinized him, checking the boxes in my mind.

1. Prince Escalus appeared to be without emotion, yet he deeply loved his sister.
2. He shouldered responsibility and took blame without whining
3. He was deeply alone and, I thought, lonely.

I *had* to find this man a good wife.

As the prince and I spoke, Friar Laurence gathered herbs for another potion. No, wait, he was examining the contents of my basket with a smile. I'd brought enough for several hearty meals, and Friar Laurence was dedicated to fine dining. As he emptied the basket, I suggested, "Why don't I invite Princess Isabella to visit us? My parents are beloved among my friends, my sisters would show her how to be a woman, my brother loves all women and—"

"Your brother?" The prince's eyes grew cold.

"Cesario. He's six." I waited for him to realize that I had no designs to bring his sister into my family by nefarious means.

Being a man, he admitted to no fault. "That's right. I believe I sent a christening gift."

"A silver cup. Our family thanks you. I promise to try to keep Cesario from teaching her to climb trees."

"Bella would not . . . But perhaps if she climbed a tree . . ." The prince rubbed his forehead. "She hides in the library. She broods so much!"

Friar Laurence lifted the concoction I had made for my mother's morning sickness and sniffed it. "Again?" Heaven knows why he sounded surprised. If you'll recall, he witnessed their impetuous passion and performed the secret marriage between Romeo and Juliet to save them from sin, as well as to unite the two warring clans of Montague and Capulet.

That plan almost foundered like an overweight galleon, and he doesn't mess with those potions anymore. At least . . . not to my knowledge.

"Again," I said to Friar Laurence. I turned back to Prince Escalus, whose face was schooled in polite disinterest in the meaning of my potion. "I could speak with Isabella if she needs more guidance, and my mother is most loving, although I deem Katherina would be a better confidant. She and Bella are almost the same age and might become friends."

"Surely they would!" The prince sounded almost cheerful.

"Because they're both female and of an age?"

"I've misspoken again?"

At his wry expression, I laughed. "The Montagues are famed for their hospitality. Let's try this and pray your lady sister finds friendship and comfort somewhere among us."

"I will so pray."

Speaking of my family reminded me . . . "Prince Escalus, I have the florin I owe you." I half thought he'd refuse it, say he'd cheated, laugh at me for offering it, then on the way home I would indeed get myself a *sorbetto*.

Instead he looked at the coin and smiled that odd half smile. "Thank you." He placed it in a hidden pocket on his doublet and walked out of the shop, and his limp, I noted, was more severe than of the previous day.

"Wait a minute!" He hadn't told me why it was his fault Duke Stephano asked for my hand in marriage. "Come back!"

As if he had heard me, he limped back in on Nurse's heels.

Nurse, the unflappable, the stoic, the daunting, rushed in, cheeks flushed, mouth agape, eyes wide with alarm.

I feared for her health. "Nurse, what is it?"

She leaned against the counter to catch her breath. "She . . . She . . ."

Prince Escalus pushed a stool under her rump. "Sit, good woman, and speak. She . . . who?"

Friar Laurence put a goblet of wine into her hand.

She drank, sputtered, wiped her hand on her gray linen sleeve. "I heard it on the street. I confirmed. I talked to her servants. It's true!"

I'd never seen her so overwrought. "Nurse, calm please." I dampened my handkerchief in a basin of water and calming flowers, wrung it out, and blotted her ruddy cheeks. "Tell us the news."

"Porcia." She wiggled her fingers above her head to indicate the absurd headdress. "Porcia was found this morning— poisoned. Dead!"

CHAPTER 19

I stood, my hand holding the pestle, frozen in shock.

Prince Escalus gripped my shoulder as if to hold me in place or give me support.

Behind me, something heavy hit the floor, rattling the glass bottles and bringing down sprinkles of dust. Turning, I saw Friar Laurence's limp and mighty bulk sprawled, arms and legs akimbo. I rushed to his side, felt his pulse in his neck. He was alive—but his eyeballs had rolled back in his head and his breathing was shallow. "Spiced wine." I held out my hand, in command without caring who obeyed.

Nurse thrust a cup in my hand.

Prince Escalus helped me lift Friar Laurence's lolling head off the floor.

I passed the wine under the good friar's nose, which twitched. He roused slowly, his eyelids fluttering, and stared into my face in confusion. With a mighty gasp, he pushed himself into a sitting position, and only quick action on my part saved the wine. He fixed his gaze on Nurse. "Porcia . . . was poisoned?"

"There is no doubt," she told him.

He put his hand on his chest, closed his eyes, and breathed.

"Do you have a pain?" I asked.

"Yes, but not such a pain as mere medicines can cure."

When I moved to take the wine away, he plucked it from my grasp. "Nevertheless . . ." He drank deeply and put the cup aside.

In a neutral tone, Prince Escalus asked, "Did you sell someone poison who you fear would have murdered Porcia?"

"No, my prince. I sell poison judiciously, to those who use it to control the pests that plague us all." To Nurse and I, Friar Laurence said, "Help me up."

When we would have obeyed, Prince Escalus brushed us aside and with his arms under Friar Laurence's armpits, he hauled him to his feet.

Friar Laurence staggered a little, put a hand on the counter to steady himself, and sat on the stool Nurse had so recently abandoned. When Prince Escalus began to speak again, Friar Laurence raised a hand. "Do not ask. I'm a friar. I cannot divulge what I hear in confession."

Prince Escalus pressed him nonetheless. "You do know something?"

"I *know* nothing, and what I suspect doesn't bear thinking about."

I could see Prince Escalus wanted to insist. He wanted to bring to bear his authority as podestà. But against the greater weight of God and Church, he had no tools.

Friar Laurence heaved himself up. "With the memory of Porcia's accusations against you, Rosie, it would be safer if you immediately returned to the Montague compound."

"When my man returns with my sedan chair, she'll go at once." Prince Escalus turned to my nurse. "You, too, will ride inside. As Friar Laurence said, Porcia's accusations against Rosie will spark malicious gossip and possibly civil unrest. You'll both stay out of sight behind the curtains, as proper and modest women should. If there's trouble, my carriers will protect you."

"Yes, my prince." Nurse curtsied.

I did the same and replied the same, but I wondered at his intensity. Was insurrection so close that Porcia's poisoning coming on the heels of Duke Stephano's stabbing could in fact cause fighting in the streets? Or during his walk through Verona, had he heard more than he admitted?

"I go now." He swept a glance across us all, then focused on me. "Until you arrive home, speak to no one. Obey me, Rosie."

As I do always, podestà of Verona.

I hear and obey, Prince Escalus.

Both would have been quiet, proper replies. Instead I snapped, "I'm not stupid!"

Nurse and Friar Laurence gave identical sighs.

Prince Escalus shook his head. "Not stupid, but unseeing and unhearing. Good day." And he was gone.

"Really," I said out loud. "Unseeing and unhearing I am not. He's the one who . . . who . . . didn't tell me why it was his fault Duke Stephano asked for my hand in marriage."

"What?" Nurse was clearly bewildered.

"Prince Escalus. He said it was his fault Duke Stephano applied to marry me. He was going to tell me why and somehow, he did not." I glared at the others, and jumped at a firm rap at the door.

A man dressed in a gentleman's finery stuck his head into the shop. I knew him, Marcellus of the critical gaze. "Lady Rosaline." He bowed. "The prince's sedan chair awaits. Prince Escalus asked me to stand guard over you as you travel through the Veronese streets. It's my privilege to do so. We leave at once." He disappeared again.

I began, "Does every man in the world think—"

"Yes, he does. I don't know why you even bother to ask!" Nurse said.

While Friar Laurence put the medicine and tonic in my basket, Nurse took my cloak off the hook and threw it over my shoulders, and we stepped into the street. The sedan chair stood close against the door. The attendants held the curtains open, protecting us from unfriendly eyes while keeping theirs averted. The wooden steps had been placed on the ground. Nurse and I climbed in. I sat on the forward-facing seat. She sat on the backward-facing seat. The basket rested on the floor between us and our knees almost touched, yet when compared to all others, this sedan chair was spacious indeed. The attendants shut the curtains and lifted us, and we moved toward the end of the alley. At least, I think we did. We sat totally surrounded by drapes and wood and ornaments that glittered. I smelled sandalwood and leather and flowers and . . . wow. Even in the near dark of total enclosure, this was opulent. I was stroking the soft leather cushions of the sedan chair when someone ripped back the curtains and screamed, "Beware, Lady Rosaline! *He* marked you when you accepted his suit!"

I caught a glimpse of wild black hair, wild green eyes, a scarred throat, and black clothing torn into floating wings that fluttered as she waved her arms—this was Miranda, the darling of the *trovatori*, the singer of great renown who had been Duke Stephano's mistress.

Nurse leaped up, hit her head on the roof, fell onto her knees in front of me, her arms spread defensively wide and her knife in one hand.

The sedan chair swayed as the bearers thumped it to the ground.

"*He* was a lover like no other, inflicting pain and passion in equal parts, and you were going to be *his* wife. Do you know what that means?" I caught a gust of sour wine on her breath. "The other wives have returned for you and you're surrounded by their essence, their malice, embodied into—"

"Jezebel!" Marcellus grabbed her from behind. "How dare you attack the Lady Rosaline."

She turned and shrieked into his face. "I do not attack! I warn! Lady Rosaline is in danger. Death stalks her and seeks to enclose her in a cold embrace." She was a talented soprano, and her projection and volume, as well as the high, pure notes she hit, forced Marcellus to stagger backward, hands over his ears. One of the bearers tackled her from behind. The others wrestled her to the ground.

These guys were more than bearers. They were protectors, defenders, guards under Marcellus's command.

Yet Miranda fought, and sang with the strength of a madwoman. "Doomed! Doomed unless you learn to search out the dead ones before they take you into their tomb to suffer restless death!"

When the guards finally lashed her arms together, they stood her up. She looked at me, her face so sorrowful that I commanded, "Let her speak."

In a soft, kind voice, quite unlike her previous soprano cries, she said, "I've seen my own doom. I have no chance. You have been chosen. Only you can contain this plague, or you and all those around you will die." As they dragged her away, she wailed, "Beware . . . !"

The curtains fell, closing us in.

Nurse dropped her outspread arms. Her prosaic words contrasted strongly with the previous melodrama. "Her wits have turned like fish in the sun." With a grunt, she got up off the floor. "My knees aren't meant for this."

She seated herself. The bearers picked up the sedan chair. We started on our way again.

I didn't know what to think. Miranda might be mad, but she believed what she said. "The trouble—" I began.

"I know the trouble. She might be mad, but Duke Stephano is stabbed. Porcia is poisoned."

"Yes, and that woman is tossed on the wild seas of love's grief."

"Or merely afloat on the wine barrels of our waterfront innkeepers." Nurse waved her hand in front of her face to ward off the odor.

"That, too, but her grief and concern seem genuine." The bearers moved so smoothly through the streets, the usual affliction of motion sickness did not take me, yet still my contemplations left me ill with worry. If Miranda thought her warnings to be sincere, and if my betrothal to Duke Stephano had caused a threat to me, well and good, I would take the risk. But to my family? To my brother and sisters? To Romeo and Juliet themselves? No, that could not be borne. "What do we tell my parents?"

"About Porcia? About Miranda's assault on the street? The truth, else someone else tells them. The prince, for instance."

"There's telling them, and there's breaking the news gently." When Nurse hesitated, I said, "How much shouting can you stand in one day?"

She sighed in exasperation. "Yes, all right. We'll do what we can to mitigate the damage. Here. I was going to give it to you when we got home, but just . . . here." She handed me a long, narrow package wrapped in paper. "You must have it before you have need of it."

In my lap, the paper fell away and in the dim light, I saw a leather holster and the hilt of a knife. I looked up at her.

Briskly she unlaced my cuff and pushed up my sleeve. She looked at the wrap around the two small wounds and tsked. "We're doing this none too soon," she said, and used leather straps to tie on the holster. "You pull the knife when you're threatened. Give it a try."

I slid my hand up my sleeve, grasped the hilt, and pulled the knife free.

"There you go. Try not to *accidentally* hurt yourself, and anyone who attacks you will be surprised when you are a warrior rather than a maiden to be raped and murdered." She looked into my eyes and with emphasis on every word, she said, "Before you pull it, you must be prepared to defend yourself, and at once. Otherwise it could be used against you."

"I know. Papà taught me that when he showed me how to use a sword."

Of course Nurse knew that, and had faithfully kept it from Mamma. "I depend on his training to give you the element of surprise."

"Yes. Thank you, dear Nurse. This is exactly what I desired." Although last night, I hadn't imagined I would want it quite this much.

CHAPTER 20

The prince's sedan chair came to a halt in front of Casa Montague. The bearers lowered it, opened the curtain, and set the steps to allow us to descend, me first, then my nurse.

Marcellus swept off his feathered cap. "My lady, we deliver you safe. I beg you forgive me for the interruption of your travels. I vow that woman will not bother you again."

I put my hand on his arm. "Sir, I beg you treat her kindly. She's far gone in grief for her lover."

"She made an attack on the sedan chair of Prince Escalus. He will render judgment, not me." He bowed again.

His chilly countenance struck an uneasy chord in me. He seemed to be a man without kindness, caring only for what was proper and judging each person by their rank. I wondered . . . would he use terror to enforce his opinion of propriety?

Would he kill?

He handed Nurse the basket. "We wait for you to safely enter your home."

I nodded. Glancing around the square, I could see curtains sway as neighbors observed the princely crest sewn on the curtains and carved onto the back of the wooden chair.

As Nurse twitched my cloak around me, she smiled in satisfaction. "That'll give 'em something to gossip about. Something besides the murder, anyway." She followed me toward the great wooden doors crowned with the Montague crest.

I lifted the great iron knocker and dropped it. The sound echoed through the spaces inside. "Couldn't we give them somebody besides me to be the object of their curiosity?"

"Porcia has done that in her death." Nurse lost her smile. "Get inside quickly before Lady Luce loses all sense of propriety and dashes out to interrogate you about today's shocking news."

Nurse and I entered quietly, as was our wont when coming from Friar Laurence's, for all in the Montague household preferred to pretend they knew not what I was doing. Despite Friar Laurence's sanctified sponsorship, when a woman is already under suspicion of killing her betrothed and possibly a mouthy contemporary, it was best not to add to the disturbance.

I discarded my cloak into Nurse's arms, and a house girl bobbed a curtsy as she received the cloak to brush. Nurse herded me toward the stairs to change out of my work clothes and into a more appropriate attire for an evening with my family, and as we climbed the first steps, the bell on the street rang decisively and a man's voice cried out, "The Princess Isabella arrives!"

"What? *Shit!* Now? I just . . ." I turned and looked helplessly at Nurse. "I invited her a mere two hours ago!"

"She's a princess. She's here." Nurse was more used to aristocratic vagaries than me.

"Prince Escalus reads me an overbearing oratory about civil unrest in Verona and getting home unseen"—I flung my hand toward the entry—"and it's okay for her to be out?"

"For the moment, she's untouched by the taint of murder," Nurse said.

"I'm untouched, too!" I tapped my chest. "Innocent, remember? If he's so worried about fighting in the streets, isn't his sister someone to protect at all costs?"

"Mayhap she's a mule like someone else I know and didn't listen!" Nurse thrust the basket at me and hurried up the stairs. "I'll round up the children and get them tidied."

"I'm not a mule," I muttered.

"Meet us back in the grand hall," Nurse instructed.

As our man Tommaso hurried toward the door, I rushed down the stairs and grabbed his arm. "Slowly. Slowly," I cautioned. "Walk with a grand and solemn pace. Take her to the grand hall and offer a seat and refreshments. We'll be there as soon as we can get ourselves"—I made a mashing gesture with my hands—"together."

Tommaso got his breath. He was young, new to his position, and he didn't know all the maneuvers involved in welcoming unexpected guests. He bowed to me. "Yes, Lady Rosie, thank you for the instruction," and he started toward the door with less speed.

Mamma had found him, a boy on the street, fighting for his life, and brought him home, where he could learn to work in a noble household. He moved up steadily for he learned quickly; my mother's astute eye had seen what was hidden beneath the grime of the city.

I ran toward my mother's room, calling, "Mamma! Mamma!"

Her maid met me. "My lord Romeo took Lady Juliet to a play."

"Now? What was he thinking?" I snarled. Then, because it wasn't the maid's fault, I said, "Good, that should distract her." I pulled the cloth off my basket and handed her the tonic and the medicine. "You know what to do with these."

She took them gingerly. "I do."

"On Lady Juliet's arrival, tell her Princess Isabella has arrived on my invitation."

The maid's eyes grew round. "Princess Isabella? I caught a glimpse of her once from a distance. She's so . . . royal!"

Lips pressed together to quell my smile, I nodded. Yes, the house of Leonardi was Verona's answer to Florence's Medici family, and the young, beautiful, reclusive Isabella was the star in a celebrity hunter's firmament.

I rushed toward my sisters' bedroom and found Nurse directing traffic while they descended into a state of wild thrashing of clothes and shoes and cranky rebellion.

Their cries attacked me as I entered. "Rosie, why is she here now?" "How could she come without notice?" "What are we supposed to do with her?"

I held my hand to my lips and waited for silence. "*I* invited Princess Isabella to visit us."

Katherina dropped her hands and glared, "Rosie!"

"You know I would have given you notice. I didn't know she would come so soon. Please, my *sorelle*, listen. The prince reports that his sister is alone as she becomes a woman."

"Ohhh." Everyone understood that.

"We, all of us, support each other. Surely we can share that support with a princess even if she arrives too soon." I smiled a quirky smile.

Katherina, always generous, said, "I'm almost dressed, I'll go to her at once."

"Take her out to the garden, teach her how to play, talk to her . . . I must change from my work clothes into something older sister suitable."

Katherina touched my hand. "You are the ultimate older sister. Find us when you can." And she was gone toward the grand hall. The others followed, running and calling.

Our home was alive with voices, song, laughter, family. I hoped we would bring Isabella comfort in her loneliness. Nurse followed me to my bedroom, stripped me out of my street clothes, and removed the scabbard and blade she'd strapped to my arm. She set that aside, then stuffed me into a gown of green velvet with embroidered gold sleeves and cuffs, elegant yet modest, simple and suitable for a quiet day at home. As she worked, she gloated. "Two sedan chairs from the podestà's household in one day. Two! Lady Luce and her haughty maid will be beside themselves with envy and curiosity!"

I shared a grin with her. "Maintain an air of mystery and drive them wild."

Nurse pushed me out the door. "You're a wicked one. I will."

I rushed down the corridors, guided by our servants' pointing fingers, past the great hall, and out to the garden tree swing, where my sisters and my brother had brought Isabella to entertain her. I stood in the shadows and observed, much as I imagined her brother would do in these circumstances.

Isabella was a slim, pale lady with blond hair and a still face that declared feelings were too much trouble to express, or perhaps even to have. She was the female embodiment of her brother, an untouchable impression of royalty, a portrait posed and waiting to be painted.

Yet my siblings saw no reason to respect that royalty. They argued that she should try the tree swing.

She refused.

They called her a whimpering goose, treated her as if she were one of our own. I thought for a few moments she would retreat, leave our home, never to be seen again, but without warning, she sat on the swing's wooden seat and with a defiant glare, pushed herself with her feet. At first it was only a slight swaying. Cesario heckled her, and she pushed higher and higher until she was reaching for the sky, then the ground, then the sky, then . . .

I took a moment to appreciate the absolute joy of her movements, her freedom, her first sensation of flying. In that moment, Princess Isabella was a child, untroubled by earthbound concerns, about the changes in her body, about the trials of the past and the tribulations to come. How lovely to see that transformation.

Until Cesario shouted, "It's my turn. My turn!"

My sisters picked up the call.

At first Isabella paid them no heed. She had not been trained to take turns. But she turned her head and heard Cesario bellowing at the top of his lungs, and observed my sisters' indignation. She dragged her feet and came to a stop.

Katherina stepped forth and explained, "Cesario is six. He gets to swing next. Then Emilia, then Imogene, then me. We all get our turns. Then you again."

Isabella stared as if Katherina was speaking a foreign language, and for a moment I feared I would have to provide mediation.

But Isabella stood. "I comprehend." She watched Katherina help Cesario onto the swing and give him a push. "You help him?"

"He's my little brother." Katherina clearly thought that was obvious.

"I try to help my brother, too," Isabella confessed, "but he's older and he doesn't think I can help."

"He's a boy," Katherina said with disdain. "They think they are *sooo* smart."

Isabella laughed, a startled explosion of sound.

A good time for me to introduce myself. I stepped forward and curtsied. "Princess Isabella, I'm Lady Rosaline. Welcome to the Montague home. I hope you're finding joy in the company of my sisters and brother."

The princess immediately reverted to her royal personage. She curtsied stiffly, inclined her head, and offered her hand. I wasn't sure if she expected me to kiss it. Instead I took it and held it between my own. "I'm glad your brother the prince extended my invitation to you, and that you came swiftly."

"He insisted I come *immediately*. I tried to tell him proper warning should be courteous, but he . . ."

"Thinks he's *sooo* smart." Deliberately I echoed Katherina's words.

Isabella smiled shyly. "Yes. Do we always have to let them think they know more than us?"

Katherina and I heaved identical sighs.

"I'm afraid so," I said.

Katherina reprovingly shook her head at me. "Rosie, you don't."

"I do!" Honesty led me to add, "As much as I'm able."

"Katherina, it's your turn!" the other children called.

Katherina hurried to the swing and hopped on. Imogene gave her a push, and soon she wore the same expression of joy Isabella had worn.

The princess looked around our lush expanse of walled garden. "You have many trees. Why doesn't your gardener put in a swing for each of you?"

"Because my mother wants us to learn to play together."

"Does she always get her way?"

"Yes."

"Is she cruel?"

"My mother?" I gave a peal of laughter. "She's the dearest woman in the world. As soon as she returns, she'll be out to greet you. You'll stay for dinner? I'll have the servants set a setting for you."

"I don't know if Escalus will approve."

"I'll send him a note." I hurried along toward the house and met my mother coming down the stone and gravel path.

She caught my arm. "The princess?"

"She's eleven. Prince Escalus is worried about her as she crosses into womanhood. I offered and he sent her . . . at once."

"He is her support? He's a cold man without understanding."

I remembered his earnest concern, and said, "Not so. He cares for her very much."

"So you say, but does he know how to show her? I think not. Poor child." Mamma hurried around me and toward the swing. "We'll show her a refuge where she may come to be surrounded by family."

I stood there, silent, alone and smiling.

"Mistress?" Gardener stood off the path in the shade of a cypress tree. He was old enough to be my grandfather and a solitary man, unused to speaking, relating more to plants than to people. He had come to know me when I was a child and now he listened politely when I directed him, allowed me to think myself in charge of the gardens, and did whatever he liked.

It was a good arrangement.

Still intoxicated with the feeling that my family would be an excellent balm for Princess Isabella's woes, I moved off the path to join him. In a small shaded alcove surrounded by tall, trimmed boxwood hedges, I asked, "What is it, Gardener?"

His shaggy eyebrows waggled ominously at me. "Mistress, I looked at the branch on the walnut tree. I have bad news. Such bad news."

"Oh no," I breathed.

The tree. The mighty walnut tree that every child in my family climbed and loved and dreamed in . . . was rotten. It would have to be taken down, and all the traditions and joy that the tree created would finish among tears and lamentation.

"The branch that broke outside your window . . . sabotage has been its untimely end."

CHAPTER 21

I had been mourning in one direction. Gardener's words jerked my head around and focused my attention on what had happened the night before to Lysander. "Sabotaged. What do you mean?"

"Someone repeatedly climbed that tree and sawed through that branch, top and bottom, until it was connected to the tree with a slim plank, deliberately creating danger for the next person who sat on the branch."

My face felt funny: stiff and unyielding, as if anger and distress had wiped normal expression away and left me unable to do more than barely move my lips. "How do you know . . . ?"

He picked up the remnants of the branch and with one shaking, gnarled finger showed me metal shards and marks of rust that had rubbed off in the doing of the deed. "Done with an iron saw, it was."

"Your iron saw?"

"No, lady. For my years of dedication, your father, Lord Romeo, gifted me with a steel saw."

I knew that. I had suggested the gift to Papà.

Gardener continued. "Its strength is that of ten iron saws, and it doesn't shed its teeth like this. I keep it hidden in my room under my mattress. Although the young gardeners beg, no one touches it but me. When I saw this destruction, I did check to make sure it's still there and safe." He spoke slowly, as a man must who daily communed with plants and seldom with people. "It is. But for all that an iron saw isn't as good, it's still an expensive piece to use to harm a good tree that produces shade every summer and walnuts every autumn. It hurts my heart to imagine what confusion and pain the tree must feel. What dungshoe would do such a cruel thing, Lady Rosie? No one under this roof, I pray!"

"I pray, also." Thoughts whirled in my mind, assessments of risk for my siblings, my parents . . . and me. "Can you tell when this was done?"

"Day of the party."

"Yesterday."

"Yes. And a year ago."

"What?"

"And five years ago."

"Someone has been sawing on that branch for . . . years?" I tried to wrap my mind around the idea that one person—or was it many persons?—had sought to harm me and my siblings. Or were they merely destructive for the sake of being destructive? "Who would have wrought such ruin over so many years?"

"Could have been anybody. The Family Montague entertains guests from near and far, even from other cities!" Clearly he didn't approve. "Could have hurt anyone. Someone did fall out of that tree. I saw the marks. Not you?"

"No."

"Not one of the little ones?"

"No."

"Do you know who?"

"Yes." I looked away.

He had to think about that, and when he did, his withered mouth grew slack with horror. "My lady, you've always been the sensible one. You haven't . . . taken sick with the family fecklessness, have you?"

The grizzled old man stared at me beseechingly, and I tried to reassure him. "The fecklessness is not so strong in me. I still harbor some semblance of sense."

"I must tell your father the truth, all the truth!"

"Could you wait a day while I consider what this means?" With one finger, I touched the fresh wound of the walnut branch. "My father, as you know, is wont to draw his sword first and think after. In this case, let *me* think on all the things that have happened since the betrothal, and see if I can de-duce—"

Too late. Romeo, my lord father, stormed down the path to-ward us, fury riding him like a snorting stallion. When he saw me, he shouted, "Do you know what they're saying?" He groped for his sword, a sword that Mamma always insisted he leave at the door. "I'll kill them all, one by one! Or take them as a group. No one can say those things about my daughter!"

I curtsied, as always, and in my stallion-soothing voice, I said, "Greetings, Papà. You're known as the greatest swords-man in Verona. Everyone would run before you rather than fight." I wasn't strictly lying. There were younger swordsmen, probably better, but my father was known for his sly skill and his love of battle. That dedication made him, even at the age of thirty-six, a power on the field. "How was the theater and the play?"

He waggled my finger in my face. "You shall not distract me."

"No, Papà." I lowered my gaze and folded my hands at my waist. "That's not my intent. I was speaking with Gardener about the walnut tree. Last night, as you can see, a branch broke."

"Not the walnut tree!" Papà put his hand to his chest and turned to Gardener. "Tell me at once, can you save the tree?"

I'd chosen incorrectly. Rather than ask about the play, I

should have remembered Papà's adoration of torrone, a candy made of egg whites, honey, and walnuts. He loved walnuts *wayyyy* more than he loved theater.

I stared pleadingly at Gardener, waiting for him to sift through his mind and say what he thought was right.

He concentrated on me, then said, dragging each word out, "The tree's healthy, lord, but the branch outside Lady Rosie's bedchamber is no longer."

Romeo sighed in relief. "As long as it's merely a branch."

Gardener dipped his head, then trudged away, dragging the branch behind him, but in his backward glance I saw a promise; I had one day before my parents knew about the visitor outside my window.

Papà said, "You used to like to creep out and sit on that one, didn't you, Rosie?"

"I did, Papà." An unexpected wave of sadness swept me. "I'll miss it."

He hugged me to his side.

I rested my head on his chest. "Which play was it?" I asked. *"Two Gentlemen of Verona."*

"Ah. Not one of my favorites. Silly men don't interest me."

"I would not expect that of you, but it's the playwright's early work, his poetry is lovely—"

I made a gagging noise.

"And it made your mother laugh."

I linked arms with him. "Then all is well in the world."

He remembered his earlier indignation, but as I'd hoped, the rage had been diffused. "No, it's not. Did you know Porcia has been poisoned?"

"I heard that."

"People are saying you work with Friar Laurence. You brew potions. You know poison."

"I'm not blind to the possibility of that gossip." Nor was Prince Escalus, obviously. "Are people gossiping about my meeting with Miranda, too?"

"Who's Miranda?" When Papà recognized the name, his eyes opened wide in consternation. "Not the singer who was Duke Stephano's mistress?"

Maybe that was one Pandora's box I should have left unopened.

"How . . . how . . . how . . ."

He was incoherent, so I took charge of the conversation and told him exactly what had happened at Friar Laurence's shop and after.

He cogitated before replying, "The prince sent you home in his sedan chair?"

"Yes."

"Afterward the princess arrived for a visit, and now that sedan chair sits outside our home and waits to carry her back to the palace?"

"Yes."

"I'm not saying this is good. Not by any means. But because of Prince Escalus's support, both last night and today, the slander will be . . . muted."

"One hopes. Does my mother know?"

"Not yet. Let's keep it from her as long as possible."

Mamma stepped around the hedge and stood, hands on hips, at the entrance of the alcove. "Keep what from me?"

CHAPTER 22

Luckily for me, she was looking at Papà. Glaring at Papà.

"Busted," he breathed.

"Yes." I wasn't any louder. When Mamma looked like that: tight-lipped, ruddy cheeks, heaving bosom, you'd be better to walk off the edge of the earth and consumed by dragons than remain within the vicinity.

"Dear heart, you know you shouldn't be upset in your condition." Papà had a way with words, and not always a good way.

"You should stick with poetry," I murmured to him.

Because, of course, Mamma took exception. "In my *condition*?"

I winced at the volume and eased backward, hoping I could pass as a boxwood until I could slip through the stiff branches and flee the vicinity.

"In my *condition*? I shouldn't be upset in my *condition*? Why should I be upset? When my husband and daughter conspire to keep some awful occurrence from me?"

Mary, Mother of God, protect me.

"An occurrence that will cause grief and death to my family and jeopardize my children? I remember what happened twenty years ago, Romeo. I was in that tomb, remember? I thought you were dead and I stabbed myself for love."

Here she goes.

Mamma bared her chest. "I have the scar to prove it!" Catching sight of me slinking away, she pointed at the ground in front of her. "Come back here, young lady!"

Shit, shit, shit. "Madam Mother, I listen and obey." I returned and toed the line.

She tapped her foot and looked between the two of us. "Well?"

I thought I'd be less likely to enrage her in the telling, so I took a breath and said, "Porcia was poisoned. There are some ugly insinuations about my confrontation with her last night complicated by my apothecary work. Papà believes our current friendly associations with Prince Escalus and Princess Bella could defuse the rumors."

"There, my true and loving lodestar. That's not so bad, is it?" Papà asked encouragingly.

"Let. Me. Think. In the space of a day, our eldest daughter, our daughter who has been repeatedly betrothed and never married, who weekly visits Friar Laurence to learn how to make potions and medicines"—clearly, this was a critique— "lost her most recent future groom to a stabbing to the heart in our own home. Because she was seen going into the garden with a knife, she is accused of killing him, and rescued only by the just intercession of Verona's prince. She publicly battles with an unpleasant woman who is dead the next day, and the good people of Verona are accusing her of"—Mamma pretended to think—"witchcraft. I did get that right, didn't I?"

I nodded glumly.

"My aging husband is going to try and skewer everyone we know in Verona to right the balance, we're dependent on Prince Escalus to save us, who, as we know, rules our republic on the sufferance of his people and on his own strength and wiliness . . . and because of *my condition*, I'm not supposed to get *excited*?"

Dear reader . . . as you know, no matter how mature you are, it never gets easier to have your mother yell at you. The barrage of words create an ongoing crisis of guilt, denial, desperate attempts at appeasement, and the pure, simple knowledge that she's only yelling because she loves you and she's off the edge of the cliff because she fears for your life and well-being.

As a response, irritation or wrath is out. You have to go with appeasement and hope that works.

I curtsied again, lower than before. "Madam Mother, at any time I'm sorry to bring travail upon you. I've done my best always to be an obedient daughter—"

Swiftly she interrupted me. "Except in the matter of marriage."

"Those earlier missteps were nothing more than chance and bad luck . . ."

She used that mother-guilt-pinning glare on me.

It worked. I looked guilty. I floundered in a sea of guilt. I bobbed to the surface to spit out a desperate, stupid, guilty comment. "I didn't know that you knew—"

"You're almost twenty and the cleverest female beneath heaven"—sarcasm dripped from her tone—"but I recognize shrewd machination when I see it."

"Wait," Papà said in confusion. "What are you two talking about? Are you saying Rosie deliberately maneuvered her early suitors to leave her and marry someone else?"

Mamma rolled her eyes at him.

This was bad. Very bad. How to explain my adroit exertions without hurting Papà's feelings and insulting Mamma? This task was beyond even my previously smug and now obviously not-so-crafty talents.

I heard a sudden burst of angry shouting out by the swing. *Saved!*

"The children are fighting. I'd better go see—" I took a step to go around them.

Mamma pointed her finger in my face. "Stay here. Even *in my condition*, my diplomacy is better than yours." She swung that finger at Papà. "You. Come with me."

He followed like a heeling dog. "But, Juliet, the suitors always fell in love with someone else. Rosie can't have arranged that!"

I put my hand on my forehead and staggered back to the alcove bench. What had happened to my happy, smug, well-ordered life? If I looked up into Verona's blue sky, would I see boxes full of disasters piled up, teetering, waiting for the slightest breeze of scandal to crash down upon my head? Surely nothing else could go wrong . . .

Hastily I crossed myself to ward off the bad luck I might have brought on myself, then jumped half out of my skin when a man's voice behind me said, "Rosaline, my love, I fear for your life!"

CHAPTER 23

"Lysander?" I turned to face him, caught a glimpse of his dazzling face hidden in the hedge, and hurriedly faced front again. It would not do to call attention to him. "What are you doing in the Montague garden? Again? Trying to get killed? Again?"

"I couldn't stay away. I came over the wall."

"How? How? The hawthorn hedge is deep and thorny."

"I bring a ladder of special making of round, hollow wood that comes with our ships from the east. It has hinges to fold it; I can carry it through the streets myself."

"Don't you get odd looks?"

"And odd comments, let me tell you! I put it on the wall, climb up, balance on the top, pull up the ladder, then place it on top of the hedge and jump into the garden, preferably somewhere soft."

Much struck, I asked, "Does it work well?"

"Mostly. Once a hinge gave way and I landed on . . . somewhere not soft."

At his tone, I gurgled with laughter.

"Limped for a week and modified all the hinges. Felt like fortune's most laughable fool. If I could get enough of that eastern wood, I could sell all the ladders."

"I have never thought of such a thing."

"You couldn't. The Montagues aren't a family famous for skulking and invention. The Montagues are famous for fighting and f—er, romance."

A smile twitched my lips. "And wine."

"The Montague wine is the envy of all the city-states and beyond." He bobbed his head in proper respect. "A single drop of their wine on my tongue is a memory to cherish forever."

Not idly, I asked, "Would you rather have me or the wine?"

"You, lady, for then . . ." He trailed off.

I chuckled softly. "For then you'd have both."

"I'm a greedy man." His tone changed, grew heavy with warning. "For that reason I had to warn you. I heard what your father said. I heard what you said. Gossip is rife on the streets. You know the peril you're in. I must help." The branches crackled as he pushed at them, sliding closer. "I must arm you."

I blinked. "Say what?" I'd had the conversation before.

"Everything that's happened since last night is a blur of horror, and it's all aimed at you. Can you see that?"

"It's been called to my attention, yes." I half turned toward him. "Nevertheless, you shouldn't be here. My father is swift with a blade and not always thoughtful beforehand. He's the best swordsman in the family, but not the only. You could be dead before you or I could explain your good intentions, and when you explained you wished to help me, you would almost certainly be skewered by one and all."

"I'd face death for you."

That was so blithely stupid, I wanted to snort in derision. It was also so romantic I took out my handkerchief and fanned my flushed face.

Yet even in an amorous tizzy, I could be prosaic. "If my kinsmen believed I had disgraced myself with you, they'd skewer me, too."

"All the more reason that you should be armed. Unlace your cuff." Lysander's intense voice raised the hair on the back of my head.

"Why?"

"I have procured a blade and holster for you." He showed me a leather holster, stamped with many designs to ward off the wicked one and with metal buckles instead of leather ties, and a blade a little longer than the one Nurse got me. Working his hands through the tangle of branches, he said, "Unlace your cuff."

I stared into his green eyes, stricken by how swiftly he'd moved to find protection for me and loving him all the more.

He stared into my eyes, also, and perhaps he found something there he hadn't seen before, for when he repeated, "Unlace your cuff," his chest rose and fell with need, and his voice was rough with passion.

I reached for my left cuff.

But sense brought me to a halt. Nurse had given me the weapon for that arm. When I changed into my present garb, believing I would be safe at home, I had discarded it, but I feared the marks of the leather binding lingered. So I switched, unlaced my right cuff, and bared my wrist.

Lysander looked at my smooth, pale skin with such pleasure, I wondered what he'd do for a glimpse of breast. It would be almost worth . . . *No, no. Don't travel that road, not even in your mind.*

He leaned out of the bushes.

As if enthralled by his splendor, a branch caught his cap, pulled it off, and held it close. His dark blond hair gleamed, tempting me to touch it, to see if it was as silky as it looked. *No, not that, either.*

He pressed a kiss on my inner wrist, a touch of soft lips against tender flesh.

I sighed with delight and gave into temptation. I slipped my fingers into his hair and pushed a strand behind his ear, lingering over the texture.

Driven to a frenzy by my gentle caress, he lunged forward to kiss my lips, to embrace me!

But the bushes gripped his waistcoat in their inexorable grasp and yanked him back.

I laughed—possibly not the best response.

After a moment, he grinned and fingered the newly created hole in his sleeve. "I commend your father on his wisdom in planting such virtuous hedges."

"I won't tell him."

"Please don't. I've heard enough to fear your father's sword." He strained to stretch out far enough to fasten the scabbard around my arm. "I have no desire to become a skewer of *porchetta*."

"Light the cooking fires!" I proclaimed.

"Heartless wench." He grinned again, leaned back with a moan, and with his handkerchief wiped a trickle of blood off his neck. "I tell you, between the thorny brambles beside your formidable garden wall and the branches on this devil plant, your virtue is kept safe."

"Perhaps you should have armed me with a hedge?"

He snorted. "Have I mentioned how much I adore your quick wit?"

"No, but you should. I'm susceptible to flattery."

"It's not flattery if it's true." In one of those lightning changes of tone, he said, "Now—should you feel in peril, you can pull the dagger out and make *porchetta* of your attacker. Try it now."

I slid my left hand up my right sleeve, grasped the hilt, slid the blade out, and lunged at the hedge. "Let him go, branches!" I commanded. To Lysander, I said, "It's not working."

"A hedge that knows its duty. That was a good thrust." Lysander sounded almost puzzled. "Have you done this before?"

My father taught me the basics of sword fighting, and my nurse demonstrated how to pull a dagger from my other sleeve, but—"I'm a fast learner." I slid the blade back into the scabbard and changed the subject before he could ask more. "Lysander, last night in the walnut tree—what *exactly* happened?"

"I'm not sure."

I would tell him of the vandalism of the tree, but first I wanted to hear what he knew. "Thoughts?"

"As I lay across the broad branch and conversed with wit and passion most meaningful, a noble goal formed in my mind, to match my unworthy lips to your ripe, lush mouth. As I inched forward, I flattered myself that you desired that glorious communion. I closed my eyes and leaned and"—the memory made him look both alarmed and disconcerted— "something hit the branch."

"Something?"

"Something big. Heavy." He took a breath. "Someone."

"You jest!"

"One of your kinsman, perhaps?"

My eyes narrowed. "Unlikely. If it was, shouting would have preceded and more shouting would have followed, and I would have been hard-pressed to save you from mincing. More like it was my nurse."

"Your nurse can climb a tree?"

"I wouldn't put it past her." Yet when I remembered how that night she had stared at me, then at the branch, I didn't believe it. "But unlikely. You're saying that the extra weight of . . .

someone . . . snapped the branch and you plummeted to the ground."

"I landed on my back. The branch landed on me."

"The other . . . person?"

"I don't think anyone else hit the ground, but the impacts knocked the breath from me, then the wit, and I rested senseless in the grass for a time out of mind. When I woke, a man was dragging me by my heels through the unlit garden. The gravel on the path scratched my head and tore my clothes." Lysander touched the back of his head with a wince. "I lifted my head to cry out, and he commanded silence on my life."

"He threatened you?"

"Indeed. With his voice and demeanor, I didn't care to test him. He asked where I was staying in Verona, and as I pulled my thoughts together, he dragged me farther and farther along the hedges. At last I told him I was staying with my uncle, and begged him to let me walk. He dropped my legs and waited while I struggled to my feet, then roughly shoved me through the garden while giving me the rundown on all the people Lord Romeo has defeated in his long and varied career with a sword."

"That's how you heard?"

"Yes, and a most impressive list it is. We arrived at a hidden door. His man awaited us, and I feared I was being handed over to an assassin."

I pressed my hand to my chest over my rapidly beating heart. "Yet you are here, now. I rejoice!"

"I rejoice, too." His dry voice lifted my spirits. "My rescuer, for I must call him that, directed that I be returned to my kinsman and I was led onto the dark street and back to the family home."

I gave voice to despair. "Lysander, why must you be of the house of Marcketti, and my enemy?"

"I'm not your enemy and I'm not the enemy of the Montagues." He surged forward, restrained again by stiff branches. "I swear to you, I have more than one reason to heal this breach!"

In a voice full of woe and crushing disappointment, I asked, "It's not just me?"

"No. Yes! I mean—" He caught sight of my smirk. "You're a vixen."

"I have my moments."

He leaned toward me. Still the trimmed boxwood branches clawed at him, held him back.

I resisted the urge to grasp him by the collar, for I could lean in, and did. My first kiss. At last! A moment to savor! An experience to explore! If all was as ecstatic as my parents had led me to believe, an experience to explore again and again!

I half closed my eyes. I viewed Lysander's perfect and handsome countenance grow nearer, and my breath tripped in anticipation. I wet my lips and felt the admiration of his gaze brush my face with the soft warmth of a puppy's head. I was ready. So ready. For this and more.

Then . . . Then! Because I was the most cursed of women, I heard running feet on the path from the house.

I couldn't believe it. I could not believe it. I stomped my foot like Emilia having a tantrum and said words no lady should know. *"Che cazzo?"*

"Rosie!" As Lysander slid back and out of sight, he sounded shocked.

To relieve my frustration a little more, I stomped my foot again, then saw that which would betray us, and whispered urgently, "Your cap!"

His arm snaked out, plucked the atrocious magenta cap from the hedge's rapacious grasp, and with only the slightest tearing sound, whisked it away.

Tommaso raced past.

I called him. "Tommaso, come back. Why are you running?"

He returned and stood gasping, holding his side. "The prince is here. Prince Escalus is here to see his sister!"

CHAPTER 24

From behind me I heard a deep groan.

Tommaso stared in confusion. "Lady Rosaline, *what*?"

"I was merely . . . clearing my throat." I stood and spread my skirts to hide any sign Lysander had disarrayed the shrubbery. "Do as I instructed you with Princess Isabella. Take Prince Escalus to the great hall and serve him refreshments. I'll bring the princess to him—"

"He comes now!" Tommaso gestured up the path.

No. My siblings were fighting, probably with Isabella, my mother was angry at me, Lysander hid in our shrubbery . . . and the prince was here? I didn't have to look up to know the boxes full of disaster had fallen on my sinful head. "Go and tell Lord Romeo and Lady Juliet at once. I'll try to delay the prince."

Tommaso bowed and stood there, all awkward legs and arms, as if the weight of the responsibility had robbed him of sense.

"They're at the swing. Go!" I urged. "Quickly!"

He ran.

I listened. The hubbub of childish shouting had calmed. I hoped my mother had worked her magic and I prayed that no one had fatally offended Princess Isabella. Or, more important, given her a shove that knocked her to the ground and dirtied her elegant gown. Stepping out on the path, I prepared to walk to meet Prince Escalus.

He was already there, striding purposefully as if he rued his decision to send his sister into our keeping.

My job: keep the chaos of her visit a secret long enough for my parents to receive the news of his arrival and deal accordingly.

I smiled widely and curtsied deeply. "My prince, what a pleasure to welcome you to our humble abode!"

He stopped. He viewed me without favor and, dare I say it, with suspicion. "I've come to escort my sister home."

"My prince, she's playing with the other children." I gestured toward the swing.

"You left her alone with your sisters and brother?" Clearly, he was offended and worried.

Which made me a little cranky and as happened sometimes, I spoke without thinking. "They're not beasts, you know."

"No, but Isabella's unused to being surrounded by rambunctious children of so many and varied ages. I thought I could trust you to remain nearby as a safeguard for her finer feelings."

"I assure you, she has no feelings finer than any of my family." That probably wasn't true, the younger kids could be savages, but he had my blood up. I forcibly reminded myself I should appease him . . . and stall him. "That said, Lord Romeo and Lady Juliet are now with my siblings and your sister."

"Why are you not with them?"

Because my father and I had discussed the current disaster, and my mother had caught us and dragged us across flickering blue coals of shame. "After our morning, I was content to allow my parents to mediate the children."

"Mediate? They required mediation?"

I got snappish again. "Yes, and some believe my skills are

subpar." I allowed myself a short breath, and before he spoke again, I added, "But all is well now. Before we join them, Prince Escalus, may I inquire what you discovered about Porcia's death?"

"As a female, you should not worry about the progress of justice in Verona."

"I'm more involved in this case than I wish to be."

Perhaps my reminder sounded brisk, for he looked up the path as if he feared for his sister's well-being, then back at me.

I smiled with false affability.

He gestured into the alcove I'd recently vacated.

Which, with Lysander lurking nearby, was not what I intended, but I could hardly complain about getting my way.

Prince Escalus waited while I seated myself, then sat beside me looking stiff and displeased. "I spoke to Porcia's husband's father and mother. The first they knew of her death was this morning when her maid's shrieks roused them. The maid told them when Porcia arrived back from last night's festivities, she violently expressed her displeasure with you, me, Duke Stephano's murder, and the events that meant she must forthwith return to her parents' home. She opened a box of sweetmeats placed upon her pillow and consumed several before retiring."

"Had the maid seen the box before?"

"No. She said she had no idea how it came to be there."

I asked the questions Prince Escalus must surely have asked. "Do we know for sure it's murder? That the sweetmeats were poisoned? Could it not have been another food or drink?"

"The maid claimed that Porcia had tossed her one piece of the candy. She might have stolen it, but I believe her, for she complained that it was the smallest piece."

I released a wry laugh. "Yes, that would be Porcia."

"That it was the smallest piece may have saved the girl's life. She was up all night, violently ill, keeping the other maids awake with her vomiting, and this morning appeared pale, drawn, and sweaty . . . and desperately afraid she'll have no place in any household after her failure to prevent Porcia's murder."

"The poor maid!" My heart contracted as I thought of her despair. "Perhaps we could take her into our household and—"

Prince Escalus turned his heavy-lidded gaze on me, and his expression was not complimentary. "You could employ a maid involved in Porcia's murder when suspicion already has been cast on you? I think not!"

"No, but—"

"She's currently traveling to my country house, where she'll be employed."

"Oh." I hadn't expected that. "That's kind of you."

"You don't have to sound so surprised." His expression, his voice, was austere.

"No, I . . ." I *was* surprised, but why? True, he was not like us, like the Montagues. We were a loud, exuberant, contentious, laughing, singing, loving and passionate family.

Prince Escalus was . . . the opposite. In every way that I knew. Yet he had learned the meaning of loyalty in a hard school, and he knew what it was to be abandoned and despairing, huddled in a dungeon, tortured and afraid. And hungry, I supposed.

I placed my hand on my chest and made a small bow. "Forgive me, my prince. Not many noblemen would care what happened to a poor girl, but you are more than the sum of most noblemen."

"I am the Prince of Verona."

I heard his unspoken words. *And I know my duty.*

He continued. "Which is why I seek justice for even such a one as Porcia. Whatever knowledge you have of her could shed light on this murder."

"Porcia's greedy fondness for sweetmeats is well known among her acquaintances."

The prince contemplated me.

I saw assessment in his gaze. "I didn't poison her, my prince. Nor did my nurse."

"No, but with that knowledge, how easily the task was done. I interrogated the household staff. No one admitted they had knowledge of the box and how it arrived in the *casa,* and when I asked, none had noted any stranger lurking in the corridors."

"I'd be suspicious of any maid or footman who pointed a finger or claimed to know about the crime. It's not in a servant's interest to know too much about such trouble."

"No. Yet they spoke fondly of their young master Troilus, who died soon after his marriage to Porcia, and not so fondly about Porcia herself. Without saying in so many words, they insinuated their master and mistress held disdain for their daughter-in-law."

"Ah, Porcia. Making friends wherever she goes." I crossed myself and added hastily, "May God rest her soul."

Prince Escalus crossed himself, also. To attract the attention of the recently dead, to mention their name, especially one who died by cruel poison, was to invite bad luck and, worse, a ghostly haunting. We had trouble enough without Porcia returning for vengeance. I'd hear the taunt of *virgin* in my sleep.

Although, with Lysander, I had hopes virginity might soon be a thing of the past. I smiled a little, then noticed the silence.

Prince Escalus watched me, heavy-lidded, far too interested in my thoughts. Or perhaps it was merely the facts of the crime that consumed him. "Whoever placed the box of sweetmeats on her pillow didn't need to walk the halls. As in so many Veronese homes, secret passages abound if one knows where to find them."

"But how would someone enter without being detected?" As soon as the words left my mouth, I knew I should have kept mum. *Really, Rosie, could you put a cork in your wine barrel?*

"The great houses are fortified against an army, yet a single person may enter easily, with guests, with staff . . . and as we both know, over the wall."

I heard an abrupt rustling behind us. A quick glance at Prince Escalus proved him oblivious and intent on his report.

He said, "There was no dissembling from Porcia's in-laws. They made it clear they had wished for an excuse to be rid of her. During my visit, her own parents arrived and were also less than pleased that she had been coming back to their home. No one seemed particularly grieved at her passing, merely shocked at the manner of it."

I would speak her name and of her reputation, but only to give Prince Escalus background in his pursuit of justice. "Make no mistake, Porcia had her circle of friends, mean girls who delighted in tormenting anyone they perceived as awkward, unstylish, unpolished—"

"A virgin?" Prince Escalus suggested blandly.

"Yes, that too." I was not amused at his reminder. "Porcia was the center of that mean-girl circle, and she was like a tick that dug under one's skin and drained one of confidence. She, like Duke Stephano, had enemies."

"Not just you?"

"Not just me."

"My investigation will continue." He stood. "I hear the approach of your family."

CHAPTER 25

How I hoped Papà and Mamma had worked their magic with the children!

I hurried after Prince Escalus onto the path and saw them leading a pack of chattering juveniles and in the midst, Princess Isabella. Her face was smudged, her hair partially unbound, her rumpled clothing bore witness to rough play. Yet she was laughing, her face alive as it had not been when she arrived.

We were as yet unseen, and Prince Escalus stopped to stare.

I didn't know what he was going to relate to, her dirty, disheveled appearance or her pleasure in the recreation, but I needn't have worried.

He said, "I see my sister has happily joined the beasts."

Sometimes he was so dry he made my mouth pucker.

At that moment, Isabella caught sight of him and broke into a run. She caught his arm and hugged it, and smiled into his face. "Brother, Lord Romeo and Lady Juliet ask that I stay for the evening meal. May I? May I please?"

For the first time, I saw him uncertain. "Surely after imposing for so many hours, it would be best if we—"

"She didn't impose!" Cesario hadn't yet thoroughly comprehended the respect owed to a prince. He stomped forward. "She's okay . . . for a girl."

Isabella pulled his hair.

Cesario grabbed her hand.

They wrestled.

Papà took them both by the elbows and chided, "If you behave with unruly enthusiasm, Prince Escalus will never allow Isabella to visit us again."

Mamma curtsied, which reminded the other girls to curtsy, and Papà and Cesario to bow. "Welcome to Casa Montague, Prince Escalus. If you can take a break from your weighty obligations, we would indeed enjoy entertaining you and your sister tonight."

"Please, Escalus. Please," Isabella begged again.

Cesario echoed her. "Please, Escalus. Please!"

"*Prince* Escalus," Papà told him. "He has a title and an important one."

"Prince Escalus," Cesario repeated. "Do I have to call you Princess Isabella?" he asked her.

"Only when you make me mad," she replied.

Emilia took her arm. "He'll have to call you Princess Isabella all the time."

The girls laughed. Cesario objected. The children passed us by and moved like a buzzing swarm of bees toward the house.

Papà said, "My prince, I add my entreaty to my lady Juliet's. If we can provide you with a moment of pleasure and lightness, do join in our informal meal."

Prince Escalus yielded. "If we're not imposing, we would be delighted to dine with your family."

I stood still and watched as they walked away, and murmured, "Dining with the beasts." For as we did when not engaged in a social occasion, the whole family dined together on one long table. Everyone talked. Everyone listened. Everyone ate. Everyone sipped wine, even the children, and gave their opinion of the scents, the flavors, the impacts. In a family of vintners, we learned early.

This night would not be the usual civilized meal presented to the prince.

I would be interested to see how he reacted.

Yet always at the back of my mind, I knew Lysander was nearby, listening, contemplating the events of the previous night and the facts gathered today, and he in his foresight had given me a great gift—a dagger.

Yes, Nurse had given me one first, but it was the thought that counts . . . and I had begun to think two weapons was none too many.

Without looking into the alcove, I put my arms behind me and lightly caressed the sleeve where beneath Lysander's scabbard rested. The touch was a silent thank-you for his thoughtfulness and a promise of a kiss not yet delivered.

The faintest whisper of a sigh answered me. Lysander had heard all; he knew I wouldn't be returning tonight.

I heard the crunch of gravel on the path, and Prince Escalus arrived at my side, startling me with his unexpected appearance. He offered my arm. "Lady Rosaline, I apologize for leaving you behind. Do come and join your family, and mine."

I stared at the crook of his elbow as if I'd never seen such a thing, then gingerly placed my hand on his sleeve. "I wonder, Prince Escalus, if you spoke with young Orlando about his rapid return to Verona after his brother's death."

"I did, indeed. After I questioned the family about Porcia's death, I visited Casa Creppa and was lucky enough to find Orlando dispersing his brother's clothing and shoes to the impoverished of Verona."

"Dispersing them? Personally? How?"

"He was throwing them out the window."

God forgive me, I laughed. "Yes, I can see him doing exactly that, and enjoying himself, too. Did he give a reason why he had come so swiftly on the heels of Duke Stephano's death?"

"He'd been to visit his parents in their cold, inhospitable

castle, and after finding them miserable and ill, in a rage he rode back to Verona to kill his brother."

In an instant, I went from amused to shocked. "Orlando freely admitted such a thing?"

"He did, but claims late last night before he rode into the city, he stopped at an inn for wine and bread and a place to sleep, and in the public room was greeted by the news of his brother's death at the hand of his latest affianced wife. He celebrated inappropriately—"

"Or appropriately."

Prince Escalus paused. "Yes. That's one way to think about it. Riding into the city in the late morning, he saw you and, he said, thanked you."

"He did. I denied it, but he made me the center of attention. It was uncomfortable." I thought again about Orlando, how openly he'd celebrated his brother's death, and the shadow I'd sensed that brooded in his spirit. "He is the heir. By his brother's death, he'll inherit everything."

"Incorrect. His father is the duke."

"Right. I forgot that."

"Orlando says he intends to reinstate his father as the head of the family."

How interesting. "Do you believe him?"

"Yes, within reason. Orlando and I will stay close until I feel certain about his character and his intentions."

I confessed, "I like him so much. I want him to be innocent. But I can't see through the shadows of the life he's lived since he left Verona."

"Nor I. If Orlando the man be who he says he is, I rejoice in him, for I need such men as an arrow in my quiver. But there's been too much desperate treachery and prowling death for me to blindly trust a boy embittered by exile and the man he's become."

Prince Escalus talked to me about shining truth and blind

justice, and when he spoke I comprehended all the difficulties he faced in his solitary trek to justice for his family and Verona.

He placed his hand on mine, pressing it to his arm, and I walked with him toward the house, away from my true love.

The silence between the prince and I felt deep and dark and brooding, out of sync with the sunny evening, the dappled leaves, the singing birds that populated our garden. In a cordial tone, he asked, "Did you notice how, in the alcove where we sat, the branches were bent and fresh leaves had fallen to the ground?"

"What? No!" That was the truth. I hadn't *noticed*. Weakly I suggested, "Perhaps the gardener trimmed the verge?"

"The smallest piece of cloth clung to the branches, and some thread of a most vibrant and ill-favored color. It almost appears that someone who wished to remain hidden skulked there for a time. I'll speak to Lord Romeo about watching for scoundrels who would climb the wall and invade the Montague home. I take my duties as podestà of Verona seriously; if one criminal can overwhelm the defenses, all can. No man should threaten you, Lady Rosaline. Or your beloved family. Or mine."

"Of course, my prince. Thank you, my prince." He was right; if Lysander could get in, others could gain access to our home and my brother and sisters could be at risk. I felt a pang at my previous disregard for the danger.

Yet . . . I would have to find a way to get word to Lysander. For soon he would try to return to me.

CHAPTER 26

The evening was as raucous as I had feared, and Prince Escalus as watchful and dignified. Yet because he was quiet, we all strained to hear what he said, and each word was measured and of interest. He brought a welcome balance to our madness, like salt to a bowl of *minestra*.

Also, and this is important, Princess Isabella had given herself over to our side, and Prince Escalus seemed to have no problem with that.

Hours later, when the meal was over and we lingered over sweet wine, Prince Escalus tore off yet another chunk of Cook's fruit and nut bread, smeared it with butter, and consumed it.

"You're very fond of that bread." Mamma's eyes sparkled. She enjoyed pleasing guests at her table.

"It's remarkable for its tastes and textures. I would have it every day if I could!" The meal had wrought a miracle; in truth, he sounded enthusiastic.

"Then Cook will gift you with a loaf to carry with you to the palace." Mamma indicated to Tommaso that it should be done. He disappeared and returned with a loaf wrapped in linen, which he presented to the prince with a bow.

The prince accepted it with many gracious thanks. He stood,

took my mother's hand, and bowed low over it. "Lady Juliet, your hospitality is matched only by your beauty. My sister and I render most sincere thanks to you and your family, and now we take our leave."

Cesario groaned. "Can't she stay? I *love* her."

Smiles slipped around the table and were swiftly hidden. It wouldn't do to hurt the little boy's feelings.

Princess Isabella, who had risen with the prince, hugged Cesario and pressed a kiss on the top of his head. "If Lord Romeo and Lady Juliet will allow, I'll have you and your sisters to the palace to play. There are gardens and so many rooms and armors, so many places for hide-and-seek!"

Cesario's eyes grew big, and he looked to our parents.

Juliet smiled. "Such an invitation would be an honor."

Cesario was a smart boy; he took Isabella's hand and bowed over it in the same elegant manner as the prince had done with our mother. Yet his enthusiastic words told all. "I can't wait to see you again!"

Among the tumult of their leaving, Prince Escalus spoke in my ear. "It would seem my suspicions were correct, and your brother has formed a *tendre* for my sister."

In a low voice to match his, I replied, "I trust the age difference to slow any romance." I knew Cesario, so I added, "Although probably not from lack of trying on his part."

Thankfully, the prince gave that quirk of a smile and he and Princess Isabella took their leave, the Princess Isabella inside the sedan chair, Prince Escalus walking beside.

I took note of the neighbors' twitching drapes and resolved to tell Nurse. Ah, the satisfaction she'd get from gloating at the servants tomorrow!

Papà helped a weary Mamma up the stairs. The kids scattered to their beds, herded by our nurse and her cadre of assistants. The servants snuffed the candles, save for one small, well-protected flame to lessen night's shadows. I stood in the entry until I was sure I was alone, then pulled the pins from my cap and *trinzale*, the net I wore over my braid, and used my fingers to loosen my hair. If I had one vanity (which was not easy when your mother was Lady Juliet Montague and whatever beauty you had was first ascribed to her), it was my hair. The rich brown rippled with tones of cool auburn and warm copper, and unbound reached to my hips. With its thick length fanned out around my shoulders, I thought myself a naiad going out to trap a mortal man.

Okay, not really. I'm not that fanciful.

It had been hours and hours, and most likely Lysander had left; the evening air was growing chilly, and he would be hungry and heedful of my warning about the swords of my kinsmen. Also, if he'd heard Prince Escalus's observations about a person skulking in the boxwood, a speedy escape would be the logical move.

Yet I wrapped myself in a fine wool cape and strolled out on the terrace to look out over the garden.

The full moon shone brightly across the paths, trees, and hedges. Stars studded the black skies, and night-blooming flowers released their heavenly scent. Tall, pointed cypress flanked each side of the terrace, dark green in the sunlight, now enigmatically casting heavy shadows that lie oppressively along the marble floors.

I leaned against the marble rail and scanned for movement. A girl could dream, and when all the garden remained empty, dream I did. Having listened to my parents my entire life—not even a pillow over my ears drowned them out—I was naturally able to envision quite a bit, and in living color, and what had previously been an annoyance was now a much-appreciated education. I wrapped my arms around myself and imagined Lysander and our coming embrace. I imagined our kiss, our whispered words, our gentle sighs, our escalating passion. . . .

When I was warm and weak in anticipation, I turned toward

the house—and a man's hulking shadow loomed by the door, backlit by the night candle.

I took a startled breath and reached for the blade in my sleeve.

The man stepped into the moonlight.

Enter stage right: Prince Escalus.

CHAPTER 27

I collapsed against the railing. "You scared me to death!"

The prince observed me; my loosened hair, my dreamy countenance, the heat that lit the air around me. "Why didn't you scream?"

"Because I . . . I'm as witless as a peahen." That was the truth. If I'd screamed, I'd have had family and retainers running to my aid. Instead I'd thought to defend myself against someone who . . . who had taken his leave. Who shouldn't be here now. "What are you doing in our house? Did you forget something?"

He paced toward me. "I want to speak to you."

"How did you know I'd be out here?"

"I did not. But the moon is full and I thought I might . . . climb the tree outside your window. It's a Montague tradition, is it not?"

I reared back. "No! Nobody . . . no! I'm insulted that you believe—"

"Your pardon." He bowed fast and low. "I believe only the best of you, Lady Rosaline. I thought to tease. I should remember that I'm bad at such a human interaction."

"You really are."

"Do you forgive me?"

"Yes. Forget it. For future reference, don't ever joke about a lady's virtue. Certainly not mine, now. I've already been threatened with a nunnery or the stake."

"Who threatened you?"

"My nurse. If you say anything else about me, she'll do more than threaten you. She'll flay you alive." I looked around. Prince Escalus seemed to have slipped back into Casa Montague without causing a ripple. There should be servants, candles, an escort, deference . . . "How did you get . . . in . . . ?"

"I have my ways."

I really had to speak to Papà about security. "The Princess Isabella is . . . well . . . ?"

"My sister enjoyed the utmost protection as she returns to our home."

"What did you want to . . . say . . . ?" With each question, I had managed to sound more and more like a braying donkey. Why? What had become of my vaulted sensibility?

I knew the answer, of course. I'd been imagining an embrace with Lysander, passion with Lysander. This love was so precious, so new, I didn't know how to conceal it. I imagined my face glowed, my eyes shone, my bosom heaved. To have Prince Escalus, this detached, unemotional man, intrude on my romantic musings felt like a trip to the celestial interrupted by a slam back to cold, hard earth.

Prince Escalus seemed to detect nothing of my turmoil. "As you're aware, I'm concerned about the attacks on Duke Stephano and Porcia."

Goodie. We were going to talk murder. So not merely a slam to the cold, hard earth, but a face full of dark and dirt and maggots. Pushing my hair back over my shoulders, I took handfuls and braided quickly and efficiently. It wouldn't do to stand before Prince Escalus in such an untamed state.

He continued. "We do not know with certainty, but I fear you are the object of these attacks, perhaps to blacken your name or to frighten you as the web of evil is constructed around you."

I shivered at his ominous choice of words, and with that, left behind the last of love's sweet glow.

"I constantly carry a concealed dagger." He pulled a worn leather scabbard from inside his brocade overcoat. "I want you to have it, to use it if needed against the villain who invades your safety, reads your fears and plays on them."

My jaw dropped.

I had already received two weapons today.

Nurse, I understood. She was a strong female and knew that women who could die under the sword needed to be prepared for violence.

Lysander, I understood. He was young and fiery, passionate and protective.

But Prince Escalus, the traditionalist, wanted *me* to protect *myself*? Rather than advising me to remain at home as a proper lady should, or explaining why I should scream rather than fight, or finding me a husband who would shelter me (when he was not beating me) . . . Prince Escalus wanted to *arm* me?

Next Prince Escalus would say that the Chinese had invented fireworks.

I had stood speechless for too long, for he asked slowly, as if giving me a chance to catch up, "Do you understand what I'm saying, Lady Rosie?"

"I . . . sure." As with Lysander, I couldn't say, *Nurse already gave me a weapon.* Nor could I say, *Lysander also already gave me a weapon.* There was only one proper response. "Thank you. I'm honored by your consideration." I stuck out my left arm, which did not at this moment have a scabbard and blade wrapped around it.

But the prince knelt at my feet. In a conversational tone, he said, "This blade is small and sharp, and has served me well."

He took my slipper-clad foot into his hand and slid his fingers up my calf.

I jumped. If this were a normal man, I'd knock him *culo* over *pentola*. But this was the Prince of Stodgy. Surely he didn't mean to—

"The scabbard buckles are here"—he gently squeezed my bare ankle—"and here"—a little farther up—"and the dagger's handle is hidden by your skirts. At the same time, it's readily available for your grasp."

The prince was touching my leg. "This is your dagger. You don't wear skirts." Possibly the most glaringly obvious comment I'd ever made, but *the prince* was rubbing his thumb over my ankle.

Chinese fireworks. Only explanation possible.

"I wear the dagger inside here." He indicated his wide-topped boots.

"I always wondered why you wore those—"

"Unfashionable boots? Yes, there's method to my madness." His hands moved on my skin, attaching the scabbard with metal buckles.

I stood very still. The leather was warm from his body, and despite the fact I knew Prince Escalus to be the most staid, proper, and may I say least exciting man in Verona, my female self sensed danger in ways I couldn't quite comprehend.

Naturally, he was unaware, and took his time buckling and explaining. "During the time before and after my father's death, I survived many attacks."

"I know." I was so tense, if a midge had buzzed my ear I would have jumped and screamed. "You give this dagger to me, and I thank you, but without it, how will you protect yourself?"

"I have other weapons, and to know my blade rests in your hand, a bulwark against future acts of violence—it's a service I'm privileged to render."

He finished attaching the scabbard, yet remained kneeling, the tips of his fingers lightly touching the back of my knee. How did they get up so far? And why had I previously never noticed how sensitive that skin was?

He looked up at me, his eyes large and dark, heavy-lidded, and they shone with an inner light that illuminated all before him, yet left him to dwell in shadow. "If I might offer the lady Rosaline advice on how to use this weapon?"

"Indeed you might. I don't know how to use a dagger strapped to my *leg*." To my arm, yes. That had today been explained twice. My leg, not so much.

Prince Escalus sprang to his feet, dagger in his grasp.

Reflexively, I stepped backward into the shadow of the tall cypress. Its sharp, woody green scent reminded me of pine and a hint of bitter orange and should have recalled the safety of home. But no safety existed in this night.

He stepped behind me, wrapped his arms around me, placed the hilt of the dagger in my hand. He curled my fingers around it and held them in his grasp. "In a fight, I find it's smart to duck *under* a punch or the swing of a sword, come up holding the knife, dive *under* the attack, and stab my assailant in the chest, abdomen, arm." Guiding my hand, my body, he thrust and thrust and thrust, first one side, then the other, then right through the middle. "Even a blow that's not fatal causes distress and distraction, and you can make the judgment to stay and finish the fight—or run away."

This felt like an embrace. Not a friendly embrace, a fighting embrace, but we were too close for comfort. I jabbed backward with my elbow and when his grip loosened, I shook him off like a dog would shake off a flea. I turned to face him. "I'd run away," I said calmly, as if I didn't hold his dagger pointed at his belly.

"And scream," he reminded me, seemingly unconcerned about any threat I might offer.

Which, to my chagrin, he probably wasn't. "And scream," I agreed.

"Very wise." He stared into my eyes, the stars behind him, his face in moonlight's shadow, and his voice wove a spell, created a hypnosis, and I was bound to this place, listening to this man. "A woman, or a youth as I once was, has no chance against a full-grown man."

"I know. I listen. I will remember." Remember what it felt to have his arms around me, remember how his hand caressed my ankle.

Holding his gaze, I flipped the dagger in the air.

He lunged for it.

I caught it by the hilt and in one smooth motion knelt and inserted it into the scabbard at my ankle.

Yes, it was foolhardy. Yes, I'm lucky I didn't skewer myself in the palm. But his casual assumption that I'd welcome his . . . What would I call them? I didn't even know. . . . Simply because we'd previously spoken without the presence of a chaperon made me sharply furious and—

Oh, like *you* wouldn't have flipped that knife, too, to make clear you should be handled . . . not at all.

The trick worked. Prince Escalus put his hand on his chest in a gesture of respect and bowed. "Where did you learn that?"

I curtsied. "My lord father would have his daughters know how to handle a blade."

"He taught you to flip a knife?" His voice rose with disbelief.

I lowered my gaze. "Perhaps we practiced that on our own." Knowing what he would say next, I added, "With a blunt blade. My young sister Imogene is the best of us children. She's wicked fast. Shall we teach Isabella the sport?"

He stared at me in horror.

I cursed my loss of temper and my thoughtless question.

Princess Isabella needed us, and now Prince Escalus would forbid her return. I intended to backtrack, to promise we'd never teach Princess Isabella such an unladylike activity, but before I could speak, from above on my balcony, Nurse called out, "Rosie, where are you?"

I stepped out from the cypress's shadow and looked up at her, a silhouette against the sky. "On the terrace."

She leaned out and spotted me. "Foolish girl, what are you doing out there? Dreaming of your one true love?"

"No!" Out here, in the moonlight, I didn't want to talk about love.

Nurse kept me in her sights and mocked, "Come to bed, you can dream as easily in your room as on the terrace."

Prince Escalus remained in the deepest shadow, watchful, unmoving.

I truly needed to reassure him about what the Montague family would teach Princess Isabella, so I called, "Anon, good Nurse," and gave her a dismissive wave of my hand.

That was a mistake.

Nurse echoed my phrase. "*Anon, good Nurse?* You dare say '*Anon, good Nurse*' to me?" Her voice rose with every word. "Hie yourself up here now, *good Rosaline*, or I'll come down to get you, and you'll be sorry!" She went inside and slammed the door.

I pressed my palm to my forehead and laughed out loud.

Prince Escalus stepped out of the shadows. "You've said 'Anon, good Nurse' to her before?" he asked in a neutral voice.

"Not I. If I remember the story rightly"—I spoke with a humor most would not comprehend—"'Anon, good Nurse' was my mother's line when she was fooling around with Papà."

It took the prince a moment to think it through, then he gave what might in another man pass as a chuckle. "Lord Romeo and Lady Juliet are rightly famous for their true and impetuous love."

"Yes." Speaking of my parents had defused the worst of a tense situation. "I must go up before Nurse arrives to beat us both about the head and shoulders, but I'd like to say—"

Prince Escalus caught my hand, bowed, placed a gentle kiss on the back of my fingers, and said, "Yes, I desire that you teach Princess Isabella how to handle a blade. The persons who murdered my father are unknown, the house of Leonardi is beset by my invisible enemies, and I would have her able to defend herself as you do."

Before I could catch my breath in surprise, he disappeared into the gardens' shadows. I turned away, believing him gone, when the breeze carried to me the faintest whisper.

"Your hair is beautiful."

I pretended I didn't hear.

CHAPTER 28

One might say I stormed into the house and up the stairs. My bedroom door stood open; as soon as I entered, Nurse slammed it shut behind me. A single door slam was to be feared. A double—one on the balcony and one here—meant I was in real trouble.

We turned on each other.

Nurse was renowned not only for her good forward sight but also for the eyes in the back of her head. "Foolish girl, I saw the man in the shadows. Who was it?"

"The prince."

It took Nurse a moment to realize she didn't comprehend or maybe simply didn't believe. "What prince?"

"Prince Escalus. How many princes do we know?"

"I thought he departed with his sister?"

"They left. He came back." I waited while Nurse realized that, even before she could scold me, her script had changed.

She lifted one finger. "How did he—?"

"I don't know. He had earlier said he'd speak to my lord father about securing the estate against an intruder. He knows a way in, I think. I'll speak to Papà also."

"What did the prince want with you?" Nurse asked.

I'm not absolutely sure. "To give me a weapon."

"A weapon?" Her voice rose.

I lifted my skirt and showed her the holster strapped to my ankle, the handle of the dagger protruding.

She stared at it. "That was good of him. Did *you* strap it on?"

She'd caught the gist of the matter. "He did."

She contemplated my ankle yet more. "The prince. Prince Escalus. Gave you a weapon. Which, I understand, he believes as I do that you're in danger. He returned to Casa Montague to gift it to you and he . . . attached it to your person himself?"

"Correct again."

She crossed her arms over her chest. "Is there more you want to tell me? *Should* tell me as the nurse who vigilantly guards your virtue?"

I ran through the odd, princely visit in my mind. "Not specifically. He showed me how to use the blade, as you did when you gave me your gift."

"Exactly as I did?"

"No, not exactly. I think he was amusing himself at my expense, mayhap testing to see if I was so advanced in age I was desperate to give up my much discussed virginity—"

"He's such a cold fish, I would have never thought. But"— she shrugged—"I suppose he is a man."

"I flipped the dagger and caught it—"

"You caught it by the hilt?"

I showed her my hands. "I'm not bleeding, am I? Yes, I caught it by the hilt and slipped it into the holster, and he bowed and asked if I'd teach his sister to defend herself, and he told me my hair was lovely." I left out the part about him kissing my hand. Nurse already gaped like a flounder.

Nurse fired up her ire. "That's another thing—why is your hair down?"

I fired back. "Nurse, I went out to dream in the moonlight of my One True Love. This is my home, my garden. I've always felt safe here. Why shouldn't I go out with my hair down?"

"Why not indeed?" Nurse plucked something from my hair and showed me a fragment of cypress.

"I still do feel safe except . . ." I reached out my hand and she grasped it. "In one night and day, love and death, family and nobility, weapons and generosity, warnings and madness. The family swirls around me, loud and exuberant, and I'm the one who they come to when their lives explode like Chinese fireworks right before their eyes—"

"Chinese fireworks? Nonsense, fireworks are the invention of Verona!"

"Now I'm standing here holding a Roman candle; it's going off in my hand and I don't know where to throw it for fear of catching the world on fire." I spoke pleadingly, asking for comfort. "Nurse, you know I'm the sensible one!"

"Yes, of course, you are. Let me help you get ready for bed." Nurse went to the fire and filled two mugs of warm wine, handed one to me, and guided me to the chair and table where the small Venetian mirror reflected my puzzled face. She loosened my makeshift braid and brushed, pulling the boar's bristles through the long lengths in soothing strokes.

I sighed, sipped, and relaxed.

"Life has found you, Lady Rosie. You couldn't hide from it forever." Nurse had the nerve to sound amused.

"Hide?" I couldn't believe her. "I haven't been hiding! How can you say that? I've been here, living as all the others do except without suffering the turmoil created by—"

"Life." She took a sip of mulled night wine and went back to brushing.

I finished as I meant to start. "Turmoil created by themselves!"

"I've prayed that you'd find something to catch you up, carry you away, enthuse you enough to make you forget all your caution." I might as well have not been speaking for all the attention Nurse paid to me.

"If I go mad with some passion, who's going to care for the household? My sisters and brother? Anyway, who says I've gone mad with passion?"

Nurse laughed, choked on the wine, and coughed until her eyes watered. "Not me. I said nothing about passion."

"I haven't gone *mad* about Lysander. I'm very sensibly aware of how ridiculous it is to fall in love at first sight."

"Hmm, yes. So you are. And the prince?"

"The prince? What about the prince? He was out there—"

"Alone with you in the moonlight—"

"Because he wanted to give me a . . ."

She was laughing.

I knew it was ridiculous. I knew, yet I couldn't comprehend what was wrong, why, how . . . Nothing made sense!

I leaned over and unbuckled the scabbard from my ankle. "Oh, shut up."

Nurse brought my nightgown and helped me change. She took Prince Escalus's weapon and placed it on a table by the door, then placed her dagger and Lysander's in other locations around the room.

She feared for my safety.

I feared for my family's safety.

I gathered my robe and slipped my arms into it.

"What are you doing?" She knew, but she asked anyway.

"As much as I would like to, this can't be put off. I must go speak to my father."

"Do you want me to accompany you?"

How creepy to think Nurse felt compelled to offer when I'd never in my life felt unsafe in Casa Montague. "No, it's a deli-

cate issue." For while I ran the household, Romeo was respon-
sible for the security of the House of Montague, and I was, in
essence, telling him he had failed.

She strapped the dagger she'd given me onto my arm, handed
me a single candlestick, and I crept through the silent house.

CHAPTER 29

As I moved toward the great double doors that marked the master's suite, I stepped on that familiar creaking piece of stone. The crack sounded loud in the quiet.

My parents' chamber door flew open and Papà stood there in his robe, sword in one hand, dagger in the other, and bellicose fire in his eyes.

I stood frozen. The candle provided a feeble illumination, I feared Papà might not immediately recognize me, and I'd seen him in action before; it would not do to make a challenging motion.

As soon as he realized who I was, he lowered his weapons. "Rosie, child. Is all well? Do you need to speak to your mother?"

Most middle of the night visits were the result of nightmares for the younger children or womanly issues for Katherina and me, so the question made sense, but I curtsied. "No, my lord father. I have something to tell you." I changed my tone to plead, "Please don't be angry, Papà."

He stepped back into the suite and murmured a reassurance to Mamma, then returned to view me with some suspicion. "When have I been angry with you, Rosie? You're so prudent there's never any need."

That sounded like dissatisfaction. Had Papà, like Nurse,

been waiting for life to sweep me off my feet? Was no one (except me) satisfied with me as I am? Had been?

"I haven't been prudent," I confessed.

"Hmm." He still didn't believe. "Let me be the judge of that."

"Lysander was here last night, as you know . . . and again today."

"Was he? Again today? To see you?"

"Yes, Papà."

"Should I plan a wedding?" He pinned me with his dark gaze. "Or a killing?"

I hastened to reassure him. "No, Papà. My virtue is safe. Lysander complimented you on your hedges and how well they restrained him."

Papà laughed, then sobered. "How did the lad get in?" I told him about the ladder and he frowned heavily. "That's a very tall wall that requires a very tall ladder and he should have been observed dragging it through the streets. I wonder if he had help?"

"I don't think so. He said something about . . . a ladder of special making."

"Ohhh. Interesting." Papà scratched at his chin and its growth of dark beard. "I've investigated Lysander. He has a reputation around Venice as the quietest of the Marcketti boys and, upon closer inquiry, the cleverest. A middle son wishing to prove himself. I don't think his appearance now, in Verona, is an accident."

Now I was suspicious. "You think he came here for what purpose?"

"A just question. I'll find out." His scrutiny strengthened. "You're in love at last, Rosie?"

"I fell in love with a pretty face, Papà. But he . . . he's funny, he's intelligent, and—"

"And he thinks you're wonderful."

"I *said* he was intelligent."

He chuckled. "Then you'll have brilliant children."

I clasped my hands before my chest. "Let's not tempt the Fates, Papà. We're a long way from that and in our family, the course of true love seldom runs smooth. Remember, the Montagues are still enemies of the Marckettis."

His face settled into grim lines. "Yes, I remember. Is that all you have to tell me, Rosie child?"

This next confession made me want to squirm. "After Prince Escalus and Princess Isabella left, the prince . . . returned."

Clearly I had startled Papà. "I saw him start down the street with the sedan chair. Why did he return?"

I asked tartly, "More to the point, how did he get in?"

"That I know. He has a key to our postern gate." Papà threw that off carelessly, as if I shouldn't be astonished.

Yet I was. "What? Why?"

"I gave it to him after Prince Escalus the elder was killed. I feared for the young man's life. I told him to keep the key close and if he had need, he could come here and the house of Montague would defend him."

Not that I expect to know everything in the family . . . but in my experience, in a family of this size, information usually leaked out. Prince Escalus the elder has been dead for eleven years, and for those eleven years Papà has quietly allowed Prince Escalus the younger to have unlimited access to our home? "That could be dangerous."

I could tell Papà wanted to pat me on the head and tell me to mind my weaving, but a man with six daughters knew better than to dismiss their acumen. "There was no danger, little one, the key's not marked and should he be taken, he would die before he gave up information on which lock it turned."

"You . . . risked so much for him?"

"For the House of Leonardi, who have long been the Montagues' allies and Verona's just rulers? Yes." Simple. Direct. Impressive, considering how cautious and protective my father could be.

I pressed a little harder. "Verona is better now. More stable. Surely he should return the key?"

"No one knows who killed his father. Someone is out there still, ready and eager to send Verona into disorder, seize power, destroy all that's noble and good and right and lawful." Papà frowned. "But you haven't told me why he returned or how you came to see him." With some humor, he said, "Please tell me he didn't play the balcony scene with you."

I looked at him, wide-eyed.

His mood changed in an instant. "I'll kill the *canaglia*." His sword rose and he started to stalk toward the stairs.

"No, Papà, no, please." I hurried after him and caught his arm. "I was on the terrace, looking at the moon."

"By yourself?"

"Yes, by myself!"

My indignation did nothing to impress him. "And?"

"Prince Escalus appeared."

"And?"

"He wanted me to carry his—"

"Baby?"

"No! Papà, stop! Sweet Virgin forbid. His dagger."

"His *dagger?"* Obviously, I'd done nothing to assuage Papà's suspicions.

"His blade. His knife. Like this!" I pushed up my sleeve and showed Papà the hilt and scabbard.

"This is his?"

"No, this is the one Nurse gave me today."

"How many weapons have you received?"

"Three. Nurse, Prince Escalus, and—"

"Lysander." Papà eyes stood half-shut, thinking thoughts that I hoped were not murderous. At last he nodded. "All were wise to be concerned about your safety. I was lax in not think-ing of it myself."

"You've hardly had time," I reassured. "Events continue apace."

"That's hardly an excuse." Reaching out, he gently pulled my knife from its scabbard. "Hilt about your palm's length, sufficient cross guard to keep you from cutting yourself, and a blade about the length of your hand."

I measured my hand on my arm. "The blade is shorter than that."

"You can wear the scabbards and daggers and still bend your elbows?"

"I can." Although Lysander's did cause discomfort.

Papà ran his thumb along both edges. "Good and sharp. A cutting and slashing blade with a nice point." He handed it back to me. "Show me the dagger at your ankle."

"I don't have it on me, but the hilt is about the same and the point is needle sharp, the blade short and thin and without edges."

"A stiletto. You could pierce a man's heart with that."

"Yes, I could." My father was warning me I might have to.

With a cautious glance toward the bedroom door, he said softly, "Tomorrow, bring your weapons and meet me between the boxwoods where we're out of sight of the house."

"The usual area?"

"Yes. I'll inspect the blades and together we'll refine your fighting skills."

I flung my arms around his neck. "Papà, thank you! It's been too long since I've practiced with you. I've missed it."

"You're a good girl, Rosie, to come to me with this." He kissed my forehead. "I vow there'll be no more visits, day or night, from gentlemen of Verona or Venice or any other city-state seeking your unchaperoned company. I hate to kill them all . . . but I will." He sounded perfectly pleasant, and perfectly sincere.

I curtsied. "My lord father, to see young men's lives and limbs severed in my name would much grieve me. Shall I write messages and—?"

"Ere the sun rises, I'll convey my thanks to them for arming you, and suggest they'd feel foolish skewered on their own blades and, failing that, on mine."

Ere the sun rises? "Like . . . now?" A swift glance at his narrowed eyes and grim mouth clarified any doubt I had.

Yes, now. I hadn't handled that as well as I'd hoped. Mamma was right; my diplomacy lacks polish. Perhaps, like my swordplay, it needed practice. Which reminded me . . . "Papà, one last thing."

"Yes?" His voice vibrated with what might have been impatience or perhaps escalating worry.

As quickly as I could, I said, "Prince Escalus wants us to teach Princess Isabella how to defend herself."

Papà stared at me and shook his head. "Of course he does."

"He could do it himself!" *Obviously.*

"No, he can't. He's her brother. She'd never listen to him. He'd have as much luck teaching her to ride a horse." As if I was about to protest, he raised an admonishing hand. "She won't be the first one of your friends I've taught to fight."

"Unlike Titania, Isabella won't fall in love with you." I curtsied again and backed away, allowing the slightest grin to warn him.

He sighed mightily. "All right, tell me. Why should I be spared this time?"

"You're old enough to be her grandfather."

"Wench!" He faked a lunge.

I turned to flee and stepped on the same cracking stone again. It repeated that sharp popping noise. I halted, one foot in the air. "My lord father, you don't fix this because it serves as a warning that someone is outside your door."

"Yes."

"You could have simply told me."

"Daughter, needing an alarm indicates caution, and I want you always to feel safe in your home."

I thought about the various creaks and groans of Casa Montague. "You have other such assurances set about."

"I'd be a fool not to, and a *grandfatherly* man with seven children and another one on the way cannot afford to be a fool." He made a shooing gesture. "Scamper back to bed now. I must speak with your mother. When I go out, she worries about a man of my *advanced* years."

"You know women swoon for one glance from your dark, Satanic eyes."

"So I constantly remind your mother."

"Does that impress her?"

"She flutters her lashes at me and I'm enslaved once more."

He returned to Mamma and I "scampered" back to my room and ignored the ache of knowing that unless the Marckettis would accept a lesser dowry for their excellent son, Lysander, I'd never know a love so true.

CHAPTER 30

Should I worry about my father confronting Lysander and Prince Escalus? I didn't think so; both of the younger men would hesitate to try to harm famed swordsman Romeo of the house of Montague, and for more reason than simply fear for their lives.

Nurse sat outside my room in a rocking chair, a candle beside her, her sewing in her lap. She looked up when I walked toward her. "I always thought when your parents had a son, he would be the cause of much labor. But Imogene can tear a gown faster than I can mend them."

I smiled. Imogene adored her pretty gowns and adored hard play. The two weren't compatible. "What did she do now?"

"She found out the walnut tree was healthy, took a celebratory climb, jumped from one branch to another, caught her sash and hung like ripe fruit until Gardener got a ladder and freed her." She sighed. "Did you get Lord Romeo straightened around?"

"I believe it was mutual." I came and sat at her feet. "Will there ever come a time when I'll have wisdom?"

She laughed and lifted my chin. "Have you merely now realized you have none?"

"This past day, the knowledge has been growing on me. Stop cackling and answer the question."

"Wisdom comes from experience and experience comes from unwise decisions, so—when you're wise in one area, you'll be tested in another."

"I was afraid you were going to say something enigmatic like that."

She started to stand.

I caught her skirt and yanked her back down. "On the way back, I was contemplating today, as one does, and I found it interesting that you never confessed what you'd discovered about Duke Stephano and his murderous tendencies."

She twitched her skirt out of my grasp. "You commanded me not to investigate."

"Yes, because for all that you're a nosy, imperious, scheming old woman, I love you." I pressed her hand. "I know better than to think you listened."

She huffed, but only a little. "I love you, too, so no, I didn't listen. I spoke to Duke Stephano's servants and his brother—all assured me he had poisoned his wives, one by one."

"Duh."

"Yet no one, not even Friar Laurence, knows who sold him the poisons."

"But surely through the years—"

"Never. Not once."

"Someone else bought them for him." Nurse had already said that no one knew—and in the case of Duke Stephano, everyone would be glad to smear him. "Or . . . or he took them from the gardener or housekeeping by stealth."

"Perhaps."

"Yet it seems a man so arrogantly proud of his poisoning habit wouldn't stoop to stealth."

"I thought that, too."

We two sat, me on the floor, her in the chair, and stared at each other.

At last she hefted herself to her feet and offered me her

hand. "I've thunk myself blind coming up with possibilities, but none that fit his character or all the circumstances. If you figure it out in your clever little mind, enlighten me. It seems if we picked up the right piece of the puzzle and put it in place, we could at once see the whole picture. As it is, with one stabbing and one poisoning, we've got no answers, a murderer or two on the loose, and like it or not, all eyes are fixed on you."

CHAPTER 31

I woke with one thought in my mind; what had come of Papà's nocturnal visits to my beloved Lysander and the inexplicable Prince Escalus?

Had Papà been diplomatic?

He could be when he chose.

Had he been abrasive?

His spoken intentions had been worrisome and involved what sounded like breaking and entering.

Had he been dramatic?

That went without saying. Melodrama defined the rhythms of my father's life.

Nurse helped me fling on a simple gown, and I hurried down the gallery to my parents' suite. There I met Mamma tiptoeing out and shutting the door behind her.

I clasped my hands at my bosom. "Is Papà . . . well?"

"Very well. He arrived home two hours ago, bruised, staggering drunk . . . and singing."

I didn't know which to broach first, but—"Singing?"

She took my arm and we walked down the stairs to a table in the atrium where the servants were setting breakfast. "As I understand it, he hammered on the Marckettis' door and shouted until Marcketti himself opened it. Romeo charged inside, laid down the first punch, demanded to speak to Lysander." She sank down in a chair. "I think that's when his nose was broken."

I sat, too, and covered my eyes in dismay. "Oh, but, Mamma! He's so pretty."

"No matter. Women will still swoon when he looks at them." She thanked the footman who delivered a basket of fresh breads, a plate of cheeses, and a variety of fruit jams.

"It's that legend of Romeo and Juliet," I said.

"It's more than that. When your Papà looks at a woman, he really looks at them, as if he appreciates them, likes them, sees their beauty." Beneath the glossy green leaves of the pin oak tree, Mamma looked as beautiful and happy as the Madonna with child. "He's like that with every woman, old and young."

I was much struck. "He is, isn't he?"

"The surprise is that *more* women haven't fallen in love with him." She tore off a chunk of Cook's dried fruit and nut bread and spread it with soft *caprino* and apricot preserves. Then she looked at the rich, brown bread in her hand and laughed softly. "Prince Escalus really loved this, didn't he? It's good to know that dour man has at least one enthusiasm."

"At least one."

Perhaps my tone revealed more than I wished, for she looked at me sharply, and a motherly question hovered on her lips.

I shrugged. "About Papà?"

As always, she was easily distracted by the subject of her Romeo. "With your Papà, it's an ongoing challenge to explain to the newly in love that he likes every woman in the world."

I took her hand. "And there's only one who is special in his heart."

"Yes." She wasn't the slightest bit modest or uncertain about her place in Papà's life.

I chose a crusty wheat roll, spread it with butter, and dribbled it with honey gathered from our lemon orchards. Taking a bite, I closed my eyes and savored the flavors of the country, and when I opened them, Mamma was smiling at me. I blurted, "Duke Stephano said if I kept eating, I'd get fat." That wasn't exactly what he'd said, but that was enough.

Mamma threw back her head and laughed. "Rosie, the only time you stop moving is when you're asleep. The day I first felt you kick, and kick, and kick, I knew you'd be busy and a help-meet to your Mamma." Slowly, she rubbed her belly as if urging quiet on this child.

"Even if I am good at mathematics?" I teased.

"Even so." She glanced up toward the suite of bedrooms that housed the children where the first rumblings of the morning rampage made themselves known. "Let us finish quickly— after the Marckettis and your Papà had thrown a few punches, Lysander arrived at the scene and my dear Romeo demanded he explain how he broke into Casa Montague. More shouting and scuffling ensued, with Marcketti Elder saying Papà had been seized by the goddess of madness. Then Lysander admitted he *had* breached the walls."

I leaned forward, listening hard, wishing I'd been there.

"Things quickly calmed down. Lysander had apparently de-signed some kind of ladder out of an odd round wood that ar-rived in one of the Marcketti merchant ships." Mamma's brow knit. "Papà said it was hollow, but as I said, when he arrived here, he was very drunk."

I chuckled at Mamma's wry tone.

"Your true love Lysander is young in years, but he holds the respect of his family. By the time that visit was over, the men had laid waste to some wines, much inferior to ours, all agreed, and some of the rancor between the houses had been less-ened."

"Go, Papà!"

"If I understood all that great slurred burble of words, he believes Lysander will go far in this world."

Pleased, I relaxed back in my seat. "Does he?"

"If my daughter is to wed him, peace between the houses would be obtained."

"Does Papà think an offer will be forthcoming?" Had I sounded too eager?

"Perhaps, but as you know, Rosie, the dowry we can offer with you will be slender, as befits our purse. To the merchant Marckettis, such a lack could be an impediment."

"So I *will* have a dowry?" That was reassuring.

"Indeed. When Papà declared to Duke Stephano you had nothing, he was simply trying to discourage the match." She sighed. "I still don't know why that didn't work."

I hid my grin in a glass of orange juice.

Mamma rapped my knuckles. "You know what I mean. He is . . . was a most greedy man. I have prayed for his soul, but first I prayed for his death. I'll have to confess that to Friar Laurence, and while he displays a generous attitude toward most of my sins, I suspect that without true contrition, I'll spend a great deal of time in prayer and penance." She looked at me with a smile. "Well worth it, too."

"We'll be on our knees together." Because while stumbling across Duke Stephano's body was gross and knowing an unknown murderer remained at large left me apprehensive and suspicious, I couldn't escape the inexplicable relief I felt at not being another of Duke Stephano's corpse brides. "Papà had wine and comradery with the Marckettis and left after an hour? Two?"

Mamma shrugged. "Something like that. I do believe there was some discussion about who Duke Stephano's murderer might be, and whether it's the same person who poisoned Porcia. No conclusions were reached, but worry expressed. A knife in the dark, and poison in the candy. Could one killer be so versatile? Or is there more than one?"

"I wish that issue didn't matter so much to me."

"I wish I believed the issue would never bother us again."

We both smeared bread in soft goat cheese, but we had lost our appetites.

I tossed my bread on my plate. "What did Papà do after the Marckettis?"

"Next my dear Romeo went to the palace to pay Prince Escalus a visit." Mamma glanced up.

The morning stampede above us increased.

"Same routine as at Casa Marcketti?"

Loud fighting mingled with cheery *Good mornings* and a loud, rhythmic thumping indicated that someone was jumping on the bed.

"Not quite," Mamma said. "He pounded on the door and shouted. The prince's guards arrested him and escorted him to the dungeon."

I was speechless for a long moment. Then I choked, "That could not have gone well."

"It's a good thing he has only one nose to break."

I dropped my face into my hands.

"Thankfully, one of the prince's trio of friends was awake, heard the shouting, and woke the prince, who came down and verified that the bruised, drunk, and bloody man was indeed Romeo Montague."

I saw no reason to raise my head. I just nodded.

"Prince Escalus took Papà into the dining room, served him cake—"

"And more wine." I wasn't really guessing.

"And they had a lively discussion about whether the prince wanted a face that looked like your Papà's, or whether he wanted to lose the wherewithal to father children."

Now I cupped my chin in my palm. "That choice seems a lose-lose."

"I believe whatever warm glow Romeo had acquired at the Marckettis dissipated in the podestà's dungeon."

"I'll bet."

Footsteps thudded on the stairs, accompanied by a loud outburst of weeping.

Mamma and I glanced in alarm toward the gallery.

Hurriedly I asked, "Which choice did Prince Escalus make?"

"He apologized profusely for interrupting your daydreams and assured my Romeo that your virtue is a rare gem, that you'd go to your marriage bed a virgin, and he is ever a friend of the Montagues."

"He appeased Papà. Very wise." I never doubted it. Prince Escalus was wise indeed. Except when he was . . . inexplicable.

"And he said . . ." Mamma took a breath as if she didn't quite know whether to repeat this.

"What, Mamma?" I asked urgently.

My siblings surged into the atrium. The girls were chattering excitedly. Cesario was the one weeping, *and* he fell down and skinned his knee and his hands.

Mamma held out her arms. "Come, little man. Tell your mommy what's wrong."

He ran to her, climbed on her lap, hid his face on her shoulder. "She said . . . Katherina said . . ."

"I told everybody we were going to have a baby!" Katherina burst out in exasperation. "And he started crying!"

"How did you know, dear?" Mamma asked her.

Katherina widened her eyes and scrunched her mouth.

"It's hard to keep a secret in this household," I advised.

"Exactly." Katherina folded her arms across her chest. "Everybody else is happy! Why isn't Cesario? He's such a baby."

Cesario lifted his head and bellowed, "I am. I am the baby!"

Everyone stared at his tear-stained, snot-nosed face.

Mamma took a napkin and wiped at him, and had him blow. Then she set him up straighter. "Are you afraid you won't be our special little boy anymore?"

His eyes filled with tears again and he nodded.

"Oh, honey." She wrapped her arms around him and rocked.

"You're our Cesario! You're not our last baby, because you're our first son. You'll be seven by the time this child is born, old enough to blow on its belly and make it laugh, teach it to walk, swing it on the swing—"

"You're going to be the big brother," I told him, emphasis on *big*.

Katherina had it figured out now, and Imogene and Emilia. They sat down around the table.

Katherina said, "I'm the big sister for all of you, and all the stuff we do—it's fun! Isn't it?"

He reluctantly nodded.

"You can hold the baby," Emilia said.

"And burp it," Imogene said.

"Can I teach it to burp real loud?" Cesario asked.

"I don't imagine I'll be able to stop you," Mamma said in resignation. "Here, eat this." She shoved her bread and cheese in his hand. Mamma was a great believer that well-fed children were happy children.

She was, of course, right. After Cesario had consumed that bread, he moved to his own chair and everyone enthusiastically broke their fast. There was much chatter about the new infant, and exchanging of stories like the time baby Emilia ate the snail and when we found baby Imogene talking to a "hoppy-hoppy" . . . which was actually a mouse.

When the most of the giggling was over, Cesario announced, "Mamma, we have enough girls. I'd like a boy."

"We'll take what God sends us," Mamma said, "and be thankful."

"What were you two talking about when we came down?" Imogene had the abilities of a small terrier dog when it came to sniffing out a story.

"Papà went out last night full of strange oaths and came in this morning looking as if . . ." Mamma struggled to articulate his state.

"As if he had been jealous in honor, sudden and quick in quarrel," I finished.

Cesario was bewildered. "What?"

Emilia translated, "He got drunk and into a fight."

"Cool," Cesario said.

"He won't think so when he wakes, bruised and hungover," Mamma answered. "Talk about mewling and puking!"

I stood. "I have much to tend to, but, Mamma, you were going to tell me what final message Papà conveyed about Prince Escalus."

Mamma rose from the table and started toward the stairs. "I can't remember what—"

I hurried after her, more curious and a little concerned. "Mamma, you must tell me what the prince said."

She stopped, sighed, faced me, and said, "He said he wished you'd stop looking at him like a stallion to be led to the proper mare for breeding."

CHAPTER 32

You know what happened next. My shouting woke Papà, who traipsed down the stairs in his robe holding his head and looking worse for wear, yelling for me to stop making so much infernal noise, while I yelled back about Prince Escalus and his conceit, and what did he mean by what he'd said?

But first Cesario clamored to see Papà's bruises, and a six-year-old Montague's clamor wins precedence over my more mature shouting, especially when our father is hungover.

When Cesario was suitably impressed at the swelling of Papà's nose and his two black eyes, Papà sank down at the table, looked at the food, moaned, and, hands on his belly, got up again.

"If you don't tell me why he said that, Papà, and what *exactly* he meant, I'll shriek again." I'd never meant a threat more sincerely.

"If it makes you feel any better, I also yelled at Prince Escalus because I knew you wouldn't play the flirt. Quite the opposite." The last he said rather sourly. "He agreed and said he misspoke, that he'd witnessed you making matches for the high and low, the mighty and the unsuspecting, and his concern now was that you contemplated him"—Papà cleared his throat and repeated what Mamma had said—"'like a stallion to be led to the proper mare for breeding.'"

"Ah." The explanation did nothing to ease my temper. I was embarrassed at being caught out and humiliated to have my excellent, well-thought-out services so rudely rejected.

Papà continued. "He requests that you cease and desist in your matchmaking as concerns him, and says he will make his own match in his own time."

"*Fine.* I don't care if he sleeps in a cold, lonely bed in his cold, lonely palace for the rest of his cold, lonely existence." I flounced around and started up the stairs, turned halfway up, and caught Papà and Mamma exchanging smirks. They hurriedly wiped their expressions as I denounced, "He can wither into old age alone and friendless, without family or joy. That'll serve him right."

Dear reader, you're right. That was possibly not my finest moment.

Papà changed his chuckle into a cough, scratched his hairy chin, and said, "As long as I'm up, I might as well give Rosie a lesson in defending herself in case of attack."

Narrow-eyed, my mother swiveled to face him.

He stared back at her.

No one said a word.

As if this was exactly what she intended, she said, "A good plan. Will you use the special swords you had made for the children?"

Shit. The woman knew everything.

"Heart of my heart," Papà said, "Rosie has her own weapons."

"Does she?" Mamma drawled.

Hastily he added, "Which I didn't give her!"

She looked up at me. "Who did give them to her?"

"Nurse, Lysander, and Prince Escalus." I off-loaded blame as fast as I could.

"I'll make a point to thank them when next I see them." She displayed strong white teeth in what should have been a smile, but looked like something else entirely. My mother, Lady Juliet

Montague, could be scary when she chose. "My lord husband, you should don more manly garb. Rosie, your gown is not your best, so sufficient unto the day. Come, children, finish your breakfasts and we'll go to the *secret practice place* in the hedges and watch Papà and Rosie take their blades to each other."

"If I do my job correctly, no steel will ever touch her," Papà declared.

"See that you do." Answering steel filled her tone.

CHAPTER 33

All the civilized world knows my father, Lord Romeo Montague, is the best swordsman within the northern city-states of Verona, Venice, Padua, and Florence. What they didn't know was that he was a man who liked children and enjoyed teaching them. To learn from my father was to laugh a lot, to watch him deliberately make a fool of himself to lessen the sting of being clumsy or slow, and, for me, to be sternly punished and then chided for losing my temper.

Let me be clear, I lost my temper with myself for being careless, and possibly as a hangover from my earlier tantrum about the prince, but in my fit I threw down my two daggers and Papà at once slashed at me with the blunted sword and left a welt across my shoulder and chest. My eyes filled with tears at the pain, but the tongue-lashing he gave me for ever letting down my guard left the real scars.

I would remember.

When I had recovered myself, I noticed the silence. Papà stood back from me. Mamma and my brother and sisters sat on benches placed around the hedges and watched without saying a word. I didn't know if they were embarrassed for me, or amazed I'd been so stupid, or more amazed that Papà had been so ruthless.

My gaze shifted to the side. Gardener watched, and I saw in him the belief I'd told Papà about the sabotaged branch, and the visitors who had populated it.

I picked my blades up off the ground, faced Papà again, and said, "Please teach me."

He leveled his most stern gaze at me. He loved me, I know, and all his intensity was focused on keeping me alive. "With a blade in your hand, you can't afford to fail. *Never* can you afford to fail in a sword fight. You have a family who loves you. You have a future. You're our oldest daughter, born of our first love. You must never ever allow someone to goad you to anger. A sword fight—any kind of fight—with a true enemy takes it down to the basics. Is it you or them? It must be you. Take up your sword. Engage your brain. Bring everything that you are and know to the battle. If someone must die, it will not be you."

"Never me," I repeated. "Engage my brain."

"Not your emotions!"

"No temper."

"You're a Montague. Of course you *have* a temper. But in a battle, that temper must be detached. Think of yourself as a blade that has been fired, pounded, folded, shaped, and slowly cooled. You have strength. You have an edge. It's not the weapon you hold in your hand that matters. You are the weapon." He viewed me with narrowed eyes. "You understand?"

I did, and I nodded.

"Now cross your blades together and meet my slice—"

We did it in slow motion, his blade swinging high above my head, then down.

"Tell me what could go wrong," he said.

As the blade slowly descended on my crossed blades, I realized, "If your swing is strong enough, you could separate my blades and slash me from above."

"Good!" he said. "If you think that might happen—"

"I use one dagger to direct your blow harmlessly off to the side."

"Then?"

I didn't have to think. I knew. "I surprise you with a thrust from the other blade"—I thrust and barely touched—"through the chest."

"That's my daughter." He touched my cheek, dropped his sword, and fell to the ground with a shout of, "I've been killed by a girl!"

My sisters leaped up and applauded.

Cesario shouted, "No, Papà! Pick up your sword!" He ran toward Papà's prone figure and pummeled his chest.

Papà wrapped him in his arms and rolled him over and over, laughing uproariously until Cesario laughed, too.

After that, Mamma allowed him to teach the younger children, and with them he was his usual cajoling, charming self, and I understood why he'd been so stern with me. I was the one in danger. I needed to control myself to save my own life . . . and the lives of everyone I loved.

CHAPTER 34

I may be a virgin (apparently a concern for *all* Verona), I may not be married or joined to a religious order as every lady of my advanced age should be, but I'm a woman of strong faith, so after a wakeful night dealing with a painful welt across the chest and a humiliating memory of my own defeat, and many long hours of trying to unsuccessfully put together pieces of reality to form a perfect picture, I determined that to church I would go to pray for guidance and for grace, and to control my temper and my tongue. My parents had been married in the crypt of Basilica di San Zeno, and there I would pray.

Again clothed in a dark, encompassing cloak with the hood pulled up, I left Casa Montague with Nurse similarly clothed and guarding my back. We stayed close to the walls and we carried our weapons, for as each day passed and Duke Stephano's murder remained unsolved, it seemed danger deepened. And indeed, as we took the first corner, Nurse touched my arm. "We're being followed."

"By who?"

"A woman dressed in black with her face veiled."

"That describes every widow in Verona. Turn here." We took an abrupt corner onto a quiet side street, then another abrupt corner, then stepped into the doorway of a home and watched, concealed by the shadows.

The widow made the first corner and kept walking.

Still we waited and watched.

She came back. She peered down our street, shook her head, turned back, shook her head again, and walked toward us. Past us.

I glanced around, too, and saw only an empty street waiting for the residents to return for their afternoon rest carrying long loaves of bread and great cuts of cheese and glorious, garlicky rounds of salumi.

Nurse and I fell in step behind her, and she twirled to face us.

It was Miranda, Duke Stephano's scarred mistress and former *trovatori* soprano.

Nurse moved behind her to close off any escape attempt.

I stepped close and spoke into her face. "Why are you following us?"

She lifted the heavy black veil from her face and glanced around as if she feared attack from all sides. Leaning close, she whispered, "Pretend you can't see me. I'm protecting you."

Nurse shoved at her shoulder. "She doesn't need your protection. She has me."

"No one can protect her from a ghost." Miranda was thinner, sadder, quieter, older, her eyes dark ringed and haunted.

"Did he do that to you?" I indicated the scar on her neck.

"Who?" Miranda's mind seemed to be drifting.

"Did Duke Stephano slash your throat?" Nurse had no patience when she feared for my life.

"No. Mayhap he ordered it, but the attack came out of the dark as I walked alone to the theater after a tryst with him. A man, thin and tall, leaped at me and used a stiletto, shouted, 'No voice, no song!' I couldn't fight him, but I could scream, and I put all my volume behind it, and people came and he ran away." Tears filled her eyes.

"Duke Stephano wanted to be rid of you," Nurse said with cruel bluntness.

Miranda glanced behind her as if Nurse herself was a ghost.

"He loved me until . . . until he saw the scar. Then he was repulsed. He liked pretty women." Miranda's gaze drifted over me. "You're pretty, but you seem so old . . ."

At least she didn't take note of my virginity. "Have you eaten today?"

"I don't remember," she said.

"Nurse, give her a coin and"—again I spoke directly into Miranda's face—"you must go at once to the market and buy food, and eat it. Not drink. Food."

Tears filled Miranda's eyes, and she bowed her head. "Lady, you're kind. You don't deserve to die."

Nurse thrust the smallest coin at her. "She's not going to die."

"I will so pray, yet death haunts us all. *Addio.*" Miranda took my hand and kissed it, then holding the coin tight in her hand, she drifted toward the market.

"Any wagers that she spends that on food?" Nurse asked me.

"I didn't tell you to give her two coins, did I? That's enough for one or the other. I hope she chooses wisely." We started once more toward the Basilica di San Zeno.

The original basilica had been damaged in *the* earthquake of old Verona. At that moment, the survivors determined to enlarge it and even now, so many years later, work progressed on the restoration. Every day, masses were said. Every day except Sunday, workmen hammered wood and chiseled stone. I'd grown up with the sounds of construction while I worshiped; I found it comforting to know so many men and women had lived and died creating this monument to God, a monument they would never live to see finished.

We'd reached the steps of the basilica when Friar Laurence hurried out, wiping his brow on his sleeve and his face droopy with worry. So anonymous was I, he walked past until I called his name. Then he cast his eyes heavenward in thanks, grabbed my arm, and dragged me along with him. "Duke Stephano's parents sent a message. We must go at once."

Nurse rushed after us. "What message, Friar?"

He kept walking, speaking back to her and then to me. "Last night, they arrived at Casa Creppa for a joyful reunion. Today they woke to find their remaining son and heir, Orlando, walking, walking, walking the corridors, eyes wide, seeing ghosts, hearing dread warnings and repeating them. They believe he's bewitched, but I suspect—"

"Poison," I said.

CHAPTER 35

After the events of these days, what else could it be but poison?

"Yes. What kind?" Friar Laurence was testing my recall of the apothecary arts. I answered promptly. "The shriveled manroot that comes on the Venetian ships from the east. From the pagans."

"And?"

"Dead man bells from the meadows and creek sides."

"And?"

"Nutmeg."

"Good. Good. There are others but more obscure. How will we know what has been used?"

"By the scents, the actions, the dilation of the pupils . . . and how quickly death follows." I remembered Orlando, the dashing young man in the market, his charm, his misplaced gratitude to me. His brother's death had freed him from a prison of exile, and brought his parents back to the heady delights of Verona. "I hope we're in time."

"If it please God." Friar Laurence panted as we climbed to the top of the hill to Casa Creppa.

The servants must have been watching for us, for the door opened as we neared and one of the younger men, not part of the staff but possibly one of Orlando's friends, rushed out. He gave me and Nurse a dismissive glance and knelt before Friar Laurence to receive his blessing. "Friar Laurence, thank you for coming so quickly. We are sore afraid."

Friar Laurence gave it. "Tell me everything, Lartius."

"It started last night." Taking Friar Laurence's arm, he assisted him up the hill. "His parents arrived from the country and he cried for happiness. He took them to the master bedroom suite, and when they had warmed their skinny old bodies by the fire and eaten a good meal and climbed into bed, he kissed them and left them to sleep. We—"

"You and he?" Friar Laurence asked.

"Yes, the two of us. We descended the stairs to the dining room and there we found Fabian and Gertrude of the house of Brambilia waiting for us."

Nurse and I exchanged glances.

"What did they want?" Friar Laurence asked.

"Money," Lartius and I said at the same time.

He nodded at me in agreement. "They came to demand Orlando repay the chest of gold coins they'd given to Duke Stephano for Titania's upkeep. Of course, Orlando knew nothing of that, nor does he have that chest or those coins, and while he tried to remain pleasant and sympathetic to their loss, they grew more and more demanding, more quarrelsome, until at last he ordered two gold candlesticks be brought from the master's bedroom. He thrust it at the Brambilias and told them to be off." Lartius added reflectively, "They were hideous candlesticks with mermaids and fish. No one will mourn their loss, but Gertrude quite relished them."

"The Brambilias proclaimed themselves satisfied and left?" Friar Laurence asked.

"Gertrude was satisfied. Fabian looked greedily at the other furnishings in the dining room." Lartius grimaced in disgust. "He left only reluctantly. Orlando confessed he knew over the next few weeks he'll face debtors demanding payment and worse, for his father, Duke Pietro, begged him to assume his role as head of the family. The old man is very feeble after the long ordeal in exile."

"I'll send a healing tonic to Duke Pietro and his good wife, and pray for their good health and recovery," Friar Laurence promised.

I crossed myself and added them to my prayers, as well.

"Orlando and I ate well and drank deep, and in our friendly good cheer Orlando seemed to forget the ugly scene." Lartius smiled as if at good memories. "We went to our beds, and when I woke up with a candle shining close to my face"—he raised his hand as if to shield his eyes—"I saw Orlando. He was muttering, 'They're coming. They're coming. Beware. They'll take us!' I thought he was sleepwalking, so I tried to wake him. I shook his shoulder and he shrieked like a ghoul, 'They're here. Look at them. They're here.'"

Friar Laurence took Lartius's arm. "You've had no signs of the madness yourself?"

"None. I am myself." Lartius pressed his hand to his forehead as if checking to see what he said was the truth.

"What happened then?" I asked.

"He . . . he . . . he wandered away, down the hall, calling the names of Duke Stephano's dead wives, hands outstretched as if to catch them." We'd reached the open door marked with the Stephano crest, where Lartius turned to Friar Laurence and in a shaking voice declared, "He's possessed!"

"By whom?" I wasn't dismissing the possibility. Everyone knows that where cruel murder stains the floorboards with blood, the ghosts do walk and seek revenge for their passing, and with so many lost to one man's greed, the dead would rise.

Lartius looked at me in alarm and spoke in a chill whisper. "Duke Stephano's ghost, of course. He fears the wives which he so coldly killed."

"Let me examine Orlando and decide," Friar Laurence said. "Other forces could be at work." He entered the house.

Lartius followed, and Nurse and I behind, and in the dark entry we found the Creppa servants, clad in black and shades of red, kneeling in various attitudes of supplication.

Curan, the man who at the betrothal party had thanked me for killing Duke Stephano, spoke for them. "Friar Laurence, take pity on our souls. Those living beings in this house live on the cliffs above hell. Flames lick at us, and we are doomed."

Friar Laurence blessed them and spoke words of comfort to them, assuring them he would move heaven and earth to protect them. He then asked that they show us where Orlando had gone.

Curan laboriously rose. "Lord Orlando was stumbling so much, we feared he would fall, so with the permission of his parents we shut him in his bedroom."

"Good, Curan. Confining him is exactly the right thing," Friar Laurence said.

Curan now faced me and in a low, urgent voice said, "My Lady Rosaline, before you enter further, forgive me, I must speak. You were betrothed to Duke Stephano, and you—"

"I did not kill him!" My denial had become automatic.

"As you say, Lady Rosaline." Curan bowed.

Lartius gasped and crossed himself. "You're Lady Rosaline of the house of Montague? You're the maiden he intended to wed?"

"She is." Curan turned back to me. "Each of Duke Stephano's wives have died. Also the young woman at the party, and Duke Stephano himself, and now his brother is possessed or driven mad. You should flee this house, flee Verona, take shelter in a convent and pray that you've outrun your fate."

Twice now he had made me the cynosure of all eyes. I thought he meant well, but what the actual Erebus did he think he would accomplish? Obviously I was here, well chaperoned, and ready to take part in this investigation, and he was announcing dire warnings that made people edge away like I carried the stain of the great pestilence on my brow.

"These women are with me and carry the protection of heaven." Friar Laurence was such a rotund, cheerful, kind and concerned man, it always surprised people—me—when he used the Voice of the Monk to chide and crush pretensions.

Certainly it worked on Curan, who cringed back like a demon faced by a crucifix.

Lartius was not so easily crushed, or perhaps he felt as if he must speak. "Please, good friar, does not Curan speak the truth? Duke Stephano acted like a rock thrown into a still pond, sending ripples and surges that overwhelmed the unwary and sent them to their dooms. Even in death he brings disaster on his family. Is it not possible for his cruel spirit to accomplish what he couldn't in life? To destroy another young woman he attached to him with the bonds of betrothal?"

Curan nodded emphatically, then cringed when Friar Laurence pointed a finger at him.

The Creppa servants murmured and cried out and prayed.

This house felt like a leper colony, a place to shun and be shunned.

"I trow it's not a spirit that brought madness to Orlando, nor a bewitching," Friar Laurence said.

"How do you know that?" Lartius asked.

"When I see him, I'll know for sure." To Curan, Friar Laurence said, "Take me to your master."

Curan hopped along, his skinny legs in their dark red tights speeding up the stairs and along the corridors to an open door . . . where Orlando's elderly parents stood in their night clothes, crying and wringing their hands. Orlando's mother turned to Friar Laurence. "He's gone. My baby's gone. My sweet boy is mad. Do something!"

I ran down the corridor in the direction of her pointing fin-ger, Friar Laurence and Nurse puffing behind me, and I found Orlando in a large, shadowy gallery, staring at a closed curtain and talking, using his hands to make his point, whatever that point might be. "I didn't do it," he said. "He was my brother. I hated him and he deserved to die every day, but I didn't kill him. I didn't kill his wives. Why am I punished? Why?" Sweat soaked his hair, and his nightshirt stuck to his back. When Friar Laurence spoke his name, he turned his head slowly, creakily, as if his neck had developed rigor mortis, and when he saw the wooden cross that hung around the good monk's neck, he screamed in high-pitched terror and fell to his knees.

Friar Laurence hastily retreated into the shadows and ges-tured me forward. I knelt beside Orlando's crumbled figure. I spoke his name in gentle tones. He lifted his face to me and something shifted in his countenance, a progress away from in-sanity and to hopeful wonder. "Lady Rosaline, are you alive?"

I touched his hand. "I am."

He snatched it in his and lifted it to his lips. He lowered his voice to the barest whisper. "Listen to me." His gaze shifted from side to side as if he saw danger lurking in the shadows. "When Leir chose you, the demons of hell escaped and drew breath on God's good earth. They're after us all. All of us who let the abomination that was Leir Stephano draw breath. Take care. When the stench of decay fills your nose, you'll know that death draws near. Lady Rosaline, take care! And God save you." He collapsed on the floor, unconscious.

Nurse dragged me backward.

Friar Laurence leaped to Orlando, pressed his finger to his throat, lifted his eyelid, and said to Lartius, "He's alive. Take him to his bed and let's see if we can give Godly help to save his life." To me, he gave the monk's gimlet eye. "Rosie, get out of this house. Go to my shop. Do not linger. Lock the door be-hind you. Wait there for me!"

I started for the door, realized Nurse wasn't behind me, turned and saw Friar Laurence admonishing her, also. He was afraid for me, as afraid as Orlando, and my mind returned to that moment when we heard about Porcia's death and Friar Laurence had fainted. What knowledge did he possess that he dare not speak, and why?

CHAPTER 36

Nurse wrapped me up in my cloak and hustled me out the Stephano family's door. We sped through Verona's now-sunny streets, heads down, doing our best to be inconspicuous, our whole goal to get to Friar Laurence's shop and to safety. The vibrant city bustled and hummed, ignorant of the scenes of horror we'd left behind, not knowing that the life of one of its bright young men depended on the grace of God and one skilled monk. Grief walked with us, and suspicion. Who had done this dreadful thing? Was it Titania's parents, wrathful at being deprived of their gold?

Or was it, as somehow seemed true, Duke Stephano's wives rising from the grave to take their vengeance on the living?

Yet when we turned onto the dark alley where the apothecaries had hung their signs, we saw a shadowy figure furtively slipping toward the end of the alley. I pushed back my hood to better see. From here, the man looked like—

"Lysander!"

When I would have rushed forward, Nurse shushed me and held me in place. "The good monk instructed you should be defended even against your own intentions, and I will so do!"

I pointed. "But that's Lysander!"

"Perhaps, but that's not our concern now." So saying she

shoved me toward Friar Laurence's shop, through the door, and after locking it behind us, she pocketed the key.

"What would Lysander be doing down here?" I went to the soot-smudged window and peered out. "What is he seeking from Toil and Trouble apothecaries?"

Nurse yanked me back. "We don't know what's down there, and we don't know if it was him."

I turned on her fiercely. "It was his cap. I know it well."

She took a breath as if to argue, let it out, and nodded.

I started for the window again.

She yanked me back again.

"I'm still cloaked and there's no light behind me. No one can see in and . . . look!" Another male figure skulked past, following Lysander's route.

This time, Nurse beat me to the window. "That looks like the prince's man, Marcellus of the house of Parisi."

The events of the morning left me suspicious and frightened, jumping to conclusions and wondering if I was overreacting . . . but afraid I was not. "Nurse, what is this conspiracy? I must go. I will go."

"Not you! To Friar Laurence I gave my oath that I would take you to his shop—"

"And you did. But this is Lysander, and Marcellus is following him."

"Or meeting him."

I struggled with that. I didn't like Marcellus . . . but yes. "He might be meeting him. But why, and why at the Toil and Trouble?"

"I don't know. I've never dared go farther than Friar Laurence's shop. The shadows there are deeper, somehow."

"You know what I fear, don't you?"

She nodded. "That Lysander is somehow involved in the murders."

"Or that Marcellus is hunting him."

"Or both." Nurse pulled up her hood and unlocked the door. Whatever was happening, she wanted to know, too. "Me first," she commanded, and slipped out, then gestured me forward. "No one in sight."

The alley dead-ended, and warm summer had left the dirt parched and hardpacked.

We moved quietly, staying close to the wall, past two more quiet, unobtrusive apothecary shops with closed doors and small, dirty windows. When we got toward the end of the alley, we stared across at the doors side by side. One was the Toil and Trouble apothecary shop . . . and one wasn't. A small sign read, LA BOCCA DEL LUPO—the wolf's mouth, and in tiny letters listed the owner as TOPO LUPO.

"What is it?" I whispered.

Nurse indicated I should remain where I was, and crept forward to look into the even filthier windows.

What was with these people with their love of dirt and darkness?

Then I looked at the Toil and Trouble and realized their windows were pristine . . . and the shop was owned by women.

The other businesses were run by men.

Oh. That answered that question.

While Nurse peered in the window, I noticed the door of the Toil and Trouble was slightly open, and through the window I could see a neat shop with nothing out of place except—

Nurse tiptoed back. "I can barely see inside, but it's clearly a public house. Dangerous, by the name of it. Lysander and Marcellus are there, sitting at a table holding glasses, heads together. They're holding a conference about something, and they don't want to be overheard."

"Hmm." I glanced at the door of the apothecary shop again.

"You can't go in. It's a sleazy place, empty except for them. I don't know how they stay in business."

"You're correct, I can't."

"You couldn't slip in unnoticed and you can't confront two grown men and ask . . . what?" Nurse did a double take. "You're not going to insist on going in?"

"I thought only the Toil and Trouble was down here. But you're right, I can't go into a public house, no matter how I long to discover what they're discussing." I started toward the open door of the Toil and Trouble. "But I can go in here."

"What? No, you can't." Nurse hurried to catch up.

"Something's wrong," I said.

"What do you mean? Why do you care? Those two women are in pact with the—"

I pushed the door open far enough to see inside.

"—Devil," Nurse finished weakly. "Is she dead?"

"So it would appear."

The woman's body was dressed all in black and stretched out on the floor, a dagger clutched in one hand and the hilt of another stuck in her throat.

"She must have given someone the wrong potion." Nurse whispered as one does in the presence of violent death . . . unless one falls on the body, in which case one screams.

The memory of Duke Stephano's cooling body beneath my palms made me shudder, and when Nurse drew me back, I went willingly—and bumped into the newcomer in the doorway.

"What are you doing here?" a woman's voice demanded sharply. "Why are you—" She caught sight of the body and gasped. "Agatha!" She shoved us out of the way and ran to kneel by the dead woman's side. Frantically she felt for a heartbeat, put her ear to the woman's chest. "Cold. She's cold." In a fury she turned on us. "What have you done?"

"We found her," I said. "If she's cold, you know we didn't do it!"

"You could have!"

I broke away from Nurse and went to kneel beside this woman. "You're Nunziatina?"

"Yes."

I extended my hands and showed them to her. "You think we killed her and stayed while the body cooled and grew rigid? No."

Nunziatina stared, wide-eyed, and nodded once, hard. "No, you're not covered in blood. If you'd stabbed her in the throat in that particular spot, you'd be coated." She choked as she gazed at her sister's bloodied body. "It spurts."

"I know," I said. "I . . . work at the apothecary shop on the corner."

Nunziatina's eyes sharpened. "Right. I've seen you. You're Lady Rosaline Montague. Infamous for the killing a few nights ago."

Reflexively I said, "I did not kill Duke Stephano."

"No. Most apothecaries are adverse to killing." Nunziatina waggled her fingers. "Although there are exceptions."

"Nor would we have returned if we'd killed her." Nurse shifted from foot to foot. She wanted to go.

"That does seem . . . unlikely. The problem is, my sister and I have learned to be careful. We're both good with our knives, and fast." With a loving touch, Nunziatina brushed the hair off Agatha's forehead. "No one easily gets close to us. So who did this? Did you see him sneak past your shop?"

"We saw two men, but they've recently arrived and they're in the"—Nurse jerked her head to the side—"La Bocca del Lupo."

I was more patient. "We just got back from a visit with Friar Laurence. We were called to Casa Creppa by Friar Laurence because a young man was going mad. Poisoned."

Nunziatina sat back on her heels. "Tell me."

I did. I told her about Orlando's behavior, his hallucinations, the way he collapsed.

Nunziatina listened closely. "He was fighting the drug. Good. If there's something to be done, Friar Laurence knows what that is. You can have hope for your friend."

Nurse moved closer. "Who's doing this, do you know?"

"It's got to be Curan," Nunziatina said.

"Curan?" I was incredulous. "He who leads the servants of Casa Creppa?"

"He comes to us . . . often. For years. First he wanted a poison to kill rats. Half our business is killing rats. Then he wanted a poison to end the infestation of flies." Nunziatina fluttered her fingers. "Everything must be the strongest, the best, the most deadly. We tell him, to kill rats you need little bits, to end an infestation you need a light hand. Yet every time . . ." Nunziatina's mouth twisted bitterly. "Then, oh then, he wanted a drug to drive someone mad. Once we sold him the rat poison, once we realized that we'd bargained with the devil, we wanted to stop, but we're the women who help other women. Difficult periods? Come to us, we'll help you. Husband who beats you? Come to us, we'll make him sorry. Your father rapes you—"

I held up my hand. "Please, no."

"You're lucky in your family. Your father's a good man." Nunziatina sighed. "I'm happy for you. But once Curan had bought from us, we were trapped. He made that clear. We were females. We were apothecaries. We're witches."

I comprehended the noose with which they'd hung themselves. They had to sell their wares to survive, and when they did, they were no longer free, for a man could accuse them— and they'd burn.

Behind us, the door creaked open wide and a large shadow fell across the shop. We all gasped, then sighed. Friar Laurence. It was Friar Laurence, and when he saw us, he broke down in tears. "Lady Rosaline, why did you leave the shop? Why . . . ?" He focused on Nunziatina, crouched beside her sister's body. "Oh, my dear. No!" At once he transformed into the much-beloved monk caring for his flock. He hurried over and knelt beside Agatha. He placed his rosary on her and prayed.

I don't know what else he did for I, too, bowed my head and prayed, but when he was done, Nunziatina took his hand and kissed it, and said, "Thank you, Friar Laurence." She had tears in her eyes, and again she stroked her sister's hair off her forehead, then ran her hand down her arm . . . and gasped. "Look. Look! There's blood on the tip of her knife. She got the bastard, whoever he was. I hope he dies from this wound."

"I do, too. I'm so sorry for your loss." I extended my hand to Nunziatina.

She grasped it. "Be careful, Lady Rosie. Mutterings rumble through the city. Duke Stephano is dead. No one cares that the bastard is dead, but men hate when a woman escapes their traps. Be wary." Nunziatina touched her forehead. "Think before you speak, before you move, before you—"

"Charge in," Nurse said.

Friar Laurence nodded.

I viewed them, kind people all. "I'll do that."

CHAPTER 37

At last Nurse got what she wanted and hustled me out of the Toil and Trouble. She veered off to peer into La Bocca del Lupo again. Lysander and Marcellus had left, although I know she would have said that regardless for she feared I'd lose my sense, go in, and ask what they were doing.

I wouldn't. That would be so bossy big sister, and that was not how I wanted Lysander to think of me. I really wouldn't allow my curiosity to get the better of me . . . I don't think.

Ah, but to be so close to Lysander and not speak! My heart ached and yearned.

When we got to Friar Laurence's shop, he led the way in, packed up the food basket I'd brought him the other day, and sent Nurse back to the Toil and Trouble with his entire pantry. "I'm too stout anyway." He patted his belly. "It's bad for the belly."

I hugged him. "Yet your heart is good and big. How is Orlando?"

"With God's grace, he'll live."

Tears sprang to my eyes. "I'm so glad. His parents deserve for him to be well, and he deserves all the best. Yet I must wonder, how did he get the poison? Nunziatina says it was Curan."

"An interesting speculation, but ultimately, no." Friar Laurence was most definite.

"From Fabian and Gertrude of the house of Brambilia, then? I'd like to think they were guilty and could be removed from society." I remembered how cruelly Gertrude had taunted me at my betrothal, and their greed in demanding a return of their gold, as if their daughter's life could be paid for in coin.

"Fabian and Gertrude are a source of trouble, indeed, and the house of Brambilia is built on the quicksand of violence and greed." Friar Laurence seemed to choose his words carefully. "But it's not them upon whom my suspicion falls."

I groped for more possibilities. "Is there a chance it was intended for Lartius?"

Friar Laurence seated himself on a stool across the table from me. "I don't believe so."

"How is all this happening?" I seated myself also.

His eyes shifted to the side. "I cannot say."

"Cannot? Or will not?"

"Don't question me." He grasped the large crucifix around his neck as if it steadied him. "I have holy duties you can't comprehend."

I gripped his arm. "You do know something. You must tell me!"

"No."

That softly spoken *no* shook me to the core. He meant it. But why?

I might ask myself, but I knew. He'd said, *I cannot divulge what I hear in confession.* For what he heard in confession was sacred, and he would never betray that trust. But if I phrased my question carefully . . . "Friar Laurence, I'll do anything to make sure my family is unharmed. How should I proceed?"

"Rosie, I don't wish to foster pride in you, but for a woman, your mind is perceptive, even gifted."

With an irony Friar Laurence had no chance of comprehending, I said, "With the generous aid from you and my parents, I have thus far managed to avoid pride in my intelligence."

"If thinking logically would have brought you to a conclusion, you'd already know what . . . has occurred, what is occurring. I'll give you the advice the head of my monastery gives us. For every problem, go to church and pray to Jesus, his Holy Virgin Mother, and to St. Zeno, who dwells in that house of the Lord and protects Verona."

I wanted to sigh in exasperation.

Then he said it differently. "After you say your prayers, still the voices in your head, and listen in your soul. When God speaks, if we listen, we can hear."

I nodded. And nodded again. When Nurse burst through the door in a rush, I stood. "Nurse, we go now to Basilica di San Zeno, where we first intended to go this morning, and there we will pray for . . . guidance."

"Let us away," Nurse said fervently. "I want no more of this alley. I fear this place."

"There's aught to fear here." I felt like the elder reassuring her.

Only an overwhelming sense of futility filled my mind. Too much had happened too quickly. I knew only that I was not guilty, yet I imagined every single person in my family, every friend, every guest could die if I couldn't follow the trail back to the person who killed us all.

Titania had died of poisoned eels, the latest in a long line of Duke Stephano's dead wives.

Duke Stephano had died from a knife in the chest.

Porcia had eaten poisoned candy.

Miranda had a slash to the throat, fear and drink had destroyed her mind, and she'd been following me. I glanced back. Was she even now following me. The black-clad and veiled figure hung back, strolling with leisurely pretense, scanning the merchant's carts.

"Do you want me to do something about her?" Nurse asked.

"No. Poor woman. If she imagines she's protecting me, there can be no harm in that."

"If she's bewitched, she won't be able to enter Basilica di San Zeno. That will tell us something."

"Do you think she's bewitched?"

"No. Driven mad by violence, love, and drink, she is, although she's walking rather straighter now. Must have used your coin for food." Nurse now sounded more pitying than disapproving. "Whoever did kill Duke Stephano has rid the world of a great evil."

"Yes." But I was still troubled, trying to track the logic of the killings even though Friar Laurence had warned against it.

Orlando had been poisoned and gone mad.

Someone had murdered the apothecary Agatha at the Toil and Trouble.

Curan seemed guilty of so much, yet . . . what had he to gain?

The summer sun shone bright and warm. The people of Verona strolled and laughed and worked and quarreled. The world continued as it had yesterday and would tomorrow . . . yet change occurred, unbidden and unwanted. I was too young for such musings, but in a week my life rocked like a boat on a raging river, and I didn't know where it would land. Or if.

Outside the basilica, workmen stood, heads together, consulting drawings of the construction, which others sawed and hammered. From the Benedictine Abbey attached to the church I could hear faint singing, praises to God.

Although the reconstruction on the church was even yet unfinished, it was glorious in its soaring columns and arches, its stained glass rose window, glorious raised presbytery, and choir with stone railing. There, the altar shone with the glory of God.

We stopped as we entered to let our sun-blinded eyes adjust, then moved into the main nave. As always, a scatter of worshippers knelt in the pews, begging for grace and forgiveness, praying for the souls of their loved ones, desiring God to answer their prayers for love, for fertility, for health.

Priests, monks, and nuns moved through the church, trimming candles, holding crying children while their parents were at prayer, kneeling with the sick and sorrowful.

Nurse and I made our ways up the center aisle to the Montague box, to the second pew where we offspring of Romeo and Juliet knelt and prayed and rose and sang. Nurse sat in the pew behind me, and I put my knees on the cold hard floor and stared at the altar. I folded my hands, I bent my head, I prayed for enlightenment. I begged God to show me the reason for all the deaths, the madness, the terrors. He knew what that reason was, and I had faith I would receive illumination. God was not so much inscrutable as expectant. The Dear Lord wanted me to use what he gave me; my mind could comprehend all if asked with the proper, humble supplication.

Yet as I knelt there and, Friar Laurence advised, opened my mind and waited, no light shone in my mind.

At last in frustration I rose. I indicated that Nurse should stay and finish her prayers, and I walked toward the crypt, the oldest and lowest level of the church. There St. Zeno rested in a sarcophagus, his face covered by a silver mask. Perhaps if I beseeched him, the patron of Verona and of fishermen, I'd know the answer Friar Laurence assured me I'd find.

I passed between the columns and went down the stairs into the dark, sunken area under the presbytery, to the very spot where my parents were married. I lifted a hand to Verona's patron saint, St. Zeno, the black bishop. "Please," I whispered.

A light sound caught my attention, a fluttering like a small bird taking wing, and I turned to see a small torn piece of tattered Fabriano paper settle onto the red marble step behind me. Hurrying over, I picked it up and read in black blotted ink, *Are you saying a prayer for dead Duke Stephano . . . and your own soon-to-be-burning-in-hell soul?*

The words had barely settled in my brain when, paper in hand, I leaped the steps in three bounds and ran backward up the aisle toward the back of the church, craning my head, trying to see who had tossed the note off the raised presbytery.

Who had written this cruel missive? Who had tossed it down at me?

I leaped onto a pew and with the added height I caught a glimpse of a veiled woman in black. She held a half-carved building stone balanced on the rail, and she pushed it over onto the step where I had bent to pick up the note.

CHAPTER 38

The stone landed hard enough to crack the stone step.

Worshippers screamed. Holy people stood, horror-stricken.

I ducked and covered my face with my arms, and marble shards struck my arms and bounced off, but the knowledge could not be avoided; if I hadn't bounded up those stairs, I would have died, crushed beneath that stone.

Nurse screamed in fear and pain, and with that I turned and jumped off the pew and to the Montague box where she knelt, holding her cupped hand to her eye. Blood seeped between her fingers, and she demanded, "Get her!"

I tried to object, but she glared from her uncovered eye and upon that unspoken demand I came to my feet and raced toward the stairs on the right that led up to the altar. At the last moment, I realized I'd chosen the wrong stairs, for the black-clad figure appeared at the bottom of the stairs to the left and fled through the columns to the door that led to the abbey.

Pulling up my hood, I chased her out of the church, down the abbey's corridor, and out onto the street. She sprinted like a rabbit . . . a rabbit who cackled maniacally as she ran. I assumed she laughed so I'd know she wasn't sorry she dropped the stone, only sorry that she'd missed.

As I ran, I tossed my hood back to better see—and I heard a

man's voice shriek, "That's Lady Rosaline Montague, the witch who stabbed Duke Stephano and poisoned Porcia!"

Suddenly I was surrounded by a crowd of Veronese citizens, silent, ominous, angry. In that instant, they had become a mob.

Where was Lysander? Where was he when I needed him? Did he not sense my desperation?

The woman in the widow's garb dodged onto a side street and vanished.

I knew better than to long for Lysander. Or the prince, for that matter. Men had their greater matters and women, if they were smart, stayed at home and minded their needles, thus ensuring their safety. Normally I scorned such sentiments. Now, in the face of such universal animosity, one understood the point of those safe prisons.

My peril grew with each rumbling of the hunting pack; it sounded as if it had cornered its prey.

I held up both hands as I backed toward the Basilica di San Zeno, afraid of the people I so loved. I spoke trippingly, "I'm Lady Rosaline, yes, but you know me as Rosie. Good citizens, I've killed no one. Good Prince Escalus himself testified to my innocence."

The same man's voice shouted, "You're a witch. You've enchanted him!"

Did he sound familiar?

More people gathered on the fringes of the crowd. Faces wore expressions of fanaticism, animosity . . . and a few cruel smiles from those who enjoyed to intimidate and terrorize. And kill?

"I am no witch, and I've enchanted no man." As I spoke, I searched for the speaker. "If I could, wouldn't I have done so before I became a withered old spinster?"

That halted their advance.

I took what felt like my first breath, but I dared not hope. Not yet, for I remembered tales of the wild mob ferocity that resulted in rape, disfigurement, fire, and death in the cruelest way possible.

Griselda Flowerseller, devoted to my kind mother, shouted, "How old are you, Rosie?"

"Nearly twenty years have passed since my birth. You know my parents. You know this to be true. Tell them!" I gestured toward the mob.

Griselda nudged her way through the crowd and faced them. "Lady Rosaline really is so old, and never once has she married."

"Get thee to a nunnery!" one of the men jeered.

Not the man who had originally shouted, and that irked me for I wanted to view the fellow whose voice sounded familiar. Where had he gone? A man had fled down the same side street as Miranda; was it him?

But I had to deal with this situation, so I looked *this* guy, Varrius Porkman, in the eyes and said, "Where I reside is for my father to decide, sir. I'm but a meek and gentle woman."

Varrius backed off . . . a little. "Humph. Yes. Meek and gentle. I wish my daughters thought as you do."

To play the meek and gentle part, I should lower my gaze, but none of his fellows had taken a step back. I stared at him boldly, keeping my chin up. "You know my father, I think. He is Lord Romeo, an honest wine merchant, a loving and guiding parent to me, a friend of your prince who walks among you daily—and a swordsman of much renown." I swept my gaze around, smiling as if I was proud of him. Which I am, but it was the threat I wanted them to hear. They could attack me, but they would suffer the wrath of Prince Escalus and Lord Romeo, and that double-edged blade made everyone take a step back.

Varrius turned to his fellows. "I've got work to do. You do, too. Get at it!" He waved an arm and they at once dispersed, leaving me shaking with relief, amazed at how speedily the menace had gathered and scattered.

Griselda watched to make sure they didn't return, then said to me, "Lady Rosaline, your mother is kind, although her flower choices are difficult to view. Now before they change their minds, scat!"

I pulled up my hood and ran toward the basilica, where I found Nurse storming out, holding her scarf to her eye.

"Are you blinded?" For if she was so wounded in my service, I'd know God had truly forsaken us.

She lifted the scarf and showed me the slice on her forehead that bled copiously. "I'll be scarred, but I will see again. Did you not catch her?"

I almost told Nurse what happened, but I knew she'd be upset that she'd sent me after the dropper of the stone, so all I said was, "Nurse, I beg your pardon, but I wasn't swift enough."

"*I'm watching you. I'm protecting you.*" Nurse mimicked Miranda. "That bitch has been planning your death every moment."

I put my arm around my beloved nurse and walked with her toward Casa Montague. "We don't know it's her. As we observed, the clothes fit the description of every widow in Verona."

"It's her." Nurse lifted the scarf from her hand and glared balefully at the blood she'd shed thereon. "Who else has an interest in killing you?"

CHAPTER 39

That was the question, wasn't it? The answer would solve all the mysteries, put our feet back on the path of normalcy, allow me to once more be a dutiful daughter, loving older sister, and surprised seeker of true love.

Although St. Zeno hadn't illuminated my mind, in his basilica events had unfolded that showed me the figure of my enemy, Duke Stephano's murderer, and a poisoner of impressive skill. I should be satisfied . . . yet when I thought of the fearful, vague, seemingly kind Miranda as she'd been when we spoke on the street, I was not.

I went to bed and should have slept the sleep of the relieved, but suspicion nudged my mind, a suspicion so absurd it made me want to laugh. What had Friar Laurence said? *If thinking logically would have brought you to a conclusion, you'd already know what . . . has occurred.*

The deaths and poisonings could not be denied.

Titania. Duke Stephano. A duo of deaths that echoed like shots fired from an iron cannon.

Then Porcia, her maid, Orlando, Agatha the Apothecary, and the attempt to kill me in my own church where my parents had wed.

Somehow, these events were united, and when my dreaming

thoughts linked all my suspicions, I woke in the night convinced I had, in fact, been given enlightenment. I couldn't sleep again, but rested on my pillow and waited for the dawn and Nurse's wakening.

To her surprise, I rose with her. I insisted on checking the cut on her forehead; the whole eye was swollen shut, and red and purple filled the sags of her eyelids above and the bags below. A cold compress of arnica and comfrey gave her ease, so she said, and she insisted on fetching our breakfast.

Meanwhile I dressed in a dark serviceable mourning gown, and on my person I strapped all the weapons given me: Nurse's blade, Lysander's blade, and the small knife presented by the prince.

When Nurse returned with fruit, cheese, and bread, I sat and ate heartily, and said, "I must go to the cemetery to pay my respects at Duke Stephano's tomb."

"Why would you do that?" Nurse asked skeptically. "You don't grieve for him."

"Do you not think it would be wise for his betrothed to pay the proper respects over his passing? Such propriety might do much to ease the buzz of speculation over my possible guilt in his death." After yesterday's incident with the mob, I wished that to be so. During my life I'd freely wandered Verona's streets and no one waylaid me. I wanted that freedom again.

"It's dangerous out there for you." She worried honestly, and in light of events, justifiably so.

"So it is, and so I go early when I'll be seen by a few, and none are prepared to do more than scowl. But they will see."

Nurse stared at me while she pondered.

I knew she wouldn't come to any conclusions, for I was thinking the unthinkable.

"Call on Lysander for protection," she suggested.

How I wish I could! But if what I believed was true . . . *was* true . . . Lysander would hesitate where I would not. No, explanations must be given, action must be taken, and I must be the one to do it.

Also, let's face it, especially in the light of day, my hunch invited laughter. I cherished my dignity and feared being teased, especially by my One True Love. "Taking Lysander to visit my betrothed who was found stabbed through the heart seems a bad idea, a reminder that all men who hear the name of Rosie Montague will find love elsewhere . . . or die."

"Yes, but—"

I offered her my outstretched arm. "With me I take the blade you so kindly gifted to me, and the blade from Lysander, and the dagger from Prince Escalus. More, I take you, who even injured as you are, is worth more than any blade." I plucked my cloak off the hook. "Are you coming?"

"I know that stubborn expression," she muttered, and joined me wrapped in her cloak before I had reached the top of the stairway.

We walked the waking streets of Verona. The merchants were setting up their stalls. The morning bell rang the hours. I breathed the river, the livestock, the fruits of summer and the early grains. Curious eyes followed us; we were a lady and her maid out alone, on foot, when we should have been asleep in our beds.

I found my breath and my steps quickening.

Nurse hurried beside me, "Gods, *femmina*, are you in a race I know not of?"

I glanced at her, and around at the frowning citizens of Verona. Would the mob form again?

No, for when we turned up the road toward the cemetery, curiosity faded. All of Verona climbed this hill to mourn their dead; the ancient cemetery stood on the eastern slope of a high hill. The oldest burials were a thousand years old, so the priests said, and the noble houses of Verona had erected white marble tombs to shelter their honored dead forever. Inside, empty marble slabs awaited their occupants. Older marble slabs acted as beds for putrefying bodies wrapped in burial clothes, skeletons that warned of every person's final end, and all the reasons why one should do good in this life so one could pass with grace into the next.

The evidence of death existed before my eyes, before everyone's eyes, and when I thought deeply on my parents' ordeal in the Capulet tomb, I'm still amazed that they woke in that tomb of contagion and death and walked away without screaming nightmares. Maybe that's why they flailed and moaned so much in their lovemaking, to keep the ghosts at bay.

Nope. Don't think about that.

I walked briskly toward the Creppa tomb. Turning to my nurse, I said, "Please stand guard while I'm inside. I wish to suffer no surprises from the outer world while I pay my respects to Duke Stephano."

Nurse looked up and down the slope of the graveyard, at the tombstones with their decreasing shadows in the rising sun, and she seemed to find solace in the coming light. "None will surprise you while I guard the entrance. Although I wish . . ."

I lifted an eyebrow at her.

"I wish I'd insisted on Lysander and his sword."

In truth, so did I, but when I next walked with Lysander, I wanted it to be not on this grim journey, but along a garden path strewn with the fragrant petals of love.

I pushed the heavy door open—no one wants to make it easy for an uneasy spirit to escape—and looked around.

A vent in the roof allowed the odors of decay to escape, although in my considered opinion, not enough odors. The tomb smelled like rotting meat, and I readily attributed that to Duke Stephano and Titania. Light entered through the same chimney-like opening high above created to pull the gases upward and leave the air pure enough for mourners to visit. I was grateful for that, too; I left the door open behind me, but one never knew when a mischievous spirit might wish to toy with a living being who willingly visited the home of the dead.

I glanced first at Duke Stephano's slab; as promised by his brother, Duke Stephano's body had been placed there without care. He wore the same clothing he had worn the night he was killed. Dried blood made the cloth black and brittle, and he would wear that expression of shock and terror forever.

I didn't care. It was not here my suspicions were directed.

I placed my handkerchief over my face to shield myself from the worst of the odors and walked toward Titania's slab.

A lady's body rested there, draped in black from head to toe, her face gleaming faintly beneath the heavy black veil.

I could have cried with relief. My absurd suspicions were unfounded. Titania had not risen to walk the earth as a wraith, haunting and murdering; she rested here on her gloomy slab in her gloomy gown, and whatever fell horrors sought to destroy me were of this world, not the next.

I walked confidently toward the corpse of Duke Stephano's last wife, my friend, and looked down at the face beneath the veil . . . and registered a few important issues.

The strong-boned face in no way resembled Titania's; this was Duke Stephano's missing mistress, Miranda. She was sturdier and taller than Titania. Her throat had been slashed. Dried blood had drenched her face, throat, and bosom, and the look of terror on her face matched the expression Duke Stephano wore in death.

I swear to you, I stared no longer than a moment, digesting these truths and making sense of them—when the heavy metal door of the tomb clanged shut, and a mighty metal bar was wedged into place beneath the handle.

With that, only the light from above illuminated the tomb, and I knew my suspicion was not so much insanity as truth, and I was in danger as I had never been in my life.

Slowly I swiveled to face . . . my friend Titania.

CHAPTER 40

Let's give up a cheer for me, who did not jump and scream.

She stood against the wall, a dark-clad, veiled, painfully thin woman, tall, yet with hunched shoulders and hands like claws.

Outside the tomb, I heard the screech as my nurse threw herself against the massive door. But the sound was muffled by stone and metal, by death and decay. This was no place for the living. Here was the place to abandon all hope and die as one is always fated to do.

I wished I could abandon hope. It would be so much easier than these next minutes promised to be. But my character was not one to fail under pressure.

"You are Titania," I said.

"Yes." She flung back her veil in a grand reveal.

I recognized her. She had been at my betrothal ball, the veiled old woman I had knocked down and remorsefully cared for. But not an old woman; emaciated, yes, skin pale yellow and shriveled like the last lemon clinging to the tree, blue eyes faded to pale gray, yet still alive and wild in her gaunt face . . . and the slash of a dagger had cut across her cheek, opening it to show bone. She'd tried to sew the wound together, but not surprisingly, she'd managed only a few large stitches of black thread.

Agatha had made her mark.

In my home, I had fostered a monster. A murderess. "You're alive, yet you're old. How is that possible? You're younger than me. Are you a demon?"

Titania laughed an exultant, wide-mouthed laugh.

Her teeth had turned amber like an old man's and seemed to hang by a thread in her red gums, and the gust of her corrosive breath convinced me she was no demon. The reek was all too human.

"Have you been so stupid, Rosie?" Titania's voice quavered as she spoke. "Have you been unable to discern my schemes?"

"I didn't often think of you," I replied truthfully. "After you died and I mourned, I had my own life and family to consider."

As if my words pained her, she spasmed and shook.

I stepped forward to . . . to assist, I guess. I mean, how stupid is that? Getting within the grasp of a woman who had killed, again and again.

But she straightened and smiled with those terrible teeth and those shrunken lips. "You're invariably kind, Rosie. It's your downfall."

"Kindness didn't carry me here." I spoke briskly, the way one does to an untrained dog of disreputable origins. "What brought me was preposterous suspicion. But not preposterous after all, for you are here, much changed, but still . . . Titania. So what I couldn't bring myself to believe . . . is true."

"Are you sure I'm not a ghost?"

Nurse pounded on the door and yelled, but in here among the black drapes and moldering bodies, the sounds seemed far away, and a quick glance at the door proved Nurse had no chance to break in—and I had no chance to break out, at least not without a fight. I knew the fight would have to occur, and having witnessed the results of Titania's skill with a dagger, I knew it would be bloody.

But first I wanted to *know*. Know why. "No ghost can wield a knife. No ghost can poison a person, and drive another mad."

I gestured at Miranda's corpse. "She knew about you. She tried to warn me. You lured her here."

"Like you, she couldn't stay away. Somehow she gathered the strength to climb the hill to her death."

Because I'd given Miranda a coin with which to buy a meal. Sweet Mary be my witness, I meant no harm!

"Do you wonder how it is I live and so many others die? Porcia. Miranda." Titania gestured toward the body reclining on her slab. "That apothecary who betrayed me with a bad potion. My darling lord and husband, Leir, who I love more than life itself . . ." She didn't use the past tense, and in these circumstances I wondered—had she somehow managed to bring him back to life? Or had she lost her mind so thoroughly she couldn't distinguish the line between life and death?

As was my wont, I answered bluntly. "No, I don't wonder. I've got that part figured out."

"No, you don't," she snapped back.

"Do you not remember who I am?" I aggressively patted my chest. Because I wanted to make a point, and because she was threatening to make me a permanent resident of Duke Stephano's tomb. I was *not* okay with that. "I *am* the daughter of Romeo and Juliet. I've heard that tale a thousand times, how my mother theatrically tossed back the potion to put her in a sleep of death for two and forty hours, all for the love of her Romeo. You adored that story. While I fake-stuck my finger down my throat, you would beg Mamma to tell it."

Titania clasped her hands in front of her emaciated chest. "True love!" she breathed.

Nurse's pounding sounded regular as a heartbeat.

"Excessive drama," I said flatly.

Titania turned on me as if I'd slandered my family. "Lady Juliet's parents were forcing her into marriage!"

"She could have sat down like a rational person and explained to them she was already married."

"They would have had Lord Romeo killed!"

"Maybe. They might have tried." Knowing them, I was doubtful. "My dad's not easy to kill, and my grandpa loves to settle arguments over a meal and a glass of good wine. The Montagues make very fine wine." Titania drew a breath to object, but I didn't give her time. "Mostly, even if they are the most melodramatic family in Verona—and late events have undermined my belief in that—after some lamenting and reproaching, they would have come around. They love Mamma, you see, and they want her to be happy."

"You are a betrayal to romance, to your bloodline!"

"I know. I'm horribly rational, but the Montagues and the Capulets love me anyway." As soon as I said it, I thought . . . *oops.* Both were true, that I'm a betrayal to my family and that they love me, but Titania's childhood had been so bleak and loveless and the lack of parental mourning at her death had been so marked, I had been perhaps less than tactless.

Time to move on. "You got the idea from my madam mother's own performance, didn't you? For some reason, you decided to use the potion to put you into a sleep of death and . . . and what? Why?"

Titania's face, so unnaturally withered, took on a malevolent cast. "You're so smart, but you can't figure out why?"

I thought through all the events that had occurred before and after she was buried. "Factoring in how quickly Duke Stephano picked a new bride—"

She pointed her finger, and I saw that her knuckles looked oversized and her nails bruised with purple. "You!"

"I would say that his interest in you was fading—"

"It wasn't fading!" She crept close to Duke Stephano's body, leaned over him, caressed his cold cheek. "Every day of our marriage, I adored him, serviced him, made him the center of my life. Then . . . then . . ." She gasped once, twice, three times. "Then he grew impatient with my worship and *shouted* at me."

I was unimpressed. "Husbands and wives do shout. I've heard that in my own house."

Nurse gave up pounding, no doubt her fists hurt, but valiantly she kept yelling.

"Not like this. He said cruel things, terrible things." Titania gazed at him as if he had this moment broken her heart. "He said that if not for me, he'd be able to take *you* to wife for the power you'd give him."

"I've heard that before. He said it." I tossed my hands in the air. "But *what* power? He could have chosen any woman in Verona. What power could I bring him?"

"He likes virgins."

When I finished grinding my teeth, which were already pretty ground down about this virginity thing, I said, "Okay. He could have chosen any *virgin* in Verona. Titania, I'm an aging spinster of a good family, but I'm no conduit to power! I wish *someone* would tell me what he thought he'd accomplish by wedding *me.*"

She shouted, "I don't know what power you could bring him. I don't care what power he thought you had. All I know is when I then told him what I'd done for him, he wasn't grateful."

"What you'd *done* for him? Like the adoration and the servicing and marriage-type stuff?" I didn't really think that's what she meant, but to what exactly did she confess?

"I loved him since he—" She paused as if unsure how—or if—to continue.

That sharpened my interest to a needle's point. "Since he what?"

"Since he visited your parents. He found me in the garden, alone and sad because your father didn't return my . . . Well. It doesn't matter why I was sad. Duke Stephano told me I was pretty and he liked me." Her voice got dreamy and childlike. "He hugged me and he kissed me and—"

"Duke Stephano visited my parents and assaulted one of our female guests?" This got worse and worse.

"He didn't assault me! He was being nice to me." She smiled faintly as if she were looking at a pretty, mythic tapestry. "He told me so."

Nice? I didn't want to know exactly what that entailed, but the picture my imagination built horrified me. "Was his first wife still alive?"

"Yes. So what? She didn't live much longer." Titania's mouth curled in satisfaction.

I'd known immutable facts about Duke Stephano, believed what all Verona believed. He had killed his wives, one by one. He'd done it for money, for sin, for cruelty. He was guilty, because no other explanation was possible. Now Titania's mania seemed more like madness, and I stated my newest notion as if it was ridiculous. Because *it* was ridiculous. Wasn't it?

Please, don't let this horrible theory be true.

"His first wife died of poison," I said. "Did *you* poison her?"

CHAPTER 41

Titania shrugged. "Why shouldn't I?"

I had to swallow revulsion before I could speak. "Because she was a pleasant woman who mitigated the worst of his—"

"He was tired of her anyway."

I was sinking into a stinking quicksand of suspicion, and all my flailing couldn't give me footing. "And . . . and the wife after?"

"I wanted him." Titania said it as if that was sufficient reason for murdering two women whose only mistake was to wed Duke Stephano. As if they had a choice—both were arranged marriages.

As I gathered my words, my thoughts, I realized Nurse had given up. Not really given up; that woman would never tamely surrender me to this horror. But she no longer pounded or shouted. She'd run for help, I presumed, and God grant she bring it quickly for the silence of this grave made a fearful noise in my head. "You got him. Duke Stephano. You married him. You had him. It didn't matter that he complained you were smothering him—"

"I didn't say smothering. How did you know he said I was smothering him?"

"I didn't know. But sounds to me as if—"

"Did he tell you I did that?"

"At our betrothal celebration, he barely spoke of you. I expect he was used to having a recently deceased wife, a situation to which you trained him"—knowing full well I should keep my tongue between my teeth, still I felt I had to point that out—"that he thought little of you."

"Not true. He did think of me."

"I recall now, he did speak of you." I was starting to relish my role as provocateur. "To your parents."

"What? *They* spoke to him? I commanded them to never approach him again. They were unworthy to wash Leir's feet." Titania's face spasmed again, and I didn't know if she suffered pains in her gut or pangs of fury. "Why did *they* presume to speak to my lord and love?"

"They paid him a yearly fee to keep you. They wanted their money back."

"They dared try to steal from my husband. I'll kill them next."

Yes, I had wished for Fabian and Gertrude Brambilia's deaths. But not quite like this. No matter how justifiably, not at the hands of their daughter. "Don't concern yourself, Titania. Orlando gave them a pair of gold candlesticks. Apparently they were from the master's bedroom and decorated with mermaids and fish, but your mother liked them and the debt is paid."

Titania so swelled with indignation, I feared she might burst and spread corruption all over the tomb. "Orlando gave my parents *my candlesticks*? He threw my beloved's belongings out the window, and he put *my candlesticks* into the hands of my parents? I'm glad I killed him."

She had answered that question. "Orlando's not dead," I informed her. Not that I knew, anyway.

"Then he'll die horribly, more horribly than anyone!"

"More horribly than you? You're a fearsome sight, Titania."

She intended to kill me; why not provoke her? "Where did you buy the potion that put you in the sleep of death? Not from Friar Laurence, I trow."

"Friar Laurence wouldn't sell me the potion. He said . . . he said no. I *did* ask him."

"Why did he say no?" I thought of Nurse running to town, screeching that someone needed to come and rescue her baby from the Stephano tomb. Then I looked at the door, built strong enough to withstand an army from without—or perhaps to keep the dead within. The bar Titania had wedged against it gave her added security. Nurse might lead the charge to free me, but unless I figured out a way to eliminate Titania and remove the bar, my liberators stood no chance—nor did I.

"When I knew I loved Duke Stephano, I went to confession and told of my sin and my intention to have him at any cost. Instead of understanding, Friar Laurence lectured me about the sin of adultery and coveting my neighbor's husband. He gave me penance!" Titania was clearly indignant. "I stopped going to confession."

Which explained Friar Laurence's distress. He knew something, suspected more, and because of his holy obligation as confessor, when questioned he could admit nothing.

"You stopped going to *Friar Laurence* to confess. You instead went to a different confessor." I wanted that clarified, for to abandon confession was a fast road to hell.

Clarification: a *faster* road to hell.

"Why would I? No confessor would understand me and the depth of my devotion." Titania spoke with scorn and disdain. "No confessor would give me absolution, and I feel no shame or sorrow. I did what I had to do to get what I want."

I could *almost* smell the brimstone as it prepared to engulf her—and no *almost* about it, I definitely could smell the stench of unwashed woman compounded by decay. Orlando had warned of death's odor; it was of Titania he spoke. Titania, who was dying . . . but too slowly to save me. "Who then sold you the poisons you gave to those you killed? Who sold the potion you yourself took?"

"Curan has contacts."

"Now we come to it. It *was* Curan." Nunziatina was right, although she didn't understand the woman who hid in the shadows and manipulated him. "He's your creature, and he'll burn for this."

"Too late. He burns now." She waved her hand toward the farthest corner of the tomb.

Dimly I saw a crumpled form with a red stockinged leg sticking out at an awkward angle. "You, um, killed him? For what reason?" I thought that was polite enough.

"Curan was supposed to poison Orlando . . . yet you tell me Orlando lived!"

"If you didn't know of Curan's failure until I told you, why eliminate him?"

"Because I knelt among the servants and heard Curan tell you to leave the city and hide in a nunnery . . . before I could kill you!"

Again and again, Titania had hidden in plain sight. "He didn't *exactly* say that."

"He did. As usual, you didn't listen. You thought that you knew better, and I can always depend on you to be your usual *I'm smarter than anyone else* self."

She might be saying things about my personality to which it would behoove me to pay attention.

She said, "You didn't hear him, but I did. Then there was the matter of my potion."

"Your potion? The, er, sleeping potion?"

"Don't play stupid, Rosie. Of course the sleeping potion! I sent him to procure it from the witches at the Toil and Trouble apothecary, and when I realized what it had done to me, I paid them a visit. Agatha said the potion should have worked. She inspected me and insisted he'd doctored the potion, probably with a dose of dragon dung, and I should be suspicious of him. She saved my life, because when he came here to bring me food and wine, he'd hidden a knife in his garments." Titania looked down and then up, and rage gave her eyes a tinge of red. "He was afraid of being caught by the Veronese authorities. He intended to betray his allegiance to me. He came to kill, and the surprise on his face when I struck first gave me great pleasure."

"You've enjoyed a lot of pleasure lately." I feared what her next pleasure would be. "If the apothecary Agatha saved your life, why did you kill her?"

Titania tsked as if I was being simple. "After I confronted Agatha, she knew for whom Curan had been buying the poisons and the potion. She could identify me. It was too bad, but she had to die." She barely breathed, she squinted as if seeing me through a fog.

A thought occurred to me—she was dying, the potion had made sure of that. If I managed to drag this out long enough, might she be easier to kill?

Two women had been trapped by their knowledge of herbal medicines, and one of them had died. Very well. Revenge should be taken.

I said, "She cut your face. The wound gapes."

"Not true. I stitched it." She pointed to the gash that didn't cover the blood and the bone of her face, and purple edges like sun-dried plums that could never be repaired.

"So you did." I cherished the hope that if I stalled long enough, Nurse would bring help, and another hope that Titania's strength and stamina would weaken to match her appearance. She was death in progress. Maybe she'd expire without any help from me?

But I had a question that I wanted answered, and if I wanted to be sure of getting a reply, I didn't dare wait on either of those events. I lifted a finger and pretended like I wasn't slowly, completely losing my temper. "One thing. The tree branch outside my bedroom where once you and I sat and talked . . . was sabotaged. Over many years, a saw was used to almost sever it. That can't have been you, can it?"

She smiled that dreadful yellow smile. "Oh yes. That was me."

"But why?" I burst forth incredulously. "It was only a few weeks ago that Duke Stephano told you he wanted to marry me. You had no previous reason to try and kill me."

"Your father . . . your father . . ."

Oh. Of course. "He didn't want you."

"He bragged about rejecting me to *you*?"

That was enough to make me mad. "He didn't reject you. *Romeo loves Juliet.* Everyone in Verona knows that as an eternal truth. Even you called it true love!"

"He bragged about rejecting me to *you*?" she repeated, so stuck in the cycle of past misery she couldn't hear anything but herself.

"No, he didn't. My lord father would never brag about such an embarrassment. I knew because"—*my mother told me*—"because it was obvious. All women commonly love him, and you've proved you're common."

She breathed heavily, deeply, and for the first time I saw blots of red color creep into those withered cheeks.

"You're common like your parents." In case I hadn't made it clear in the first place.

Beneath the skin, Titania bled and it made me wonder what else was happening internally. Whatever that potion had been, it behaved like a slow-acting poison. Could I make Titania talk long enough to die from a slow seepage of blood from all the parts of her body?

She gave me the side-eye; I think she saw through my machinations and wanted to make me bleed beneath the skin, also.

She said, "I stole a saw and starting cutting on the tree.

Years it took me, and no accidents occurred, but finally, *finally* that night of your betrothal to *my* husband, I made it happen. I took it through far enough that it broke underneath your lover."

She could have killed Lysander.

"Your lover." She spat the words in a spray of red spittle. "The man for whom you betrayed my husband."

Lysander, mi amante! I had hoped to see you again. The sorrowful pang that struck me caught me by surprise: no future, no love, no husband, no family . . . *No time for that now. Concentrate!* "Wait. I'm confused. You wanted me to be loyal to your husband? To Duke Stephano? I didn't want him, and I thought you didn't want me to have him!"

"You stupid whore. Any woman he chose had to die. Any woman who wanted him had to die. Any brother who hated him had to die." The red blots of color exploded in red stars on her cheeks. "Leir Stephano is mine."

"Forever. Not much longer now until you join him." My words slithered through the silence of the tomb.

"I know . . ." Her faded eyes, so large in her face, stared fixedly at me. "Do you know why I cut that tree outside your window? Because your father loved you. Because your brother and sisters climbed the tree. Because I hoped one of you would fall and break your neck and your father and mother would—"

Enraged, I attacked.

CHAPTER 42

Papà would have shouted at me for being stupid.

He needn't have bothered. As soon as Titania pulled Duke Stephano's sword from underneath his robes, I knew I'd suffer for my failure.

She slashed.

I sprang back.

She sliced my neck and my chest. The sword was sharp. My clothes fell apart. Warm blood slithered down my skin. The copper scent of it filled my nose. Through my own lack of control, I had been injured. I deserved to die, but I determined I must live, for if she continued, before she died, she would kill everyone: Romeo and Juliet, my sisters, my little brother, the unborn sibling, my friends, the podestà, and Lysander, my One True Love.

As my father said, a man's sword was too long for a woman, too large for her hands, and that gave me an advantage which I recognized and exploited. As Titania swung again, the sword directed from above, I pulled my blades from the sheaths on my arms and met her blade.

The two knives met hers with a clash of steel that rang through the tomb.

"That is a man's sword." Knowing it would infuriate her, I

made my tone instructional. "The blade is too long for you, the hilt too large for your hands."

She glanced at the sword and faltered.

I leaped in and used the tip of one dagger to cut her chest.

She screamed in anticipation of pain.

But my arms and blade weren't long enough to take a chunk of flesh. All I got was her bodice strings. I leaped back, then feigned forward and found myself staring at the steely blinking point of her blade.

"This is my husband's sword," she said fervently. "It's right and just that you should die upon it."

I leaned back, thinking fast, and spoke almost without thinking. Anything to keep the fight going until I could figure out the way to win. "That's a thought, a terrible thought for me, but here's one for you—the clumsiness of the sword in your hands gives me the advantage."

She went on a slashing spree, using the edge left, right, overhead, slamming at me while I parried and moved and sought a way to take command of the situation. Her face, so awful in its vicious concentration, heated and grew sweaty, sagging like a wax candle melting in the flame of combat. Yet still she struck, and that sword and her long arms gave her every advantage, and I . . . I was bleeding. I was gasping, growing weaker. I had killed myself with my stupid angry attack on her. I had to do something to give myself a moment to rest, to think, so I said quite calmly, "Wait a sundial minute."

I startled her. She faltered. *"What?"*

Nonchalantly, I lowered my blades as if our fight had been nothing but a brief interruption in our conversation. I said, "Ultimately, I comprehend your motives for the string of murders you committed—unholy love and jealousy. But, Titania— why the potion for you? Why appear to die?"

She stood there and blinked at me as if she had to separate each of my words to have them make sense.

"Nice follow-up, by the way." As if unconcerned, I dabbed at the blood trickling down my bodice with my sleeve, then glanced up. "Titania, if you don't tell me, no one will ever know."

"No one will ever know anyway, because you're going to die here!"

"That may well be true, but don't you want to tell someone about your clever plan?" My performance could have persuaded Beelzebub himself to take a test flight to heaven. "What did your apparent death gain you with Duke Stephano?"

Titania glanced around as if seeking approval from the dead. Uncertainly, she said, "I . . . I believed I'd be asleep forty and two hours."

"Like my mother." I managed to sound as if I approved of such madness.

"Yes, like your mother. That would give Leir time to realize what a great mistake he'd made by scorning my love. By shouting at me." She gained confidence as she spoke. "But when I woke, it should have been daylight. It was dark. So dark. At first I feared I was blind. Then I saw the stars"—she pointed at the sky vent—"and knew something had gone wrong. Was I awake too early? Too late? I wanted drink and food. Water and wine that Curan had promised me, and bread and cheese. I tried to stand and . . . I fell. My knees couldn't support me. My head swam. I vomited, but there was nothing in my stomach. I groped my way across the stone floor . . ." She painted a vivid nightmare picture of this tomb, a woman slowly dying by her own hand, and justice's inevitable retribution.

"I can't imagine." But too clearly I could, for I, too, would die here unless I got very clever very quickly.

She continued. "I found the jug and drank, and at last revived. I tried to eat, but the bread was hard and the cheese cracked, I could not. I opened the door and breathed the night air, looked down on Verona and wondered how all could be so bright with torches and music and laughter when I had so recently been laid to rest on a marble slab." Her faded eyes gazed at some scene I couldn't imagine. "Yet I knew, I *knew* my most loving husband now realized how much he mourned me."

"That's why you . . ." At last I understood. She'd faked death to make Duke Stephano suffer the pangs of loss and longing. A girl's stupid trick and one of such delusion, I wanted to shake my head, pat her shoulder, and say, *Oh, honey.* Instead, I leaned against one of the marble slabs—I would have liked to sit, to rest a moment before starting to fight once more, but the resident corpse took up too much room—and asked, "What did you do next?"

"I went home. I went to Casa Creppa where I had lived. I knew what I would find. A house shrouded in mourning cloth. Our servants speaking in hushed tones of my passing, and a master prostrate with grief." Before I could ask, *How did that work out?* she turned on me like a virago. "Do you know what I found instead?"

"The opposite?" I made my tone friendly and instructional. "You know, Titania, that was your fault. Your killings of Duke Stephano's wives accustomed the household to tragedy. You couldn't expect the servants and Duke Stephano to mourn every single time one of his wives succumbed to death. Especially since I suspect you weren't a popular mistress."

Without warning, she leaped at me.

I barely caught and off-sided her stroke. Maybe it was time to back off from the truth-telling. Titania didn't seem to take it well.

She began to mutter in the drained, lifeless voice. "Time to end it. Time for blood and woe, the end of false friendship and broken dreams."

I'm the oldest in the family. I know how to speak firmly with a slap in my voice. "Titania! Tell me what happened next. You found a bed in Casa Creppa and laid down to rest?"

Still she muttered, "No more youth, no more laughter, only a long sleep of death and contagion—"

"Titania!" I slammed her sword with my dagger. "I visited Casa Creppa with Friar Laurence. Everyone there is frightened for their lives and souls. What horrendous acts did you perform?"

As if the memory made her tired, she lowered her sword.

Her lack of attention to me meant that she really wasn't afraid of me and my knives. Although I wanted to slap her for such disregard, I told myself that was a good thing.

"I rested," she said. "I don't know how long. Days, I think. When I roused, I found food and drink. Here and there in the house. Bowls in the halls outside the master's bedroom. Loaves for the workmen who were stripping away all evidence of Leir's love for me. They saw me. The servants did. They saw me. They were afraid. I didn't understand why. I spoke to them encouragingly. I was myself. Yet they screamed and ran."

"Because they thought you were dead? Because you'd convinced them you were dead?" Those red eyes glared at me, and I added mildly, "Just a suggestion."

"Even Curan feared me. For good reason, as we have discussed."

I nodded.

"He fell to his knees when he saw me. He trembled, then declared his devotion to me, did as I bid him, and I believed him true." She cast a contemptuous glance at the still and awkward pile of clothes and flesh in the corner. "I don't play the fool often, and I always take revenge."

"You wear the cloak of magnificent madness well."

She preened. "Thank you."

Clearly, Titania had lost her ability to sense sarcasm.

Or did she ever possess one? Probably not. "I'm speculating here, but what you imagined was that when Duke Stephano saw you and realized you were indeed alive, it would be the most glorious, loving, triumphant moment of your life."

"I followed the sprightliest music, the loudest laughter, the brightest torches to . . . Casa Montague, mingled with the guests at the door, and found myself at . . ." Titania took a quivering breath. "At the betrothal party of my husband and my best friend."

"I didn't want that union. You understand that?"

"You didn't want my husband?" Her breath smelled like her lungs burned blood. "The man who I treasured, to whom I gave everything? For shame. Shame to you for not recognizing the treasure you were offered!"

I couldn't win. If I wanted him, I betrayed her. If I eschewed him, I failed to value the unworthy man who held her heart.

I had to face the truth; I was perpetually on the defensive. Against her advantages, skill would avail me nothing. I couldn't win this battle unless I gave her what she wanted so desperately.

Victory.

I had to let Titania win.

But I couldn't make it easy. She had to work for it. She had to deserve it. She had to *believe*.

I barely caught and off-sided one of her strokes, then slapped her sword with my other dagger. The clang sounded throughout the tomb like the mighty church bell that caused the faithful to worship, and her sword wavered. I wanted to follow up with a close-in slash, but I forced myself to swerve away as if dancing on blue coals, giving her time to recover.

Recover she did, and once more she slashed sideways.

I ducked barely in time.

The lack of impact threw her off balance. She spun and stumbled.

Again I barely held myself back, and right that I did so for she came around so quickly I realized she feigned the stumble. If I'd moved in, she would have finished me.

I whispered, "You heard Duke Stephano summon me into the garden and you followed him. While Porcia delayed me, you revealed yourself to him and . . . ?"

"I threw back my veil and he . . . he didn't recognize me." She sounded like a child who'd seen their brightest dream broken.

Even I felt sorry for her. "Perhaps the torch lights distorted you."

"I was like the sun. I shone with love for him. I had killed myself for him. He should have seen me, embraced me, thanked God for my life! But he didn't know me. And when I said, 'I'm Titania. I'm alive, Husband!' do you know what he said?"

I shook my head. Honestly, I couldn't imagine.

"He . . . he . . . he laughed. Then he looked. Looked close. He laughed again, wildly. He said I was horrible, a ghoul, a walking corpse. He shrank from me. He didn't appreciate me, what I'd done for him."

"He had to die." I dabbed my sleeve at the blood that still trickled from the wound on my chest.

"No. No! I didn't mean to kill him, but he . . . he kept laughing, as if I was a bad jest, a joke he didn't like to see and . . . and nothing was as I imagined. I told him what I'd done for him. Killed his wives. He complained I was the reason he was despised and suspected. He didn't comprehend the depth and breadth of my love. That I'd risked my soul to have him." Thick yellow tears trickled like pus down Titania's emaciated cheeks. She didn't bother to wipe them away. "He was horrified. Terrified. He said I was hideous. He didn't want me back. He commanded me to return to hell. He cursed me. He called me a hag. I had to . . . I had to murder him. I had to take the knife from his belt and . . . put it into his chest. Stop his heart." She wailed like the ghoul he called her, "He had no heart!"

Dear God in heaven. The irony of it. Duke Stephano had been hated for murdering his three wives—and he was innocent. He had seduced a child and created a demon, a demon that had haunted him the rest of his life, killing his wives, providing unending misery to him, and destroying any chance he had for redemption. Finally, in blasphemous outrage, that demon had murdered him.

Some sins lash with a long, stinging tail that poisons and kills.

"You doused the torch," I said, "and left him for me to find."

"Yes."

"When you came back in after you killed him, you sought me and heard Porcia." I remembered the stains on the old lady's gloves. "And you heard what she said about taking him for herself. That's why you killed her."

Her sorrow burned away in the flames of hellish fury. "He's mine!"

Confused by the past and present, unable to see the difference between life and death . . . if I could hold Titania off long enough, her mind and body would collapse into rubble, leaving me alone on the field of battle.

But I couldn't wait. I had to end this now. My wound stung, and moment by moment I grew fainter and the need to put an end to this struggle with hellish, naked villainy more imperative.

"Titania." I knelt on the cold stone floor. I chose my position and my words carefully. "You must forgive me. Grant me mercy. Your husband was yours and yours alone. *Is* yours. Please don't kill me." My gaze flicked up at her.

For one moment, she looked almost sane.

That would not do. Her sanity was a fleeting thing, the danger she posed to my family was boundless. This had to end now. "I don't want to die for a union that I disdained and that didn't occur."

I felt the blast as the heat of her temper exploded. "You disdain the man I love."

I crouched closer to the floor, bent my head, and pretended to tremble. "I could never want your husband. He's yours! I'm weak and at your mercy. Please, please don't kill me." With one hand on my chest and the other behind me . . . on my ankle . . . I crawled forward, getting as close to her as I could.

She gave voice to all the madness and cruelty she'd learned in her short life. "More than anyone else, I'm going to enjoy killing you."

As she lifted her sword high, I rose and with the prince's knife secure in my palm, I drove the blade into her chest, into her heart.

She paused, almost as if surprise held her in place. Her gaze met mine.

I leaped back.

With no grace, no life, no hope of redemption, she fell to the floor.

It was over.

I looked at my hand in distaste. Titania's blood dripped off the blade, onto my skin. Hastily I dropped the dagger and backed away from the body. From outside the door, I heard Nurse's voice once more shout, "Rosie! Rosie!"

Hammering commenced and rapidly intensified, becoming a rhythmic thumping.

For a moment, I didn't understand. Then I did.

Nurse had fetched help. They were using . . . something . . . to break down the door.

No need. I could open it. I found I staggered when I walked; it was a very odd thing to realize my knees couldn't keep me steady. When I got close, I shouted, "Stand back." Only it wasn't a shout, it was a whisper. My head swam, and I had to lean my hand on the wall and draw a breath before I could try again. "Stand back!" This time I put some volume behind it.

Silence rewarded me.

Someone pounded on the door more rapidly, more softly, and Nurse sobbed, "Rosie, oh my Rosie!" She was beating on it with her hands.

"Anon, good Nurse." I smiled as I said the phrase of my mother. "Be calm. I'll let you in." Using both hands, I moved the mighty metal bar from beneath the handle, turned it, and flung wide the door. Sunshine beamed in. Fresh air and freedom. A crowd of people, but the only person I could see was Nurse.

I pitched forward into her arms. "Take me from this place," I begged. "I'm not yet ready for the tomb."

CHAPTER 43

The sword that Titania used to strike at me dripped with Duke Stephano's putrefaction. My wound developed an infection, and so it was Duke Stephano and Titania did almost kill me. In fact, my Nurse to this day claims that not long after she entered the tomb, I died to the world and only her efforts brought me back from the other side of heaven. I know not what she meant; I remember nothing beyond that time when the stiletto pierced Titania's chest and for one short moment, her eyes returned to sanity and sorrow.

A persistent weakness followed my terrible fever, and thus it was a month before, at last, I could sit up in bed and eat soft grains enhanced with duck egg and nettles, and drink watered wine. I knew how sick I'd been when my mother laid eyes on me, ran and kissed and hugged me, and her tears trickled into my hair. That more than anything healed me—and convinced me I must control my unfortunate temper.

More weeks passed before my siblings were allowed to visit me, and they were hushed and in awe. That upset me almost to tears, and Nurse encouraged them to act like the wild animals they were, which made me laugh almost to tears.

I cried easily.

Not long after, Princess Isabella came to pay an official visit.

She understood her role was princess, not the child who played with my siblings. She brought healing foods from the palace kitchen (no better than compost, by the way, but she meant well), she spoke soothing and encouraging words, she praised me for my heroism in stopping such an evil villain. It was odd to encounter royalty when one was used to the child, but of course she'd been trained in her duties and she executed them well.

Even better, when she finished her visit with me, I heard the other children meet her in the corridor. She must have easily discarded her imperial demeanor, for they carried her away in a glorious babble of laughter and teasing. Soon Papà would teach her the sword work he'd taught me and the other children, and she would be safer than ever before in her young life.

I relaxed, for all was right with my world.

When I had the strength to walk with help, down the steps and into the atrium to sit under the lemon tree, I at last felt like myself. There the sun fed my soul strength and hope.

On the table before me sat an olive wood board decorated with enticing tidbits of food: figs, apples and cheese, bread, shaved smoked meats, and salumis. The colors and the scents of the food strengthened my body even as it enticed my soul with the pleasures of the flesh.

Nurse sat at my left side and my mother at my right, and they smiled and wiped their eyes as if I'd died and been reborn.

Maybe I had been.

Papà joined us with Emilia and Cesario trailing behind. Mamma's belly was now large enough for her to place her goblet on it, and we laughed to see the child try to kick it off.

"That one will be a ball player," Nurse predicted.

"I'm sure she will," Papà said. A outcry of protest occurred, although not from Cesario, and Papà shook his head. "What do I need another son for? I have this sturdy fellow—"

One did not brag of health, and to avert the evil eye, Nurse pulled Cesario close and lightly spit on his head.

"And a daughter who sallies forth to fight evil and injustice when she could simply trust her father to handle it!" He glared at me. He'd made no secret of his indignation.

"Papà, I would have. Really! But the idea that Titania was alive seemed so ridiculous. Even now, even with this"—I indicated my bright red, not-quite-healed scar—"I can hardly believe it."

Mamma nodded. "You know she's right, Romeo."

"She almost died from being right." Papà would never stop grumbling.

"I couldn't rest until I was sure. I am sorry, Papà." I made apologetic puppy eyes at him. "You'd have dealt with Titania in better ways, I'm sure."

"Humph." He crossed his arms over his chest and leaned back in his chair.

Emilia scooched next to me and grinned, and I saw she'd lost another tooth. Soon she'd have a mouth full of adult teeth and a body to match, and my baby sister would be grown. I wrapped my arms around her and hugged. She understood even if Papà pretended not to.

Time to change the subject. "How is Orlando?" I asked.

Mamma said, "With Friar Laurence's help, he's recovered. His parents are so grateful they donated a large sum to the monastery, and a young artist is creating a statue of them as angels praising God."

"Good." I smiled. "Good. Orlando deserves to live and be happy. Perhaps if he's lucky, I'll find him a wife."

"Your talent for matchmaking is unsurpassed," Nurse agreed.

"But, Rosie, not for yourself," Mamma said. "You're the family keepsake, a treasure for us to cherish all our lives. We'll keep you here in safety and, I promise, we'll never again try to match you with a bridegroom."

I never imagined such a result from my escapade. They'd decided to keep me home and safe? B-but . . . "No bridegroom? Mamma, what about Lysander? Is he not worthy? Or does he not now show true interest in the wedding of me?"

Mamma took my hand and held it. "I told you, child, our lackluster dowry might not entice the Marcketti family into a joining with ours, and so it is. The elder Marckettis did in fact approach us with a suggestion of marriage, yet when the negotiations began and they heard what we can settle on you, they backed away."

Papà lost his sulky expression, leaned forward, and said earnestly, "I'm sorry, Rosie, I believe Lysander is most perturbed with their foolishness."

"Indeed, Lysander has been most faithful in his visitations." Mamma nodded significantly at Nurse.

"Nevertheless, the suit does not progress," Papà said.

"Oh." Oh. Where a few months ago my whole self was dedicated to remaining within the Montague household, I was now downcast at the prospect. With Lysander I would have liked to live through the joys and trials of love. I would have gladly borne his beautiful children. Now I must make do with mathematics and household management and caring for my siblings and making matches for them and every other worthy aristocrat and underling in Verona.

Not Prince Escalus, I told myself hastily. He'd rejected my help in no uncertain terms.

"I'm tired." It was true; an hour spent walking with help, sitting up and eating—that was all I could do. My parents looked concerned; Nurse leaped forward to help me to my feet.

I hoped I had the strength to get back up the stairs without resting halfway. I did make it back to my bed, but barely, where I immediately fell asleep.

When I woke it was night, and I found a vast malaise spread

over me like a smothering blanket. I didn't want to rise, not ever again, but alas, the body makes its demands and we obey. I slid to my feet and found the chamber pot and used it and, after checking to see that Nurse was asleep, wrapped a blanket around my shoulders and followed the strip of moonlight across the floor to the balcony.

The night garden postured in dramatic shades of black and white, with elongated shadows and brilliant shining leaves that fluttered in the autumn's first cool breeze. Close to the house, torches flamed in their sconces. I sank down on the chaise and tried to concentrate on being here, now, and not in some sad and lonely future.

The whistle, when I heard it, sounded like a charming bird trying to attract a mate. It made me smile.

Yet when it didn't stop, when it went on and on, I was torn between wringing the bird's neck and giving it to Cook for soup, and shooing a female bird in the ridiculous bird's direction. Finally, as I contemplated how much I loved well-roasted fowl, a little rock flew up in a high arc over the rail and bounced across the floor.

CHAPTER 44

I stared at the pebble, confused . . . but only a moment. I bounded to my feet, pain, melancholy, and exhaustion forgotten. I reached the railing, leaned over, and stared, searching . . . searching.

"Rosie!" Lysander's voice, speaking from the ground.

Half laughing, half sobbing, I sagged on the stone. "It is you I have longed to see."

"Don't," he begged. "Don't! Wait. Darling girl, don't cry." He shimmied up the tree, branch by branch. But the perch outside my window was gone, ruined by Titania's malicious acts, so Lysander stood on a broad branch farther down, straining to reach up to me.

I leaned down, straining also, but our fingertips could not . . . quite . . . touch.

In a voice of rampant indignation, he asked, "Did you hear that my jackass of an uncle refused to enter into negotiations for your hand in marriage?"

I tensed and withdrew my hand. "I did."

"Because of the dowry." He made the word sound like a curse. "Like we need the money! The Marckettis are the most prosperous merchant family in Venice. We're wildly, vulgarly rich."

I smiled at him in an unexpected and charmed gust of amusement.

"Listen." He crawled up the side of the tree, hanging on to tiny branches. "I've been here every night, waiting for you to recover."

Knowing he'd been here cheered me. "You were never caught?"

"I told you I'm a master at skulking. Although perhaps not the master I believed, for after the first two nights, I found a small repast waiting for me at that table." He pointed to the table on the terrace.

I looked and saw the remains of a small loaf of bread, some cheese, and a cluster of grapes.

He said, "So perhaps someone in your family suspected my presence."

"My parents like you very much."

He looked delighted. "Did they say so? I shall have a conceit."

"You may have as many conceits as you wish, but please remember, Romeo and Juliet hate only their mortal enemies, and if the Montagues make a deal with the Marckettis, that's another mortal enemy turned to ally."

"Your parents like everyone."

"Not *everyone*," I assured him. "But mostly."

He sagged. "You do feel better, don't you?"

"I do. Now." The sight of Lysander, working his way up that tree, trying to get closer to me, made me cheerful. And cheer made me stronger.

"Listen. Someone has to correct this situation. You and me are meant to be together."

I now expected to hear something about running away from our families, a wedding performed by a devious monk, a life of poverty and love until Lysander's inventive genius gave us wealth.

Instead he continued. "And you're the one to do it."

"Me?" What about his inventive genius? "What do you mean?"

"I love you. The first time I saw your face . . . after I ran into you and knocked you down . . . your face knocked me down, too. Not literally, but—"

"I understand." I loved the way he stammered. "I felt that way, too. You're so perfect."

"I'm a man like any other."

"Not true. I've never fallen in love at first sight with another man."

He hung by one arm on a narrow branch, his other arm wrapped around the trunk, grinning at me in the light from my room. "We love each other, you and me."

"We do, don't we?" What a delight this was.

"What we need is an intelligent mind working for us who has made other . . . matches. Betrothals."

He definitely was talking about me. "You want me to make a match for you?"

"With the proper maiden . . . whose name is Rosie." He crawled a little farther, managed to get to a branch above my head, and reached down toward me.

I reached up toward him.

We still couldn't . . . quite . . . touch.

I couldn't continue to reach. I remained weak, tired. I withered down onto the floor.

"Rosie! No, please, be well." He swung his legs off the branch. "I'll jump down to you!"

Nurse, a strong, hearty woman sworn to protect my virginity, charged out of the door where she had been listening. "You will not, young man! You stay where you are!" Reaching down, she hauled me to my feet and helped me to the chaise.

Lysander swung himself back up onto the branch. "Please, Nurse, you must help us."

"Yes, yes. True love. Young love. Blah, blah." Nurse's scorn could scour dried egg off an iron pan. "Rosie was the only person in the family not totally besotted by passion . . . then you came along. What do you want her to do?"

"I want her to figure out how we can wed." Lysander sounded so confident!

"I . . . can't. Not right now." Beside my head, I made a fluttery motion with my fingers. "I haven't the ability to connect one thought to another and"—I was embarrassed to admit this—"I still suffer from weakness."

Nurse sighed loudly. "Fine. I'll do it." She pointed at Lysander. "Two nights hence, Lord Romeo is having a dinner party wherein he'll discuss with your father, Duke of the Marckettis of Verona, the possibility of selling wine to them as a fine export across the known world."

"I know this is true. I arranged that meeting."

All was now clear. "When you met with Marcellus?" I asked. "In the public house near Friar Laurence's shop?"

"Yes. I was hoping to see you, but I guess bad timing." Lysander hung his head down to look right at me. "I'll be a good husband to you, Rosie. I'm more than a pretty face."

I tried to look solemn as I agreed, "I fear this is true."

Nurse continued on in an authoritative tone. "On that night when Verona's clock strikes eight, you'll meet Rosie in the Montague garden at the fountain. The two of you will proceed to the grotto near the swing. You know where I mean."

Lysander and I both nodded.

"There you will indulge yourselves in a passionate embrace."

"Sounds good!" I felt better already.

"But her virtuous reputation!" Lysander was plainly worried.

Nurse bent a glare on him that should have withered him like an autumn leaf. "I have Rosie's virtuous reputation well protected and well documented, and I'll be the one who runs to Lord Romeo and cries that my charge has disappeared into the garden with Lysander of the Marckettis and he must come with me to save her virtue."

"We'll be caught in the dark together," I said.

"I'll beg forgiveness and her hand in marriage," Lysander said.

Now we comprehended the brilliance of Nurse's plan!

"My father will be the guest of the Montagues. He most sincerely wants to be the exporter of Montagues' fine wines. When Lord Romeo points his sword at my throat and declares me a dead man, and I beg to wed his daughter, my father will yield for love of me—and for the profit he foresees by this union. Oh, Nurse!" Lysander swung down from his branch, his hand outstretched.

My nurse, heartier, taller, and stronger than me, reached up and slapped his hand.

They smiled at each other, and I smiled at them both. Two people who loved me, dedicated to creating the life I desired for me.

I adored them.

As if something had caught her eye, Nurse jerked her head and looked over the railing.

"What is it?" I asked.

"I thought I saw someone down there, skulking in the shadows." Nurse swept her gaze all around.

Lysander used his perch to view the garden.

"What is that?" Nurse pointed at a black silhouette that loomed in the dark hedges.

"Nothing." But Lysander slid down the trunk much faster than he'd climbed up. As soon as he reached the ground, he stalked around the perimeter of the light, looking into the shadows and paying special care to the area Nurse had indicated. Looking up, he spread his arms wide. "We're alone in the night."

Nurse shushed him.

He lowered his voice. "Farewell, my sweet Rosie. Two nights hence, we'll meet in the garden and I'll at last hold you in my arms and kiss your sweet lips, and before the night is over, you'll be betrothed to a man worthy of your clever self."

I kissed my fingers and watched him kiss his, and he disappeared into the depths of our yard.

"He's right," Nurse said. "He's good at skulking." Yet before she helped me back to bed, again she scanned the shadows, and as she did, she shook her head.

I spent the next two days in bed, eating nourishing foods, drinking watered wine until I sloshed, stretching and regaining my strength. I had to be able to meet Lysander in the garden at the proper moment, and I had to go by myself so Nurse could alert my father, Lord Romeo, that I was in danger of losing my virtue to Lysander. After we were caught, the rest would play out. My father would point the sword at Lysander's throat. I would kneel and swear he respected me still and beg for his life. Duke Marcketti would be forced to agree to our betrothal. And we would live happily ever after.

That night, I thanked Nurse with all my heart for the brilliance of her foolproof plan, and in my prayers I thanked the blessed Virgin Mary herself and all the saints that I'd soon be properly wedded, bedded, and rid of this irksome virginity.

CHAPTER 45

On the appointed night, Nurse had dressed me in three petti-coats, bound me in three chemises, put me into my most re-strictive bodice, and strapped the two daggers on my arms and the blade on my ankle. She added my heaviest sleeves, my tightest cuffs, and she muttered all the while. When I asked what she was doing, she answered, "You've been ill. It's cold out there. I fear for your health."

"Me too, dragging all this weight around!"

I jested, but she folded her lips into a tight line, then burst out, "Lysander is a virile man. You're a young woman in love. There isn't enough clothing in the world if passion takes you!"

"Nurse, we're not my parents. We're mature adults in con-trol of ourselves." I thought this would be a comforting re-minder.

Instead she snorted. Loudly. Yet she bore the scar on her forehead from the sabotage in Basilica di San Zeno, and I trusted her.

Now I stood by the fountain, waiting for Lysander to ap-pear. The torches lit the flow of water from the laughing cupid's tiny penis, and he looked so joyful about his naughty spray I smiled at him and hoped a naiad would join him and free him from the stone. The night air's chill spoke of the coming winter, but I wasn't cold. All those petticoats, you know, plus a cloak and perhaps a fever of excitement.

I had arrived a little early, which was foolish, for it gave me time to imagine one disaster after another. But not much time, for I heard a hiss, faced the darkened path through the hedges, and saw a masculine hand, clad in a leather glove, beckon me.

I smiled in relief and excitement, reached out and twined my fingers in his, and as he pulled me I ran with him.

Dear reader, I confess I giggled. After all, a girl can only once enjoy an escapade like this.

The moon was no more than a sliver, the stars twinkled brightly, his hand grasping mine was firm and warm, even through the glove. He stopped halfway to our tryst spot, pulled me close, and covered my mouth with his.

My first kiss.

Finally.

The lip press, the tongue probe. The taste of him in my mouth, the scent of his breath. This kiss was interesting and I liked it, but the heavens still slipped slowly across the stars, time continued as it had before . . . and may I say how relieved I was to kiss my love and still be Rosie, plain practical Rosie. I wasn't like my parents. Love had not blindsided me, recreated me, made me a stranger to myself.

I suspected he might be moving in for another try, and we really didn't have time. I knew Nurse was worried and would rouse my father and the Marckettis to immediate action.

As was natural to me, I took up the reins. "We'd better get to the bench and set ourselves up to be discovered."

He slid his hand around my waist, pulled me close to his side, and led me toward the spot.

"You have very good night vision." My voice perhaps had an approving tone, but who could blame me? It boded well for our future progeny.

My night vision, too, improved as we moved along the path,

and I recognized when the hedges gave way to the designated sitting area. He led me to the marble bench and, still holding me, sank down on it.

"I've been trying to figure out the best way to look disheveled and passionate without embarrassing ourselves. What do you think of—"

He quite firmly took charge.

After a moment of surprise, I realized that made sense. No doubt he had experience in the art of love. Men did. But as he gently turned me to recline sideways across his lap and bent to kiss me again, it also occurred to me perhaps Nurse was right. He intended to take advantage of this clever plan and teach me to sip and appreciate the wine of love.

I was willing. Startled, but willing.

My head fit in the crook of his arm. His hand rested on my breast, which would have been very exciting if I wasn't so swaddled in layers. He used his free hand to press on my belly and bent to kiss my lips.

The first kiss had been a plate of pale flat bread and dried apricots. Enjoyable, nourishing, but not memorable.

This kiss was risen bread stuffed with apricots and walnuts fresh from the tree and seasoned with cinnamon. This kiss was a treat that filled my lungs and heart with strength and my belly with joy. This was taste and sensation, freedom and surprise. My eyes closed. I found my hands creeping up into his shoulder-length hair—he had eschewed his horrible cap—and holding him in place for the pleasure of his kissing. He hovered over me, passionate and laughing, sincere and reverent.

This was the loss of self I feared. Yet I welcomed it, too, for to touch another person's soul was to banish loneliness. How better to do that except through . . . this kiss. This passion. This escalating exaltation.

Abruptly he slid me off his lap, placed me flat on my back on the bench, the cool marble cradling my head. He placed a knee beside my hip, bent, held me and kissed my mouth, my throat, my ears, my hands. He placed my hands on my breasts and pressed and fondled, guiding me, letting me know that all the fabric meant to be a barricade was nothing more than an enticement. Through my own palms I fed passion from him through me, and I wanted more. I moved my legs restlessly, bent my knees, pressed the bottoms of my slippered feet to the bench.

He reacted at once, reaching under my skirt, running his hand up from my ankle to my thigh . . .

At that touch, I broke out of my passionate trance. My eyes popped open.

I still couldn't see his face, but I knew who this man wasn't— it *wasn't* Lysander—and I knew who it was.

Prince Escalus.

I said, "You bastard!" and I kicked hard at his gut.

He stumbled backward.

I sat up on my elbows, blinked, and—

CHAPTER 46

The glare of torches blinded me.

I closed my eyes, turned my head away, gave myself a moment to adjust, and turned back toward the torches.

You have never heard a group of men so silent. My father, Lord Marcketti, Prince Escalus's men, Dion, Marcellus, and Holofernes, not to mention a half dozen of the most influential men of Verona. And my nurse.

They all stared as if mesmerized by the scene.

I faced the figure at the back of the opening, the man I'd kicked aside, and pointed at him. At Prince Escalus, who stood crumpled, holding his male parts as if I'd ruined his chances for progeny. As I hoped I had.

Without thought or sense, I ranted, "He touched my leg. I recognized his touch. He strapped that dagger on my ankle and that was fine. Not really, but his intentions were good. I think. But this! I knew it was him. How did he think I'd be fooled? His hand—" I stopped talking. Because it occurred to me the silence remained profound. I looked to the back of the crowd of men, met Nurse's eyes, and she stared, mouth open, as if she couldn't believe her eyes.

At that moment, I saw myself as these men saw me. Stretched

out on a bench like a side of Nonna's porchetta, fully dressed, yes, but lamenting that a man had touched my leg . . . and complaining that I remembered his touch, that it had happened before.

Verdict: virtue destroyed, doomed to a nunnery as a penitent whore.

Because a man had touched my leg.

Touched my leg twice.

Where is the justice in that?

At that moment, Prince Escalus recovered himself. He took a strained breath, straightened, and strode around the bench toward my father and his sword, which was now pointed at his throat.

Cut him open!

I didn't say that. I really really wanted to, but I'd said enough. Instead, I eased myself into a seated position and clutched the bench hard in my hands. The cool marble should have melted, so enraged was I, but the world remained as it had been. Stone was stone, men were men—and I was the world's worst fool.

Prince Escalus, the weasel, knelt before my father and with hands outstretched in supplication, said, "Lord Romeo, your daughter Rosaline is the fairest maiden in Verona. Her virtue remains intact, and what appears to be a scandal is none of her making. The chance to hold her in my arms was too much temptation for your prince—"

Yeah, make sure you point out you're the prince. That'll make it all better.

"—and her compliance is the result of trickeries on my part. Therefore I beg you grant me the hand of Fair Rosaline of the Montagues, to take to wed so that we may live happily as man and wife for all our days."

"Um, sure." Papà appeared to be winded by all these events.

I understood how he felt.

Yet one question pounded at my mind: *Where is Lysander?*

Men were exchanging glances, at one another, at me, at Nurse, whose foolproof plan had resulted in . . . in . . . this?

Papà picked up on the very thread that interested me. "Trickeries on your part?" His sword remained pointed at Prince Escalus's throat. "What trickeries?"

Silently I asked again: *Where is Lysander?*

No, I didn't say that out loud, either. I had regained some modicum of sense.

Prince Escalus said, "Fair Rosaline is but a simple maiden who knows not how desperate a man's desires may make him."

That was no answer, which I now realized was a good thing. Because if I was guessing, Prince Escalus or one of his men had been the shadow Nurse had glimpsed in the garden while she laid out her brilliant plan for Lysander and I, and admitting that would do nothing to help my badly damaged reputation.

Also . . . a simple maiden? Simple as in not too clever? Did he think I had no wit stirring?

With one fingertip, Prince Escalus cautiously pushed the tip of Papà's sword aside. "Let us go into your warm and welcoming home, and there drink a toast to the union of two of Verona's greatest houses, the Montagues and the Leonardis. And dare I hope, to the successful agreement between the Montagues and the noble house of Marcketti?"

Papà allowed Prince Escalus the motion, and reluctantly sheathed his sword. "Gentlemen, I beg you, do go back to the dining hall. I'll escort my daughter and her nurse to her quarters to ensue no more *trickeries* occur."

I recognized his expression. He was no longer dumbfounded; he was calculating how best to get out of this situation with the least damage to the Montagues. I was, I thought, in for a scolding. Which I expected when I enthusiastically agreed to this escapade, but for Lysander's sake, I would have gladly borne it. I now not so gladly allowed Nurse to help me into my cloak, and walked behind my father as he strode toward our family's private entrance. He led me into the atrium, ablaze with torches, and to the base of the stairs that led to my bedroom, and waited for me there. When I had taken the first step, he caught my hand. I stopped and faced him.

"Daughter, I didn't realize you'd had the good sense to catch the Prince of Verona." I didn't know if humor or bemusement infused his tone.

"I didn't. He caught me!" I was still so angry that I knew I hadn't taken in the significance of the events. I couldn't have Lysander. I would have Prince Escalus. In one gamble that had been assured to pay off, I had lost all: independence, home, and dare I say it?

Virginity.

I couldn't comprehend Prince Escalus.

I *could not* believe this.

"I didn't realize the podestà would have the sense, either." Papà stood, thinking deeply, if the crease between his brows was any indication. "This night isn't over for you yet. Nurse, wrap her up in a blanket, give her something warm to drink, and keep her here in the atrium for a little while longer." He looked into my eyes. "You won't sleep now, anyway. Stay and wait."

He was gone, walking toward the dining hall, where men's voices rose and fell and more and more wine-driven cheer drove the sounds.

He was right. I wouldn't sleep, not until the fire of fury had died and I could forget, at least for a moment, that whole passionate, humiliating, humbling ordeal.

Nurse brought a blanket, put it around my hunched shoulders. The torches burned, the stars burned, and I burned. It was one big damned flaming circle of unity.

She placed a chair beside the table where I'd eaten with Mamma. "Sit," she urged.

"I can't." I was too stiff with outrage.

"I didn't betray you." Nurse stood behind me and smoothed my hair. "I thought it was Lysander. Not Prince Escalus. I knew that night after he and Princess Isabella dined with us, he'd found you on the terrace, but you said it was to deliver the dagger, not to—"

I shot her a glance that should have stabbed her through the heart.

Indeed, she blanched. She knelt, took my hands. "My lady, I did not, I did not betray you."

"Yet I think tonight you should let me sit alone and wait for . . . whatever comes next. For I am . . . angry with everyone, even you, and I know most unfairly, yet . . . I am."

She bent her head over my hands. I felt her hot tears drop onto my skin. I didn't care. My heart was broken, my gut burned, and I was cold to the bone. "Get up," I said.

Still weeping, she did, and walked toward the stairs. "I'll send Tommaso with a tincture of *camomilla*."

"I don't like *camomilla*." Even if I did, I'd choke on it.

"You don't have to drink it," she said, "but will you sleep without it?"

"If you give me enough wine—Oh, fine. Send the *camomilla*." My chest heaved as I tried to get enough breath to both speak and survive this ordeal. "Nurse!"

"Lady Rosie?" She sounded hopeful that I'd called her back.

Yet I did still wish to be alone until . . . Well, until I wasn't. "Thank you for not saying it could have been worse, that the prince kindly saved my reputation and wishes to marry me. It's the truth, but I don't know if I could have borne to hear you say it."

"I wouldn't. Yes, it's the truth, and yes, in their dishonor, men have been praising themselves in such ways since the Garden of Eden. Nevertheless, my lady, I weep for you." She glanced behind me and disappeared toward the kitchen.

And . . . enter stage left.

Prince Escalus.

Again.

CHAPTER 47

My now future husband seemed a dark, silent phantom against the wall, but I finally realized he excelled at blending into the shadows.

I sank down on the chair Nurse had set for me, propped my elbow up on the marble tabletop—which was frigid, by the way, but I wanted to present a relaxed, authoritative mien. "Prince Escalus." I beckoned him to approach.

Yes, yes, you're right. Without a long sword with a sharp point and a fast running head start, I couldn't have kept him from approaching. But by God, I wasn't going to approach him, not even to slam my foot into his privates again, not even for the pleasure that would give me.

Let me correct myself. The *great* pleasure it would give me.

"Lady Rosie." He moved forward into the light.

I'll give him credit. He walked lightly, as if trying with silence not to annoy me. He didn't look smug as most men would when faced with the woman who encouraged him to kiss so wildly and returned that kiss with such enthusiasm.

Please remember, this was no significant praise, for I'd never before enjoyed a lover's kiss. I couldn't compare it to anything, could I?

But never mind that. I asked that which was foremost in my mind, "Where is Lysander?"

"He was unavoidably detained, but quite safe." His voice was pitched low and had a reassuring tone.

Like that was going to soothe me. "Detained being the operative word?"

Prince Escalus said nothing, by which I concluded we were done discussing my One True Love, Lysander. I could see how the subject might make the sucking louse feel less noble and more like a rooting swine.

I smiled with patently false amiability. "Prince Escalus, you have concluded the bargaining for my hand and body in marriage?"

A patter of footsteps sounded on the walk, and Nurse appeared, carrying a steaming cup and a small plate of biscotti. She hesitated until I gestured her forward, then placed them within reach of my grasp. "I'll remain close. If you need me, you have only to call."

"Thank you, Nurse, but there's no need. My reputation is ruined. Nothing worse can happen." As soon as I said it, I knew myself ridiculous since I was still technically a virgin, but it did feel as if this night, every life I'd hoped to live had been ended, and I groped down a dark tunnel blind and alone.

Nurse aimed herself between us and curtsied.

Prince Escalus placed his hand on his chest and bowed, not ignoring Nurse but his attention clearly on me. "The deal is struck, Lady Rosaline. Your reputation is intact. You are to be mine, as you said, hand, body, and any other parts you wish to bring to our marriage bed."

I took a sip from the cup of stewed *camomilla* weeds that were supposed to calm me, then placed it on the table because *blech*. "Why?"

He tilted his head. "Why?" he repeated as if he didn't understand the question.

I knew perfectly he did, but I felt compelled to spell it out. "All the reasons that applied to Duke Stephano's inexplicable proposal to me also apply to you. My family has little dowry to settle on me, I'm outspoken, I'm now twenty years old (we'd celebrated my birthday during my illness), ancient among the current crop of—"

"Virgins?" He inserted the word as if it was the only one he knew.

I spoke with chill ill humor. "Quite. But tonight was a deliberate ruse to close all other avenues to me. Except the convent, and that's a route I'll not take unless forced. You're rich, you're respectable, you're influential. You could have any maiden in the land. So why me?"

"I've been watching you for quite a while." As he explained, he watched my face most intently. "It started after I saw you maneuver your way out of your third betrothal, and it occurred to me you'd make a master diplomat. That's a very useful trait for the podestà's wife."

"My third betrothal was almost three years ago." He'd been watching me for three years? "How . . . creepy."

"While I considered the possibility of you as wife and whether your bad temper would cause more havoc than your diplomatic skills could fix, your parents betrothed you again."

"I remember. That one was a fast turnaround."

"He was a wealthy young man and would have been an asset to your family, so you matched him to your own sister. Again, a brilliant and statesmanlike move." His admiring tone might have been flattering, if I'd been in the mood to be flattered.

"That was almost exactly two years ago."

"At that point I had to deal with the issues caused in Venice by the Acquasassos. They fomented revolt, and the Venetians wanted them gone, and they wanted Verona to take them back." He grimaced. "I had to negotiate mightily to keep them in exile. Due to those actions, I had no time to bother with marriage, and I told myself I could relax. I believed you could dodge any potential threat of marriage without any help from me. As you did. Unfortunately, while I waited for the time to woo you, I began to notice other admirable traits about you."

"Did you?" Talk about sweep a girl off her feet with all the sweet talk. "What would those be?"

"I like your family."

"My family."

"You must know they're charming."

"Yes, I like them, too."

"You're close with them all, your parents and siblings, so as your husband, I'd have to spend time with them. It's a good thing to like your in-laws."

"Um-hmm." I wanted to point out that my family was not one of my admirable qualities, but I'd clenched my jaws. Surely this couldn't get worse?

"Plus I knew Isabella needed more in her life than a too-busy elder brother."

Worse. Much, much worse.

Oblivious, he continued. "You're efficient. You direct your parents' household through calm and crisis, seemingly without malfunction. The kitchens here are exemplary, and mine at the palace need a firm hand."

I nodded and ran my hand back and forth over the cold marble table, trying to cool my . . . my everything, and to remind myself that making a fist and pounding it on the table would result in possible injury and not really much satisfactory noise.

"An addendum to your family situation is the fertility your parents have shown. As podestà, I not only need to have a male heir, but the palace is large and empty. I'd like to fill it with children's laughter."

Let's see. He wanted to marry me for my diplomatic skills, to fill his need for a family with the ready-built Montagues, my housekeeping skills, and for my womb, which he assumed would be generous. I unclenched my jaws to ask, "Anything else?"

"Your breasts are perfect, exactly the size to fit into the palm of my hand."

I sharply looked up and found his gaze, not on my nipples, which were hard—no, no, not because I was secretly aroused, but because it was cold out here and getting colder—but into my eyes.

He had that inscrutable expression on his face, the one he had perfected with much practice. "But there was still the issue of your temper, which I noted broke out repeatedly, and you do shout." Consideringly, he said, "All your family does, but in that issue only you are of concern to me."

"Wouldn't want to disturb the podestà unduly." I sounded so cordial! So sincere! As if I wasn't wondering how much harder I could kick him in the hairy hangers!

"Next I did as I so often do when faced with an important choice." He seemed to think he was imparting something of great importance to me. "I made a list."

I couldn't tear my eyes away from his. "A list."

"I take a parchment and a quill, and with ink I divide the paper in half"—he indicated top to bottom—"and then a line near the top, creating four uneven boxes. In the two small top boxes, I wrote, 'Reasons to wed Lady Rosie' and 'Reasons not to wed Lady Rosie.' In the larger boxes, I listed all the reasons, pro and con, for our union to proceed or not."

Friar Laurence and my parents had pointed out my logic and methodical faults.

This guy had them beat by cubits. He was so pedantic he could make your eyes roll into the back of your head—except that he was talking about *me*. Me, as if I were a cipher to be figured and the answer, once found, would be immutable.

"You ask, why am I telling you this?" Apparently not even he was completely oblivious to the insult he offered me. "Do you remember I told you that I was the reason Duke Stephano wanted to marry you? For power?"

I did remember. Prince Escalus had said so in Friar Laurence's shop and then Nurse had run in with news of Porcia's death. Now I made an inspired guess. "You're not going to tell me that you left your list sitting around and Duke Stephano found it, read it, and—"

Prince Escalus was already nodding his head.

"He decided he'd have power over you if he took possession first and used me to control you? Because you made a list that commended my family, my diplomatic skill, and my tits and those reasons would make me a suitable wife for the podestà?" My voice was rising. "Are you jesting?"

He conceded, "There might have been a few more items on the list that convinced him he'd be holding me by the short hairs."

"What short hairs? The ones on the back of your head? Or—" Then I got it and blushed. "Oh."

"Duke Stephano didn't share my thoughtful habit of waiting on events. As soon as Titania was dead"—the prince paused as if unsure how to phrase this—"the first time, he made the deal with your father and by the time I'd heard of it, it was too late."

"He who hesitates—"

"Yes, I lost. I wasn't worried—"

Remembering the way he'd announced our betrothal at the party, I allowed my sarcasm to overflow. "I could tell."

"Because I intended to remove you from Duke Stephano's sphere by whatever nefarious but necessary means were required."

CHAPTER 48

"As you did Lysander," I snapped.

"I would've handled Duke Stephano differently," Prince Escalus assured me.

I accused him. "You were rougher with Lysander because he's a younger son of a distant family."

Prince Escalus lowered his gaze, and when he lifted it, the glint in his dark eyes might have been described as implacable. "Quite the contrary. Duke Stephano dared to try and take what was mine, to harm what was mine, believing my intent to maintain Verona's peace made me a coward. I'd have taught him his mistake. He'd have begged for exile."

I wanted to take issue with Prince Escalus's claiming of me as *his*, but among all the issues here, that was the lesser. Moreover, I'd realized I was wrong about the glint in his eyes. That wasn't implacability. That was danger.

"Your betrothal to Duke Stephano was nothing more than a technical difficulty and as with his death, unimportant. Man and wife are one," Prince Escalus said, "and since Titania killed him, one might say he's now dead by his own hand."

Sadly, I touched the scar on my chest, realized I had imitated my mother, and hastily lowered my hand.

"The real loss came when you met Lysander and fell in love.

I could fight Duke Stephano and end your engagement, but I can't untangle an emotional attachment."

"You're pretty smart . . . for a man."

From his expression, my words were unintelligible. Then he made that grimace that might be taken as a half grin, and I realized he got it. Probably he thought I was trying to be funny, though.

"Your attachment to Lysander was an obstacle which took concentrated thought on my part. I'd met him before and of course I was aware he was in the city. It's my business to know. My observations and reports of Lysander were that he was an intelligent, honorable man out to prove himself. When the two of you fell in love, I had to consider whether to step aside and to see if love at first sight would blossom." That grimace was definitely a half grin. "Because nothing bad ever comes of love at first sight, right?"

I startled. That sounded so much like something I'd said in the past. . . .

"I thought I could give you up. I thought I'd have to. Then that night, you trusted me to save you from the charges of Duke Stephano's stabbing. I offered to help you, give you a chance to join with Lysander, to become betrothed and wed. You refused."

"At that moment, I thought him shallow. I quickly learned better."

"And . . ." Prince Escalus looked down at his feet.

"And . . . ?"

He looked up into my eyes. "You teased me."

"I teased you?" Baffled, I asked, "About what?"

"About Porcia's obnoxious reminders of your virginity." He pulled something out of a hidden pocket close to his heart and showed it to me.

It was a coin. "What . . . oh!" The florin he'd won from me—

by cheating, not that I was holding a grudge. "Does no one ever tease you?"

"No."

"Never?"

"No. Not since my father was murdered, not since my mother died, not since I was tortured and mutilated, not since I won back Verona and banished the Acquasassos. No one has dared."

I really wanted to suggest that if he wasn't always such a grim, humorless stick he might make a few friends, but while I was angry, somehow that seemed like too low a blow. "That's why you decided to marry me? Because I teased you?"

"That, and the fact you trusted me to save you from the accusation of murder. Those were the deciding factors." He slipped the coin back into his pocket. "But mostly the teasing."

I remembered distinctly that I was merely trying to make him less grim.

No good deed goes unpunished.

"I was annoyed when I realized you were eyeing me the way you eyed your other fiancés, as if you were measuring me for the cloth of marriage—and you weren't reaching with the correct conclusion."

"The correct conclusion being what?"

He raised his eyebrows as if I was being obtuse.

"Oh, me and you." I shook my head. "No, it would have taken me a long time to pair *us.*"

"I'd learned my lesson. No more waiting for the elderly spinster Lady Rosaline to be un-betrothed." He held his hand palm up and slowly closed it into a fist. "If I wanted her, I'd have to claim her any way I could."

"You spied on me and overheard the plan with Lysander."

"I came to climb the walnut tree and woo you as seems a tradition in your family."

For the first time in the whole conversation, I grinned. "That would have been something to see!"

My amusement seemed to annoy him. "What I overheard caused my plan to change."

I realized that as we'd been speaking, the prince had been stealthily approaching me, gliding forward like a hunter intent on capturing a unicorn. The sneaky bastard.

He took the final step and knelt beside me.

I allowed him to take my hand.

In case you're wondering why, it had recently been borne in on me that Prince Escalus would do whatever it took to get his way, including wrestle with me. He might even *want* to wrestle with me, but that contest I was destined to lose.

Also, I'd had enough physical action with the prince tonight. Enough physical action for a lifetime, although at this point that seemed wistful thinking.

Prince Escalus lifted my hand to his lips and spoke. "You believe I shouldn't have used such a dishonorable ruse to secure you." He put his lips on my fingernails. "To secure this hand." His lips moved against my skin, then gradually he turned my wrist until my palm was up. "When I stood in that tomb where you had defended yourself against a long sword using only three daggers. You said . . ."

"What did I say?"

"You don't remember?"

"I don't remember anything after I . . . stabbed Titania."

"When your nurse revived you, you said, 'I had to kill Titania. She was going to hurt my family. She was going to hurt my friends. She would never stop. I had to stop her.' Then you slipped back out of consciousness." He closed his eyes and lightly put his lips to my palm. I felt his lips move as he said, "I knew I had never been in the presence of such bravery, such loyalty, such character." He pressed a kiss into my palm, folded my fingers over it and, lifting his head, he stared into my eyes. "I want you for who you are, and I'll do anything to have you and keep you safe." Rising from his knees, he guided my fist to my chest, over my heart. "Parting is such sweet sorrow, so hold my kiss close tonight, and release it not 'til it be morrow."

I watched Prince Escalus, my new lord and master, stride across the atrium toward the front entrance.

Shit. *Poetry*. He quoted *poetry*. To me. As if I was a woman who would swoon over the rhyming phrases, the tender sentiments. He doesn't understand that I've never liked poetry. Poetry reminds me too much of my parents, their wild impetuous youthful love and all the drama that has unfolded from it. Drama and life, children and laughter, family and closeness.

Neither the prince nor I were wild and impetuous, and certainly not youthful, so why was he quoting *poetry* as if we were?

From behind me, Nurse cautiously whispered, "Lady Rosaline, will you come away to bed?"

I nodded and rose, walked to the stairway and climbed it, let her help me out of the layers of clothing and into bed. There I stared at the ceiling and thought I had evaded marriage before, surely I could do so again . . . although never had I encountered so worthy an opponent as Prince Escalus . . .

Nurse asked, "What did he give you, my lady?"

"What?" I stared blankly.

"In your hand." She indicated my clenched fist. "What did he give you?"

I realized I still held that kiss pressed to my chest over my heart. "Something to think about."

AUTHOR'S NOTE

One day I said to my younger daughter, Arwen, "I'd like to write a book that springs off of a story so iconic everyone knows it without having it explained, like Pride and Prejudice or —"

She said, "The Daughter of Romeo and Juliet."

I said, as does every single person who hears it, "Romeo and Juliet are dead." I promptly realized that although *Romeo and Juliet* is a hallowed story, it's also a work of fiction and fiction is not history. In fact, Shakespeare borrowed the plot of this play and dramatically changed the story while doing so.

As Shakespearean scholar Mary Bly, aka *New York Times* bestseller Eloisa James, says, "Literary theft was second nature to Shakespeare; he shaped *Romeo and Juliet* from a poem by Arthur Brooke, who took the plot from a story by Matteo Bandello. Brooke disapproved of Romeo and Juliet's 'unhonest desire,' so Shakespeare didn't hesitate to shake up that chestnut, just as Christina has done. He would have approved!"

Sitting down, I wrote the first four pages. It was as if Rosie had been lurking in my subconscious for her story to be told. Arwen and I brainstormed key elements of the story—another of her brilliant suggestions was that Rosie would fall in love at first sight as her parents did, and be thoroughly chagrinned about it.

Then I put those pages away. Because I'm a working writer and (like Rosie) a sensible person. Who would want to read such an unusual story set in a unique setting?

So while The Daughter of Romeo and Juliet silently bubbled like the yeast in Juliet's fruit bread, Fate in the shape of New York Times bestseller Susan Elizabeth Phillips took over. She emailed after an exchange of wit between her, New York Times bestseller Jayne Ann Krentz, and me, and said, "You're funny. You should write romantic comedy." We exchanged more wit, then I sent the four pages to Susan and Jayne. They more or less demanded I continue, and with their encouragement The Daughter of Romeo and Juliet (as I then called it,) became an entire manuscript.

I sent pages to my agent, Annelise Robey, who called and assured me that she could sell it. Her quote was something like, "After I picked myself up off the floor . . ." She did sell the book to the visionary John Scognamiglio at Kensington Books.

As I wrote, I researched Romeo and Juliet, and the natural first question I googled was, *When did Romeo and Juliet take place?* To my astonishment, Google announced it took place somewhere in the 14th or 15th century. Two hundred years! In other words, late medieval or early Renaissance Verona. A lot happened in those two hundred years. As I researched further, I discovered that while little is known of Shakespeare's life, it's extremely unlikely he ever left the mighty island of England. That makes Verona a mythical romantic destination for him. So following his lead, The Daughter of Romeo and Juliet (now *A Daughter of Fair Verona*) is a work of fiction based on a work of fiction, set in mythic Verona.

Who am I to dare revise the revered tale of *Romeo and Juliet?*

I'm a groundling, a.k.a. a plebeian, an audience member at Shakespeare's Globe who stands in the yard to watch the play. I'm the person for whom he wrote touching flights of romantic poetry, coarse jokes, and created characters to be laughed at or feared. I am his audience.

So accept my invitation to join me in the yard to view the further adventures of Rosie Montague, her parents Romeo and Juliet, the gorgeous Lysander and the mysterious Prince Escalus, and all the cast and characters of *A Daughter of Fair Verona.*

Want to know more about Rosie Montague and her future adventures and misadventures? Visit the website created for the series, DaughterofMontague.com, where you'll discover sneak peeks of upcoming stories, clips from the audiobook, the recipe for Juliet's fruit and nut bread, and photos, videos and commentary from my visit to present day Verona.

Until next time, happy reading!

Warmly,

Christina Dodd
New York Times bestselling author

Would you like to recreate Juliet's fruit and nut bread?
It's easy and delicious!
You can find the recipe on Christina's website,
ChristinaDodd.com, and on her special website for the
Daughter of Montague series,
DaughterofMontague.com

A DAUGHTER OF
FAIR VERONA

ABOUT THIS GUIDE

The suggested questions are included to enhance your group's
reading of Christina Dodd's *A Daughter of Fair Verona*!

DISCUSSION QUESTIONS

1. The premise of A DAUGHTER OF FAIR VERONA is that Romeo and Juliet did not die in the tomb but instead enjoyed a normal, happy life with their many children. Do you like this outcome? Do you feel that it's more likely their impetuous union would lead to an unhappy marriage? What results of such young love have you seen in your life?

2. Have you ever felt the all-consuming teenage passion of Romeo and Juliet? Can you imagine marrying the person you fell in love with at thirteen years of age? In your opinion, how would that union have turned out in today's society?

3. Rosie's life has been so saturated with the Romeo and Juliet romantic legend that, at the beginning of the story, she's stubbornly opposed to falling in love. Do you consider that an expected reaction? How would you react to being a child of such famed and venerated lovers?

4. For the most part, Rosie speaks to the reader in a contemporary voice and in fact is lamentably bad at the poetry that epitomizes Shakespeare's tragic romance, *Romeo and Juliet*. In your opinion, does her flippant sarcasm add or detract from the story told in A DAUGHTER OF FAIR VERONA? Do you feel you related to Rosie more because of the lack of Shakespeare's Elizabethan language?

5. The stories of Romeo and Juliet and of Rosie Montague are set in a time where marriages were arranged and bro-

kered by a woman's parents. Imagine you were living in such a culture: What would your reaction be to a marriage brokered by your parents? Would it be akin to Rosie's attempts to escape matrimony, or would you accept the match? Discuss the factors that would lead to your decision.

6. On page 1, Rosie sarcastically says, "Nothing bad ever came of love at first sight, right?" Yet despite her opposition to falling in love, at her betrothal ball, Rosie runs into Lysander and, like her parents, is instantly smitten. Do you believe in love at first sight? What do you think are the chances of union based on passion and visual attraction surviving?

7. Have you known a gossipmonger like Porcia? How would you/did you handle her constant barrage of insults and accusations?

8. Prince Escalus is intent on proving Rosie innocent of the murder at her betrothal ball. As you read that scene, did you believe the remote prince was motivated by his quest for justice and his desire to keep Verona's peace? Now that you've finished the book and know more about his character, what do you see as his true motivations?

9. The author considered many titles for this first work in the Daughter of Montague series before settling on A DAUGHTER OF FAIR VERONA. What alternate titles would you give this story?

10. In a film adaptation of this story, who would you cast as the pragmatic Rosie? The intelligent and romantic Lysander? The enigmatic Prince Escalus? The wicked Duke

Stephano? And, of course, the now-in-their-thirties Romeo and Juliet?

11. In order to research the setting of this story, the author visited Verona, Italy, one of the less visited, yet most beautiful cities in Europe. After reading this story, would you visit fair Verona? Knowing that *Romeo and Juliet* is a work of fiction, would you visit the tourist sites (notably Juliet's house with her statue and the iconic balcony) dedicated to the doomed lovers?

12. How would you describe the story to convince a potential reader to read A DAUGHTER OF FAIR VERONA? Would you call it a historical work of fiction based on a Shakespearean work of fiction? A murder mystery? A coming of age story? A humorous take on a legendary tale? What scenes would you cite as memorable?

13. A DAUGHTER OF FAIR VERONA's cover is striking with its bold colors and symbolic use of daggers, skulls, asps, roses, and a cross cleverly placed into the title. Do you think it aptly conveys an impression of the story told within? If you were tapped to design a cover based on such an iconic story, what elements would you include?

14. Most historians agree that William Shakespeare never left the British Isles, yet he chose Verona as the setting for three of his plays: *Romeo and Juliet, Two Gentlemen of Verona* and, in part, *The Taming of the Shrew*. He wrote of faraway places, places that to him would have been as exotic as any fantasy world created today. Given his love for setting his stories in Italy, do you think he traveled there in his lifetime? What known attributes about Italy do you think motivated his use of the setting?

15. Overall, what is your take on the liberties the author took with the most famous and cherished Shakespearean play, *Romeo and Juliet*? How would you tweak the most known love story of all time?